PRAISE

Pike Island

"The perfect follow-up to Wirt's thrilling *Just Stay Away*, *Pike Island* delivers a breakneck read from the first chapter all the way to Wirt's delivery of the best twist I've read this year. I loved this book!"
—Elle Marr, Amazon Charts bestselling author of *The Alone Time* and *Your Dark Secrets*

"With shades of *House of Cards* and *I Know What You Did Last Summer*, Tony Wirt's *Pike Island* elegantly dances between past and present, gradually cracking open to reveal the 'real' story behind a picture-perfect politician on a meteoric rise and the boyhood secrets he's worked hard to bury. Wirt's immersive writing, clever twists, and layered examinations of loyalty, greed, and ambition's darkest corners will make you want to read this pulse-pounding, utterly satisfying thriller in one sitting."
—Kathleen Willett, author of *Anything for a Friend*

"*Pike Island* is everything you want in a thriller. A compelling plot, great characters, and a storyline that sweeps you along. I devoured it in a single sitting. Absolutely loved it."
—Cate Quinn, author of *The Clinic*

Just Stay Away

"Nobody believes Craig when he insists nine-year-old Levi is the source of the mayhem in his life—which is regrettable, as Levi might be a troublemaker worse than *Baby Teeth*'s Hanna (so says the author of *Baby Teeth*). *Just Stay Away* is a tense page-turner that literally had me reading with my shoulders hunched."
—Zoje Stage, bestselling author of *Baby Teeth* and *Mothered*

"Cancel your plans and find a good chair because once you start *Just Stay Away*, you won't be able to stop. A psychological game of cat and mouse evolves between a writer and his daughter's creepy new friend in this superbly plotted, fantastically immersive domestic thriller. From the characters to the writing to the pitch-perfect ending, Wirt delivers on every level."
—Mindy Mejia, bestselling author of *Everything You Want Me to Be* and *To Catch a Storm*

"A relentlessly creepy and dangerously addictive read, *Just Stay Away* will have you checking your locks and jumping at shadows once you've finished. Using the unique perspective of a stay-at-home dad, Tony Wirt expertly crafts an atmosphere of ever-increasing isolation, claustrophobia, and gaslighting to ramp up from a sinister simmer into a full-blown nightmare. In doing so, Wirt explores gender roles, masculinity, and boyhood in the profound ways you find in the best of the genre. An absolute must-read—if you dare!"
—Brianna Labuskes, *Wall Street Journal* bestselling author of *A Familiar Sight*

"In *Just Stay Away*, Wirt flawlessly weaves tension into everyday domestic life. The protagonist, Craig, finds himself in a suspenseful game of cat and mouse with a neighborhood child that will leave you wondering, What would you do to protect those you love?"
—Elle Grawl, author of *One of Those Faces* and *What Still Burns*

A Necessary Act

Underground Book Reviews 2017 Novel of the Year, Reader's Choice

"I literally could not put this book down. As far as thrillers and crime novels go, it ticked every box for me while also managing to be unique in its concept and style. Great characters, genuine bellyaching tension, and an ending that both surprises and satisfies . . . and yet is left wide, wide open . . . I truly hope there is more to come."

—Underground Book Reviews

"*A Necessary Act* grabbed me by the throat and refused to let go—even after I turned the last page!"

—C. H. Armstrong, author of *The Edge of Nowhere*

"This book is filled with creepy and suspenseful moments that are sure to get anyone's heart pumping. Just leave the lights on."

—*Rochester Magazine*

SILENT CREEK

ALSO BY TONY WIRT

A Necessary Act

Just Stay Away

Pike Island

SILENT CREEK

TONY WIRT

THOMAS & MERCER

This is a work of fiction. Names, characters, organizations, places, events, and incidents are either products of the author's imagination or are used fictitiously. Otherwise, any resemblance to actual persons, living or dead, is purely coincidental.

Text copyright © 2025 by Tony Wirt
All rights reserved.

No part of this book may be reproduced, or stored in a retrieval system, or transmitted in any form or by any means, electronic, mechanical, photocopying, recording, or otherwise, without express written permission of the publisher.

Published by Thomas & Mercer, Seattle
www.apub.com

Amazon, the Amazon logo, and Thomas & Mercer are trademarks of Amazon.com, Inc., or its affiliates.

EU product safety contact:
Amazon Media EU S. à r.l.
38, avenue John F. Kennedy, L-1855 Luxembourg
amazonpublishing-gpsr@amazon.com

ISBN-13: 9781662530111 (paperback)
ISBN-13: 9781662530104 (digital)

Cover design by David Drummond
Cover image: © Likman Uladzimir, © N. Rotteveel / Shutterstock; © Pierre-Olivier Valiquette / Getty

Printed in the United States of America

To my parents,
Thanks for always welcoming me back home.

Chapter One

"I'll take that, Mom."

Jim fought to keep the frustration out of his voice. He'd repeatedly told his mom she didn't need to help him haul boxes in from the truck, but every time he turned around, she had something in her hands.

Not that he didn't appreciate the help, but the word BEDROOM was clearly scrawled across the cardboard in his blocky handwriting, and she was carrying it into the bathroom.

Maybe she hadn't noticed, or maybe she simply wanted to get as many boxes inside the house before her only son realized what he was doing and changed his mind about moving home.

Or maybe she's confused.

Gail McCann had always been a little flighty, but Jim had no clue how bad it had gotten until he'd come home for his dad's funeral. He'd tried to pass it off as grief but could tell even before Pastor Mader pulled him aside that his mother was not well. She'd tell the same story three times in a night, ask questions that he'd answered just minutes before. But when he'd told her it was time to leave for the church and she asked why, there was no denying it.

He gently ushered his mother down the hall. "I told you, don't worry about the boxes, Mom. I can handle it. Besides, Kyle Erikson is coming over. You remember him, right? We used to play basketball together."

"Of course I know Kyle." Her eyes darkened in a way that showed contempt for the question but didn't necessarily confirm she was telling the truth.

How long had his father let this go on? Ignoring the signs, covering for her lapses, refusing to take his wife to a doctor when something could have been done to slow the process. Instead choosing to deflect and hide because to James McCann II, getting help would be showing weakness or some other macho bullshit. It was the same when Jim's knee gave out for the final time and shuttered his basketball career for good. Dad couldn't fathom why his son wasn't willing to undergo a fourth surgery and grueling rehab to chase down a dream he'd woken from years before.

Deep breath.

It was easy to blame Dad for Mom's condition, but if he did, Jim had to eat some himself. How many years had it been since he'd come home to visit? If he hadn't begged off holiday invites with flimsy excuses, maybe they wouldn't have stopped coming. He could have recognized what was going on with his mom in time to do something. But he hadn't, and now his dad was dead of a heart attack and he was back in Silent Creek, Minnesota, moving into his mom's house and his dad's office at McCann LP, which supplied propane and heating oil to a wide swath of southern Minnesota.

Jim left his mom in the kitchen and went back outside to grab another box. A gray Jeep Grand Cherokee was parked alongside the curb. The driver's side door popped open.

"I never thought I'd see the day." Kyle stepped around his car with a pair of work gloves in his hand and a smile on his face. He stuck his other hand out, then pulled Jim into a bro hug on the sidewalk. "Jimmy McCann, back in the Creek."

Inseparable as kids, he and Kyle had drifted apart during college. They both started at the University of Minnesota together, but basketball took up most of Jim's time and Kyle ended up dropping out after freshman year. Emails and texts kept them in contact for a while, but after Jim moved out East, that dried up too. They'd caught up a bit at the funeral, but that was mostly condolences and pleasantries. Before that, Jim hadn't talked to his old friend in years.

Kyle's hair was starting to thin on top, and his middle was doughier. He definitely looked older than Jim, whose six-foot-nine frame was built on an athlete's metabolism. Kyle had been working at McCann LP since he'd dropped out of college and worked his way up to the number-two spot in the company by the time Jim's dad died. From the conversations they'd had, Kyle made it sound like he'd been running the day-to-day operations for a while. That was good because Jim was coming in with no knowledge of the propane business. James had expected his son to come back for a job at the company after his basketball career ended, but returning to Silent Creek had been the furthest thing from his mind. When Jim took a job at some Gopher alumnus's medical-device company out in Boston, Dad took it as a middle finger directed right at him.

Whether he'd meant it to be or not didn't matter now because his dad was dead and Jim was back, carrying boxes into the house he'd grown up in and done everything to avoid since graduating from high school.

"I appreciate the help," Jim said. "Mom wants to, of course, but you know . . ."

"Dude, it's what old friends do." Kyle pulled on his work gloves and grabbed a box from the back of the rental truck. "How's she handling all this?"

Jim glanced back at the house before reaching for a box of his own. "Fine, I think, but it's hard to tell sometimes. You'll ask her something, and she'll answer vaguely, so you aren't sure if she understands or not. But if you follow up, she'll get upset."

"You want me to give Carrie a call? See if she can come over and help out? Maybe hang out with her?"

"That's okay," Jim said. Not that he'd thought of Carrie Erikson, née Gustafson, much over the years, but he had been legitimately surprised when he heard his high school best friend was marrying Jim's high school

3

girlfriend. Like with Kyle, Jim hadn't kept in touch with Carrie at all, which was probably common for most high school relationships.

It was a little strange to see them together at the funeral, but it didn't bother Jim at all. Any feelings he'd had for Carrie had been left behind long ago, and funeral conversations were awkward by nature, so he attributed any weirdness to their circumstances.

Jim adjusted his hold on the box in his arms and walked up to the house alongside Kyle.

"So, do you have a plan for when you want to come to work?" Kyle stopped at the front step. "No rush, obviously."

Jim put his box down so he could open the front door. "I was thinking I could come in on Monday, start getting the feel of the place, you know, meet people and introduce myself."

"Take your time and get settled. I've been running that place for years, so I can keep my hands on the wheel for as long as you want. Seriously, take a week or two if you want," Kyle said. "Besides, you don't have to introduce yourself to anybody in Silent Creek."

As if pushed into their conversation by a stage manager, the mail carrier walked up behind them. "Hi, Jimmy!"

Jim turned around and saw an older guy with a gray mustache and the light-blue button-up shirt of the USPS. He looked familiar, but Jim couldn't find his name. "Hey . . . how're you doing?"

"Real good!" he said. "I'd heard you were moving back. That's great."

Jim wasn't quite sure how to respond to this relative stranger's excitement, so he simply smiled and nodded.

"You know, my granddaughter started playing basketball. She's only in fourth grade but already says she wants to play varsity when she gets older. Just the other day I was telling her about you, how even though you were from tiny, little Silent Creek, you were so good you got to go on and play in college. Maybe someday she'll be the next Jimmy Buckets."

Jim never really liked that nickname, and in his mind, it had aged like fish in the sun over the last fifteen years. When he decided to move back, part of him hoped at least that had been forgotten. That people would get to know him for who he was now, not whatever legend the *Silent Creek Signal* had painted of him back in high school.

He forced a good-natured chuckle. "If she works hard, hopefully she can be better."

That brought a real laugh from the mail carrier. "She's not *that* good. She's quick but not very tall. I was telling her she needs to work on . . ."

The words droned on as Jim's vision blurred and his mind wandered in a way he hoped wasn't obvious. Jim told himself the guy was just being nice, but years of having the same conversations over and over again had worn on him. As soon as the guy stopped talking long enough for a breath, Jim jumped in.

"Well, hey, good seeing you, but I don't want to keep you from your route."

The guy looked surprised to be reminded he was on the clock.

"Yeah, I better get." He gave a familiar long pause, and Jim knew what was coming next. "Do you think I could get an autograph for my granddaughter? She'd be so excited."

Jim couldn't imagine a nine-year-old girl caring about a signature from a guy who last touched a basketball in the early 2000s, but he smiled and agreed.

Unfortunately, they didn't have anything handy to sign, but that didn't deter the man, who dug up a pen and a piece of someone else's junk mail.

Jim scrawled his name across the back of a Pottery Barn flyer, and the mail carrier took it back like Moses receiving the stone tablets.

He thanked Jim repeatedly before handing him a stack of mail and moving on to the next house.

"Did he have you sign someone's mail?" Kyle asked as soon as the guy was out of earshot.

Jim tried to shrug it off.

"First day back home and you're committing felonies."

They went inside, and Jim dropped the mail on the little table by the door before following Kyle toward the back of the house.

"You know, since we're talking about basketball—" Kyle was cut off by the sound of shattering glass from the kitchen. Jim took off down the hall, worried he was going to walk in on a bloody floor and have to cart his mom off to the emergency room.

His mom stood in the middle of the kitchen, shards of glass on the linoleum all around her.

"What happened?" Jim asked. "You okay?"

Gail pulled her hand away from her mouth and tried to shake some color back into her face. "I'm fine. It was an accident. It's fine."

She started toward the cabinet that had housed their broom for as long as Jim could remember.

"Wait! I'll get it." Jim looked at the pieces of glass scattered between her stocking feet and the broom. They were bigger than anything that could have come from a glass. Looked like a bowl or something. "Careful . . ." He snuck around the perimeter and pulled the broom out. Long arms helped him reach over and sweep the biggest chunks toward him. "What were you doing?"

Gail followed the newly swept trail over to her son. "I was going to make you boys something to eat and . . ."

"That's okay, Mrs. McCann," Kyle said. "You don't need to go to any fuss over me."

She looked past Jim at his friend and smiled politely, but her face didn't betray whether she recognized him or not. "It's no fuss. You guys are probably hungry."

"It's 10:00 a.m., Mom. We're good." Jim swept up the remaining glass and dumped it in the garbage. He looked around for any flashes of light but didn't see any.

"I'll call Carrie and have her bring over some of her tomatoes for you," Kyle said. "You know how good her garden is. We're absolutely swimming in them."

"That would be nice," Gail said. "Her stuff makes such good salads. I used to make one for James's lunch every day."

"Are you sure about that, Mom?" James McCann was a born-and-bred Minnesotan who considered turkey a vegetable, and the fact that his mom was reminiscing about making salads for him was the most worrying thing she'd said yet. "I never saw Dad eat anything green in his life."

"Actually, we both did, if you can believe it," Kyle said. "Carrie put me on a diet this summer and somehow convinced your dad to do it too. She grows it all in the backyard, and we kept your mom fully stocked. Not sure how much your dad liked it, but at least he tried."

The thought of his dad eating lettuce flabbergasted Jim.

"You good?" Kyle asked.

Jim shook the confusion from his head. "Yeah . . . hard to picture, I guess."

They made sure Gail was occupied and there was no more glass on the floor before heading out for another load.

The morning sun was getting going as they stepped out into the yard and headed over to the truck.

"So, anyway, like I was saying . . ." Kyle said. "I've got something you may be interested in."

Jim stared into the back of the rental van, debating what to take next. "What's that?"

"You know I've been coaching varsity the last five seasons, and John Pederson has been my assistant coach the whole time."

He had heard Kyle was coaching boys' basketball at Silent Creek High School but hadn't given much thought to who he was doing it with. Coach Pederson had been an assistant back when they played. "He's still alive?"

"Barely," Kyle said. "But that's the point. He wants to be done, but there is nobody else out there who knows anything. I mean, apparently Joel Dillon said he'd do it, but he doesn't know shit about basketball. He never even played."

Jim saw where this was going before Kyle asked, and he looked into the back of the truck to see if there was a place to hide among the boxes.

"So I was thinking, if you were looking for something to do . . ."

The morning clouds had parted, and the sun felt like a spotlight cooking Jim at center stage. He wanted to say not only *no*, but *no way in hell.* It was, literally, the last thing on earth he wanted to do. That offer was everything he feared about moving back to Silent Creek, a continuation of basketball being the center of his life, sucking in everything around it like a black hole, until there was nothing left.

The silence apparently hung longer than he'd realized.

"Well, what do you say?"

Jim stood at the open door of the truck and felt sweat bead down his back.

"Yeah, I don't know about that. I mean, I've got to get up to speed down at McCann and . . . you know . . ." His trail off didn't sound definitive and left the door wide open for Kyle to kick through.

"Oh, come on, man. We've sucked for the past few years, but I've finally got some talent this season. And if I can get Pederson out of there and get a real assistant?" He was worked up. In salesman mode. "Jimmy Buckets and K-Dogg back coaching the Beavers to the state tournament . . . it's a freaking movie, dude."

No, it wasn't a movie. *Jimmy Buckets* was a nickname he'd been trying to shed for years. And no one had ever called Kyle *K-Dogg*.

"It'll be great. You already know the plays and everything."

"You're still running those same sets we did back in the day? Memphis and Tennessee?" It sounded more dismissive than Jim had intended, and Kyle caught it.

"Yeah, but that's because it's all anybody around here knows. That's why I need you. I want to modernize things. Add new wrinkles. If you bring some Big Ten–level schemes in, man, the guys would love that."

There was no way he was going to coach. That was a nonstarter, no matter how much Kyle wanted it, but he had to find a way to let his old friend down easy. Jim scanned the truck for something he could carry in by himself and get away from the sales pitch. Give him time to think up an excuse. He reached down and picked up a box marked for the living room.

Kyle swooped past and grabbed the first box he saw, then added a second on top.

"Just think about it, okay? You want to get settled first, fine. Just don't say no yet."

He agreed to get Kyle off his back, even though there was no way he was changing his mind.

Jim had left basketball behind long ago, but it sure seemed like Silent Creek hadn't.

Chapter Two

Kyle and Carrie's backyard was massive. A bountiful vegetable garden stretched all along its width. Multicolored flower beds surrounded the house and the fences along the property line.

Jim tried to stand off to the side, clutching a Styrofoam plate with a burger that was somehow both charred and undercooked, offering a hopefully-not-forced smile to everyone Kyle invited over.

It reminded him of those alumni-club dinners he'd had to do back at the University of Minnesota. Some hotel ballroom full of fat donors who went to the U thirty years ago, still dressed in maroon and gold, and based way too much of their identity on a game played by nineteen-year-old kids. But you had to be polite. Grin and bear it because you never knew if the old guy in front of you was thinking of cutting a million-dollar check to help build a new weight room. Because, when it came down to it, you were nothing more than a show pony to them. You'd smile for the picture they would plaster up on the walls of their dentist office or law firm.

Jim wondered how many walls he still adorned or if his unmet expectations had banished him in favor of younger players who hadn't committed the sin of suffering debilitating knee injuries.

"Jimmy B.!"

Kyle hollered from halfway across the yard, beer in one hand and the other around the shoulder of another guy Jim didn't recognize. He'd already tap-danced around a few people who he couldn't initially place, but he was relatively sure this was an actual introduction. The guy's salt-and-pepper hair looked premature. Jim figured he wasn't too much older than he was. Definitely in the window where he'd at least look familiar if they'd met before.

Kyle clapped the guy on his shoulder and pointed his beer at Jim.

"Marc Langmore, lemme introduce my ole high school buddy."

"The man, the myth, the legend." Marc extended his hand, and Jim swallowed hard before swapping his plate over to his left and shaking hands.

"Jim McCann." Not Jimmy Buckets and certainly not Jimmy B. "Nice to meet you."

"Marc's the principal over at SCHS," Kyle said.

"Nice." Jim only said that because he didn't know what else to say. George Wilbur had been the principal at Silent Creek back when Jim and Kyle were in school and had served for twenty-five years before that. Jim had assumed he was still there because nothing ever changed in this town. In comparison, Marc looked a little young to be a principal, but maybe that smattering of gray wasn't as premature as he'd assumed. "How long have you been there?"

"This is my sixth year," Marc said.

"Marc's the guy who hired me to coach, even though I'm not a teacher," Kyle said.

Jim fought hard to keep his face neutral. Kyle had brought up his offer pretty much every time they'd spoken since the day he'd moved in, and Jim was running out of ways to politely decline.

"I asked him about you being my assistant, and they're cool with it." Kyle took a swig of his beer. Budweiser, not Bud Light like they used to drink in high school. Probably why his stomach was starting to peek out over his belt.

"We usually offer the position to faculty first—it can make some things easier—but there's no hard-and-fast rule about it. Anyone can be considered," Marc said. "And, given your qualifications and history with the team, I'm pretty sure the town would be ecstatic to have you back in the gym."

Jim was stammering his way toward an excuse when Carrie called out for Kyle from their patio door.

"Ugh," Kyle said, then made some weird motion like he was pressing pause on the conversation. "I'll be right back."

Marc stayed while Kyle retreated to find more buns or ketchup or whatever, and Jim figured he should rip the Band-Aid off while he could.

"I'm not going to be able to help out with the team this year. I'm taking my dad's spot over at McCann, and if I'm honest, I've got no clue what I'm doing. And then there's my mom . . ." Jim looked at Marc and realized he was starting to spill his guts out to a man he'd just met.

"I understand." His voice was sincere, but Jim could see the disappointment in his eyes. "Life can get really busy, especially when you're dealing with major overhauls. My condolences on your father, by the way. I can't say I knew him, but certainly knew of him. Sounded like a good man."

Marc Langmore definitely didn't know him if that's what he thought. Then again, it's what you say to be polite, so Jim let it pass.

"Thanks."

Silence hung between them without Kyle's beer-fueled enthusiasm there to steer the boat.

"So, you're taking over the business?"

"Yeah," Jim said. "We'll see how it goes. I was in medical sales out in Boston. All I had to do was show up and tell the doctors about the newest version of the equipment they were already using, but running things? I took a few business classes at the U, but honestly, I'm not sure how qualified I am to do this. Dad always wanted me to come back and work for him, but . . ."

"Sometimes it isn't the right fit."

Jim looked down at him. "Exactly." Even if it wouldn't change a thing, it was nice to hear what was going through his head from someone else. "But now that he's gone, my mom needs someone around." He wasn't sure how widely known his mother's condition was—hell, *he* hadn't had a clue until he came back for the funeral.

He wasn't sure how much he should be sharing. "She's got some health issues, so I've got to be around for that. There's no way I'd be able to commit to practices, games . . ."

Marc held up his hands with a polite smile. "Say no more."

"Thanks." Jim didn't know why he was offering excuses, because he didn't need to justify his decision to anyone. Even if he had the time, he had no desire to get back in that gym. He'd given this town everything he had for four years, and he didn't owe anyone a damn thing.

They stood silently long enough for Jim to take a bite of his forgotten burger. He looked around the yard and noticed at least three sets of eyeballs on him. Some familiar, some not, all making him feel like he was floating around in a fishbowl.

"I was at that game your freshman year when you dropped twenty-seven on Michigan State."

It felt like a betrayal, which was weird because they didn't know each other and all the man was doing was giving Jim a compliment.

"Oh yeah? That was a fun one." Jim had used some version of that response at least a hundred times in his life, but hadn't dusted it off in a while. Out East, where only the college-basketball die hards and Minnesota transplants remembered his once-promising, injury-derailed career, he could be himself, not some character from the past.

It had been nice.

"Man, you guys were good that year," Marc said. His gaze wandered, as if he were watching a replay in his head. "Too bad."

Anger swept through Jim as fast as the pain had when he'd landed awkwardly against Ohio State two weeks after the game Marc so fondly remembered. The guy wasn't concerned with the torn ACL and MCL that required a full reconstruction. He didn't consider the sleepless nights when the painkillers weren't strong enough, or how hard it was trying to get to class on crutches in the middle of winter.

No, Marc was lamenting the fact that he hadn't gotten to watch his favorite team roll into the NCAA tournament that year.

Sorry about your knee, but I was really looking forward to watching that.

"What was Coach Cellucci really like? Us fans see him on the bench and in press conferences and stuff, but . . . is he always that intense? Like in practice and the locker room?"

Jim took a deep breath and scanned the yard for any sort of rescue. Kyle was nowhere to be seen, and he didn't know anyone else.

"Yeah, Coach was pretty passionate."

"I'll say," Langmore said with a laugh. "I used to love it when he'd get all riled up working the refs."

It wasn't only the refs who were the targets of his wrath. Jim flashed back to the time he'd found himself out of position on defense during one of his first practices and Coach stopped everything to deliver the most impressive string of expletives he'd ever heard. It was the first time he'd thought maybe he was just a small-town kid, completely out of his depth at the Big Ten level. He'd wanted to go home then but knew if he did, it would be the same thing from his father. Maybe not as red faced as what Coach Cellucci was delivering, but the message would be the same.

Disappointment.

As Langmore droned on about his old college coach, Jim stuffed the rest of his underwhelming burger in his mouth so he could use his empty plate as an excuse to escape at the first chance he got. As if on cue, his left knee barked at him on the first step. A constant reminder, like the surgeons had placed a little shard of glass in there during one of his three surgeries.

He tossed his plate in the garbage and looked down the table. He wasn't hungry, but if he'd used food as an excuse to abandon Marc, he should probably grab something else. Two others—somewhat familiar but he didn't remember their names—were picking their way along the spread. He gave them a polite nod.

Jim pulled a grocery store chocolate chip cookie from a plastic tray and headed for the open cooler at the end of the table.

He needed a beer.

A case worth of Budweiser was tucked into the ice, and Jim eventually settled for one when his hand got too cold digging for something better. He stood up and almost bumped into a woman reaching down for a beer of her own.

"Ope, sorry." Barely a week in Minnesota and his accent was already creeping back.

She rooted past the Bud Heavy, elbow deep in ice, as Jim watched. He didn't recognize her, and something about her didn't look like Silent Creek anyway. Brown hair pulled back into a ponytail, yet somehow more modern than it should be, and her tan skin hinted at a background beyond a ten-square-mile tract of land in Norway.

Jim could see goose bumps creeping up her biceps as she continued probing through the ice.

"There's only Budweiser in there," he said, seconds before she pulled a Wild Berry Truly from the depths of the cooler. She popped the top and raised an eyebrow as she took a drink.

"You've gotta be persistent," the woman said.

He shifted his beer to his left hand and extended his right. "Jim McCann."

"Kelli Alexander." Her hand was still cold from the ice.

"It's nice to meet you, Kelli." He wanted to say more, something clever, but his brain wasn't ready to go beyond the same boring conversations he'd had since moving back, so the silence hung.

Awkwardly.

Jim figured he had about five seconds before she took her hard seltzer and walked away. He couldn't let that happen.

"So . . . how'd you end up here?" She side-eyed him, and Jim felt the embarrassment of his stupid question bloom on the back of his neck and clog up his speech. She was tall—nowhere near his own six-foot-nine frame, but she didn't have to crane her neck to look up at him. "I mean, how do you know Kyle and Carrie?"

"I work with Carrie," Kelli said.

"Oh yeah? You a teacher, or . . ."

"Elementary art."

"Nice." Jim needed something beyond banal small talk to grab her interest, but his conversation skills had atrophied. Since he'd moved back, he hadn't said much beyond *Thank you for your condolences* or *Yeah, I remember that game too.* But here was this person who didn't have a clue who he was, a person willing to have a conversation that didn't revolve around funerals or 2008 high school basketball, and his verbal well was dry.

"I just moved to town," Jim said. "Well, back to town, I guess. I grew up here."

"Yo, J. B.!" Kyle's voice was as loud as the first time he'd beckoned to him from across the yard, and the abbreviated nickname was somehow more annoying. Jim wanted to ignore it, but Kelli had heard it too.

"J. B.?" Her eyebrow cocked enough to show she knew there was a story behind those letters, and most likely one that bothered him.

"It's nothing, just—"

"Jimmy!" Kyle pressed. "C'mere for a sec."

He didn't have time to come up with an excuse; Kelli nodded and walked away. She found Carrie at the end of the barbecue buffet and helped restock the plastic utensils.

Kyle was still waving him over, so Jim shuffled across the grass to be part of his friend's look-who-I-know show-and-tell.

He immediately forgot the guy's name but told all the stories Kyle wanted him to. Kelli disappeared into the house with Carrie, but Jim noticed when she came back carrying two packages of hot dog buns.

After putting in what he considered an appropriate amount of time, he used his empty beer can as an excuse to peel off from Kyle and whoever he'd wanted to impress.

Kelli had wandered to the far side of the lawn by the flower beds and was talking to the principal Kyle had introduced him to earlier. The wheels in his head spun for a bit before they clicked.

Langmore.

Jim bypassed the cooler and headed over.

"Hey, Jimmy," Principal Langmore said.

Time to nip this in the bud.

"Actually, I usually go by Jim."

"Oh . . . sorry, Jim."

"I thought it was J. B.?" Kelli's voice had some taunt in it. Nothing mean, but a hint of an edge.

Jim rolled his eyes. Exaggerating, but still playful. He hoped it had come off like that, anyway. "An old nickname. Hard to shake, I guess."

"You know, you two probably have a lot in common," Principal Langmore said. "Kelli here was a ballplayer too. She's coaching the girls' team this year."

That explained her height. Jim smiled and realized it was the first time basketball had been mentioned and he hadn't cringed. "Oh yeah?"

"It's my first year, so we'll see how it goes," Kelli said.

"We've got some good kids, so we're excited to have her on board," Langmore said.

Jim tried to ignore him without looking rude. "Did you play in college?"

"Just DII." There was no shame in her voice, even as she downplayed her experience. "Four years at Concordia."

Before he could respond, a loud buzz popped up behind his ear and Jim jumped, afraid he was about to get stung by a bee. Kelli laughed as a hummingbird darted back to the flower bed by the fence.

Jim felt the embarrassment fade away as they watched the tiny bird work its way down a cluster of pink flowers.

"Carrie's gardens are pretty impressive," Jim said. "I mean, I don't know anything about plants, but they look good."

Kelli smiled. "I want to get some of that foxglove at my place and see if I can attract some hummingbirds."

"Hummingbirds like foxglove?" Jim said. "Isn't it poisonous?"

"I thought you didn't know anything about plants?"

"It's the plant the Rake uses to kill the first kid in that Decemberists song on *Hazards of Love*." It took Jim a second to realize talking about indie folk songs revolving around child murder may not make the impression he was hoping for. "I mean . . . it's not just about . . . it's this whole indie rock-opera thing about a woman who falls in love with a guy who can change into a deer, and . . . you know what, please forget I said any of that."

"No, please go on." Jim could see the laughter she was barely holding back. "Tell me about the child-murdering, deer opera song."

Her playful tone helped dissipate some of the humiliation. "It's actually a great album. You'd like it."

"I'm sure."

"No, really. I saw them earlier this year at the Orpheum back in Boston. Fantastic show. If they ever come around . . ." Jim remembered he was in Silent Creek, where the biggest music event was a cover band who played Lynyrd Skynyrd at the Fourth of July Fest. "Maybe up in Minneapolis or something."

They kept talking for a while. At some point, Langmore realized he was a third wheel and excused himself.

Jim and Kelli barely noticed. They spent the next few hours talking about anything and everything next to the flowers, Jim invested in a conversation for the first time since he'd come back to Silent Creek.

Kelli had grown up on the Iron Range, where girls were more likely to be found on the ice than in the gym. But Kelli grew up shooting threes and earned a scholarship. After some persistent digging, Jim got her to admit she'd left as the school's all-time leader in three-pointers made.

They kept going until the backyard was empty, then helped Kyle and Carrie clean up.

When all the food was wrapped up and the tables were back in the garage, Jim still wanted to talk, but didn't want to push it. Besides, his mom had been home alone all afternoon, and he should probably check on her.

He helped Kyle carry a load of chairs down into the basement. When they came back up, Kelli was gone. Jim hadn't gotten her contact information. He was bummed, but not despondent.

In a town that small, he'd have no trouble finding her again.

Chapter Three

Two weeks later, Jim sat behind his father's old desk, Kyle in the chair across from him, well into their second hour of "orientation."

But he wasn't listening.

He was staring at himself.

The far wall was covered in pictures of Jim, and it had legitimately thrown him when he'd first come in. There was their Silent Creek High School team picture from his senior year. A picture of him dunking against Albert Lea, recognizable because the local paper used it any chance they could—his dad must have bought a copy from them. There was a picture of him sitting at a press table next to his parents, signing his National Letter of Intent with a brand-new maroon-and-gold hat crooked on his head, and a shot of Jim and his mother on Parents' Day.

The wall was a monument to his former glory, and it was unnerving. Not that it was strange for a parent to have pictures of their kid up in the workplace, but Jim had barely spoken with his father since his basketball career had crashed and burned. His dad had acted like his injury wasn't a tragic accident, but a failure of character. As if hard work and gumption could've overcome shredded ligaments if he'd simply wanted it enough. Like it was some sort of act of rebellion against a father who had pushed his son hard from day one.

Jim would take them all down before he went home that night.

"So other than that, there isn't too much pressing that you need to do right now." Kyle was still talking, so Jim tried to feign interest.

"That's good then. It sounds like you've got things pretty well under control."

"You're in good hands, my friend. To be honest, I've been running this thing for years." Kyle chuckled to himself. "When I started, I don't even think your dad had contracts or anything. *A handshake's all I need.* It took a while, but eventually he trusted me enough to organize our financials a little better. Honestly, the last few years I think he was just happy he didn't have to worry about it."

That's exactly what Jim had hoped to hear. He still had no idea what his long-term plans were, so ideally he'd be able to float along until he got that figured out.

Much of that depended on his mother. He'd originally hoped to get her in an assisted living facility, but none of the places he'd contacted were keen on bringing someone in with encroaching dementia. The last place suggested he start looking for a memory-care unit. He wasn't ready to go that route and didn't dare mention it to his mother anyway. She probably didn't need that level of care.

Yet.

In the meantime, he was stuck in Silent Creek, trying to fill his dad's shoes at McCann LP the best he could.

"There are a few things I need you to sign off on, though." Kyle reached into a folder and pushed a small stack of papers across the desk.

Jim stared at the lines that said *owner* below them.

"Yeah . . . okay. Can't you do it? I mean, it feels weird, you know? First day."

Kyle smirked across the desk. "You're the boss man, my friend. I may do all the work, but it's your name that's gotta go on the checks."

Jim scrawled his name across the bottom of the page, then stopped as he pushed it back. "Shit. Um . . . do you have another?"

"What? Why?"

Jim had signed his name so many times in his life it was second nature, but like a lot of athletes, he had a distinct and separate way of signing official documents.

He'd just autographed their supply order.

Kyle laughed when Jim explained. "The distributor doesn't give a shit, man. Hell, dude will probably frame it."

Embarrassment heated the back of Jim's neck as Kyle stuffed the forms back into a folder.

"There's one other thing you need to sign off on," Kyle said. "We've got to let somebody go."

"You mean fire someone? Jesus Christ, it's my first day, and you want me to fire somebody?"

Kyle disregarded Jim's concern. "It's not a big deal. I've got everything put together. You just need to sign the final paperwork."

Jim slumped back into his chair and pushed away from the desk. "Yeah, but I literally just got here. How's that going to look?"

"Like you're the boss doing your job? Your dad made the decision a while back, but these things take time to get ducks in a row and before we could get things finalized . . ." Kyle trailed off and left the reason unsaid. "Anyway, I've got all that taken care of. All you need to do is sign off on it."

Kyle pushed another piece of paper across the desk. Jim looked down, and the name Colton Reid jumped out before he read anything else.

"You're kidding me."

"You remember him."

"Yeah, I didn't realize he worked here."

"We were really short a while back, so your dad hired him to drive a truck." There was a hint of history in Kyle's voice. Considering what things had been like in high school, Jim honestly expected more. "He figured he wouldn't have to interact with anyone, but that didn't change the fact that he's still got a . . . challenging personality."

Jim looked back at his friend for an explanation, but there wasn't one. Kyle's feelings about Colton Reid had always been well known and obviously hadn't changed over the years.

"Okay, so why are we getting rid of him? Did he do something?"

Kyle wore an oddly confused look. "Don't worry about it."

The pen felt heavy in Jim's hand.

"I'm going to fire a guy, I need to know why."

Kyle took a slightly impatient breath before speaking. As bored as Jim had been listening to him explain the ins and outs of the business, Kyle was probably equally frustrated having to hold his hand all day. "Honestly, it was a mistake to hire him in the first place, and your dad realized that pretty early on. But—like I said—we had to make sure we had all the proper documentation and everything, so it took a while. Trust me, it's all there."

"Okay, but what—"

"It's all the same stuff the guy's been doing his whole life. You of all people should understand this. We were desperate for people, so we took a chance and brought him on. It didn't work, and we're no longer desperate, so we're rectifying the mistake. Your dad was gonna do this weeks ago, but obviously that couldn't happen, and we can't let it drag out any longer. If you're gonna be the boss, you gotta do the dirty work sometimes."

Jim stared down at the paperwork in front of him. It felt weird to have that much power over someone else's life, butKyle was right. Like it or not, that's the boss's job.

He scrawled his business signature across the line and pushed it back across the desk. "Do I have to call him or anything?"

Kyle stood and scooped up the papers, along with the weight that had settled over Jim's desk. "Like I said, I'll take care of it. Don't worry."

Jim thanked him, secretly glad he wouldn't have to do it. With their shared history, it would certainly be awkward. But while he'd been gone, Kyle and Colton had been living in the same town for years and presumably interacted enough that whatever stupid high school grudges once existed were long gone. Besides, Kyle had experience in this type of stuff.

Better to let him handle it professionally.

"So, Friday night . . ." Kyle said. "You in?"

He and Carrie had invited him over for dinner, but Jim had been noncommittal so far. With all the chaos bouncing around between moving back home, getting thrust in front of the family business, and figuring out what to do with his mom, Jim wasn't sure he needed another night at Kyle's.

"Yeah, thanks . . . we'll see."

Kyle waved him off. "Come on. I'll grill up some steaks while it's still warm enough to be outside."

"I don't know," Jim said. "I'm still trying to get settled in, you know? Between all this and Mom . . ."

"It'll be fun." Kyle's expression showed no sign that he comprehended or accepted Jim's polite decline. He held up the paperwork terminating Colton Reid's employment with McCann LP. "And I'll handle this, don't worry."

Jim watched him leave the office, and his eyes caught on the team picture on the wall behind him. *2008 South Minnesota Conference Champions* emblazoned across the bottom. He stood in the middle of the back row, a goofy teenage look on his face while Kyle stood next to him beaming a five-hundred-watt smile.

A redheaded kid stood at the far end of the row. Not as tall as Jim, but towering over the rest of the team. There was no smile on the kid's face, and he seemed to stare through time and across the office at Jim.

As if he knew he was going to be fired that day.

Chapter Four

"Get some eggs."

The refrigerated air reached out from the shelves and brushed Jim's arms as he pushed the metal cart. His mom walked in front, the grand marshal of the grocery store, pointing out items for her son to grab.

Thing was, they already had eggs. An entire carton in the fridge back home. Jim had seen them that morning.

He reached over and plucked a carton off the shelf. It was easier to just do it. They'd keep.

Jim continued after his mom, loading up their cart with whatever she asked for. He struggled with how much to correct her when she got confused. Sometimes she said thanks and carried on like it was no big deal. Sometimes she snapped back like he'd personally insulted her.

Depended on the day.

He—they—really needed to talk to someone. A doctor would be able to figure out what was going on inside his mother's head and tell him how to handle it. There may even be some things they could do—therapy, medications—to slow her descent. He'd spent a lot of time on the internet looking at options, but Dr. Google wasn't a substitute for a real live MD.

"What kind of milk do you usually get?" Jim asked.

Gail looked back at him like he'd asked her for the capital of Guatemala. "Just regular milk."

He opened his mouth to ask again, then reached over for a gallon of 1 percent.

Jim needed to make an appointment with someone, but when it came down to it, he was afraid. About not only what the doctor would say, but how he would talk to his mother about it.

How do you tell someone you think they are losing their marbles?

They pressed through the refrigerated aisle and turned back to the bread. A hulk of a man stood down by the English muffins.

It took Jim a second to realize who it was, and by the time he did, his mom was wandering down the aisle toward Colton Reid.

"*Mom.*" His voice was a hiss that seemed to bounce off every variety of bread on the shelves. She looked back at him, face slapped with annoyance, and kept going.

Jim slipped around the cart and headed after her, hurrying but doing whatever he could to keep his six-foot-nine frame incognito. Luckily something caught her eye, and she stopped.

Raisin bread. He'd never seen anything other than Country Hearth Cracked Wheat in his parents' bread drawer, but Gail studied the loaf in front of her like she was about to make a major life change.

Jim sidled up to her and couldn't help but glance down at Colton. His frame hadn't changed, only it carried a lot more weight than it had back in high school. He could tell there was still muscle underneath, though, the same way he knew a pointy chin lived under that bushy beard.

Fortunately, Colton hadn't noticed them. Not that Jim was afraid or anything; he just didn't want to deal with the baggage that came with such a conversation. It felt like he was trying to cross a river on new, untested ice. He spotted the cracked wheat and grabbed a loaf.

"Got it." His voice was quiet, but he hoped normal. "Can we head back this way? I forgot to get something."

"What?" Her voice boomed down the aisle. Jim couldn't help but glance past her, where Colton's sunken eyes pulled him in like honeybees to an abandoned soda can.

Or, if he were going for accuracy, hornets.

"Um . . ."

Gail followed her son's gaze and turned down the aisle. "Who's that?"

Jim didn't have time to come up with an answer before Colton sauntered down the aisle toward them.

"It's nobody," he mumbled.

"Now that's no way to talk about an old friend." Colton's smile was wide enough under his scraggly beard they could see the spot where his incisor was supposed to be.

Jim didn't want to say anything, but he could see his mom trying to place Colton, unsure if she should know him or not, and it felt cruel to let her spin her wheels that way. "Yeah, sorry. Mom, this is Colton Reid."

The name didn't appear to register with her, which didn't necessarily mean anything. The only way she'd know him was through basketball, and he'd only been on the team a few weeks.

"I played basketball with your boy here." His voice dripped with sugar but still left a bitter taste in Jim's mouth.

"Back in high school." Jim's mention of his school days brought the tug of a smile to her mouth. "Colton was on the team for a bit during my senior year."

"That's right." Colton slowly shifted his gaze from Gail up to Jim. "Just a little bit."

The man's eyes were intrusive, as if they drilled right through the lock on Jim's thoughts and laid them bare to the world, and it took Jim a second to shake the feeling. "Mom, why don't you keep going, and I'll catch up in a sec? I need to talk to Colton real quick."

Jim waited until his mom was down the aisle before turning back to Colton.

Colton held hard eye contact, and Jim thought he smelled something on his breath.

"So, Colton . . . How you doing?" It was a default question born out of upper-Midwestern politeness and the fact that Jim didn't have a clue what else to say.

Colton's grin widened, and his eyebrows arched in incredulity.

"Yeah, sorry," Jim said. "I know how that probably sounds coming from me."

The silence between them agreed.

"You know how it is. As much as you'd like to keep everyone, sometimes the numbers are the numbers and you've got to make tough decisions. Honestly, it wasn't even my decision. This was in the works before I even got here. But then Dad had his heart attack and . . ." Jim didn't like the way he sounded, and Colton clearly didn't like what he'd said.

"At least take credit for it." He wasn't speaking loudly, but his voice filled the entire aisle. "Pawning it off on your dead dad? That's a bad look."

"I'm telling you, I—" Jim felt himself floundering, and it pissed him off. Colton was right about one thing. Jim was the boss at McCann, and it was time to start acting like it. "I'm sorry, but these things happen."

Colton took a step closer, and Jim had to fight the urge to retreat.

"Well now, they don't seem to happen to *everybody*, do they? Funny how that works, isn't it?" Colton winked at him, but there was nothing playful about it. He held eye contact for another few seconds, like he was daring Jim to say something, before turning back down the aisle.

Jim shifted, and his three-time surgically repaired knee twinged, as if trying to prove that things did indeed happen to Jim McCann. He shifted his weight to the other side as the movie of the life he should have had flashed across his thoughts.

He wanted to let Colton go, hope things would cool down with time, but figured it was best to get it out here and let whatever wound Colton felt between them scab over. "If you've got something you want to say to me, now's your chance. I'm right here, and I'm listening. But let's work it out so we can both move on. I'm not looking for any trouble here."

Colton stopped and slowly turned back with a grin widened well past the black hole where his incisor should have been. It pulled at Jim, held him, unwilling to let him break free.

"Well, that's too bad, because you don't always gotta go looking for trouble, Jimmy. Sometimes trouble finds you."

Chapter Five

Jim pulled into the driveway of his parents' house and parked on the left side. He sat behind the wheel, staring at the garage door in front of him. His father's Ford F-150 truck was still sitting in there, another thing Jim had to figure out how to deal with. He should sell it but didn't know how to broach the subject with his mom. Unfortunately, winter was coming, and he wasn't excited about leaving his own car outside every night so a monument to his father could sit in the relative warmth of the garage.

He dropped back into the headrest and let out a heavy sigh. Jim allowed himself to fret in silence for a moment before flushing it away and concentrating on the one positive that had come from that day.

He had a date to prep for.

Despite his earlier predictions, it had been harder to find Kelli's number than he'd expected.

The logical move would have been to ask Carrie. She worked with her at the school, and they were obviously friendly enough that she'd invited Kelli to the cookout, but it felt weird asking his old girlfriend for another woman's number. It was stupid and juvenile—they'd broken up years ago, and she'd moved on and gotten married—but he still couldn't shake the awkwardness.

He could have asked Kyle but didn't want to put up with the relentless teasing that would bring.

Without those two, his only option would've been lurking outside the school like a creep in the hopes of bumping into her, so he was thrilled when he pulled in to fill up on the way home from work and saw Kelli filling her Subaru Outback on the other side of the pump. She looked happy enough to see him again that he forgot about begging off dinner at Kyle and Carrie's and asked if she wanted to get together that night.

She waited just long enough to make him squirm before accepting.

Jim smiled to himself, popped out of his car, and headed inside.

The smells coming from his mother's kitchen hit Jim with a wave of nostalgia as he walked through the door. It was a strange combination of cocktail wienies, ham salad, and store-bought ice that kids around the Midwest knew meant one thing.

Bridge club.

His mom and her friend Helen Anderson bustled between Crock-Pots with the grace of longtime synchronized swimmers. Helen noticed Jim as she dug through a cabinet for the pitcher that had held water at every function in that house the last forty years.

"Oh hello, Jimmy."

"Hey, Mrs. Anderson."

She waved away his ingrained formality. "You're grown now, Jimmy. You can call me Helen."

He thought about telling her the same thing about calling him Jimmy but instead forced a chuckle and reached over to pluck a pickle off his mother's ancient crystal relish tray. "Old habits die hard, I guess."

He looked over at the kitchen table, where his mom was busying herself with baskets of crackers and stacks of paper plates. She hadn't acknowledged his arrival, but in fairness she'd always had a laser focus when in hostess mode.

"Expecting company tonight?"

Gail didn't answer.

"The girls are coming to play bridge," Helen said. "I figured I would come over and help your mom set up."

"Thank you for that," Jim said. "It's nice to know Mom has some help."

Helen patted his arm and turned back to the table to help sort plastic utensils.

"Did you want something to eat, James?" The only time Gail used his full name was when he was in trouble as a kid. His dad had held title on that name. Jim chose to ignore it and noticed Helen ignoring it too.

"No, Mom, I'm actually heading out to meet someone."

His mom didn't react, but he saw Helen's ears perk up.

Jim hustled out of the kitchen before he had to answer any questions.

The only clothes Jim had unpacked were work clothes and shorts to wear around the house, so he started peeling the tape off cardboard boxes in hopes of finding something decent to wear. A juvenile excitement ate at his stomach as he did, and it made him chuckle.

He spent too much time looking for a black merino polo, then threw it on top of the first pair of jeans he found and headed back into the kitchen. There were a dozen places back in Boston Jim would have loved to take Kelli on their first date, but options in Silent Creek were few and good options were nonexistent. Eventually they'd agreed to meet at the North Star around seven.

The fact that his mom was having friends over for cards relieved any guilt he had about going out.

He stood in the doorway for a minute before saying goodbye, watching Helen and his mother lay out the spread in the same way it had been done every other time they had company. Jim wondered how much her friends knew about his mom's condition. More than he did, most likely. Her friends had probably been picking up on signs for years, helping out where they could without ever saying anything. To her or his dad, anyway. There were certainly whispers behind closed doors.

It was the Minnesota way.

The fact that Helen had come early to help told him all he needed to know. His mom had set out a spread for card club so many times she could probably do it in her sleep, and Helen knew that. Yet she'd come anyway. To help, sure, but more likely to keep an eye on her. Make sure nothing bad happened.

Also the Minnesota way.

Jim thanked Helen and snatched another pickle from the relish tray before giving his mom a kiss and heading out.

The burgers at the North Star tasted the exact same, and a familiar mist of grease and cheap beer hung in the air. As much as he'd dreaded taking Kelli to a small-town dive bar, Jim quickly realized location didn't matter. They had been there for over an hour already, and the Friday-night crowd was slowly getting louder. The cracked vinyl bench creaked as he leaned forward on his elbows.

He didn't want to miss a word of what Kelli was saying.

They'd picked up right where they'd left off in Kyle and Carrie's backyard, and it was once again a welcome respite to the crush of emotions and frustration that had battered him since he moved back.

They talked basketball some, but it wasn't reminiscing about big wins or tournament runs. They swapped stories from road trips, locker room pranks, and behind-the-scenes things that only a fellow player would understand. Jim was a little self-conscious about the level of luxury he'd traveled in at the Division I level, compared to the cramped van rides that Kelli had endured at Concordia, but she had a lot of fond memories of midnight gas stations and entire position groups piling into a single hotel room.

But mostly, Kelli told stories about growing up on the Iron Range with her three sisters, while Jim told tales from the school where she now taught art.

He was halfway through a story before he realized he'd added more information than he'd intended.

"Hold on." A look of shock crept across Kelli's face. The small scar that popped up from the top of her lip got a little whiter as her jaw dropped. "You and Carrie dated in high school?"

Jim felt the red invade his face as her words evaporated into the small-town-bar air. He hadn't specifically hidden it from her; he just hadn't brought it up. Everyone else in town knew anyway, so it wasn't something he was used to telling anyone.

"Um . . ."

Kelli threw back her head and cackled. "No way! That is *hilarious*."

Her reaction diffused the tension that had built at the back of Jim's neck. He leaned into the booth and ran his hand through his light-brown hair.

"Yeah, well . . . that was a long time ago."

"So your high school girlfriend went out and married your high school best friend." Kelli picked up her glass and drained the last inch that had been sitting there for a while. "Was that weird?"

Jim reached down and took a sip from his own glass. "Not really. I guess they started dating when Kyle moved back after freshman year."

"Wait . . . what do you mean, moved back?"

"He started at Minnesota with me," Jim said. "Well, not *with* me, you know, but at the same time. I think he thought we'd be able to room together and everything, but Coach always had the freshmen live together in the dorms so the older guys could show us the ropes and all that. I felt bad, but you know how little time you get outside of team stuff. I guess he never really found his own thing there and left after the first year. Came back here and commuted to Riverland Community College, then finished up at Mankato State."

"And started dating your old girlfriend, apparently," Kelli said.

"Yeah, I guess. I didn't even know they were together until my mom told me they were getting married."

Something caught Kelli's eye behind him, and she waved. "Speak of the devil."

Jim turned back to the front door and saw Kyle and Carrie walk in. It took a second, but Kyle noticed them and made a beeline to the booth. Jim cringed at the smirk his friend wore as he sauntered up to them.

"So much for going to bed early tonight, eh?"

The heat of embarrassment climbed up Jim's neck again, and Kelli gave him a side-eye across the table. "What do you mean?"

Kyle nudged Jim over and plopped down beside him while Carrie slid in next to Kelli.

"We invited Jimmy Buckets here over for dinner, but he said he was worn out from the week and begged off." Kyle shifted his gaze between Jim and Kelli about three times. "Looks like he had better plans."

Kyle—and Kelli—were obviously enjoying the embarrassment that was radiating off Jim, while Carrie seemed more uncomfortable.

"I *was* planning on that, but—"

"I saw him at the gas station on my way home from school and dragged him out," Kelli said.

"Mom is hosting card club," Jim said. "So I figured it was better to get out of the way."

"Your mom still make that taco dip?" Kyle asked. "Man, I could eat that stuff all night."

Jim resigned himself to the fact that even though she was still across the booth from him, his night with Kelli Alexander was effectively over. She must have realized it, too, but snuck a reassuring wink at him as Kyle started telling another story from their high school days.

"Speaking of high school," Kelli said, shifting the focus to Carrie. "What color did you wear?"

Carrie's eyebrows crinkled in the same way Jim remembered from when they'd studied together. "What do you mean?"

"When you and Jim went to *PROM*!" Kelli hit the last word hard enough that it let loose a torrent of laughter from her.

"Oh God." Carrie dropped her face into her hands.

"Was it hot pink? Were there ruffles? There were, weren't there." Kelli looked across the table and grabbed Jim's hand, which threw him for a loop. "Did you wear a matching tie and cummerbund? Are there pictures? Tell me there are pictures."

Kyle let out a laugh. "I'm gonna go get some beers." He squeezed out of the booth and swayed just enough to show it wouldn't be his first of the night. Jim tried to offer him some money, but he'd already weaved his way into the rapidly growing crowd.

"How did you know?" Carrie asked.

Kelli nodded across the table. "He let it slip telling old high school stories."

Carrie looked a little embarrassed, but nothing terrible, which helped keep the awkwardness down. "Yeah, that was a while ago."

Kelli kept asking questions, mostly digging for embarrassing stories. Jim, for his part, kept quiet and his head down.

He'd said enough.

Eventually Kyle emerged from the crowd and dropped four bottles of Miller Lite in the middle of the table. The impact forced an eruption of foam from the one closest to Jim, so he snatched it up and made sure it went in his mouth as opposed to on the table.

"Take a look at who's at the bar." Kyle slid into the booth beside Jim and jerked his head back the way he'd come.

Jim craned his neck to see through the bodies that filled the North Star, and eventually a group split enough that he could see Colton Reid sitting on a stool at the end of the bar. He quick pulled his attention back to the booth, afraid to get caught looking.

"Did he see you? Say anything?"

Kyle shook his head as Kelli looked back over her shoulder. "Who?"

"Colton Reid." Kyle practically spat his name on the table.

"He worked at McCann," Jim said. "But we had to let him go this week."

Kelli gave an awkward grimace. "Yikes. Why did you fire him?"

Jim opened his mouth to respond but realized he still didn't know, so he looked over at Kyle.

"Guy's a psycho." From the tone of his voice, it appeared Kyle had had enough beer to turn off his filter. "Always has been."

"What did he do?"

Kyle took a long pull from his beer and nodded at his wife. "You remember him, right?" He pointed his bottle across the booth at Kelli. "Tell her."

Carrie gave an awkward pause before speaking. "He's always had problems." Her husband snorted from across the table, but she ignored it. "He was in and out of school a lot—suspended, expelled, whatever. His dad was . . . I'll just say he didn't have a very stable homelife."

"Sounds sad," Kelli said.

"Sure, but it's not like he was some choirboy. He's been arrested for assault *multiple* times. Literally fresh out of prison when your dad hired him."

That didn't sound like something his father would do, but the last thing Jim wanted was to bring his dad into this conversation, so he said nothing.

"If he's so bad, why did you hire him at McCann?" Jim could tell Kelli wasn't impressed with Kyle's lack of empathy, but she did a decent job hiding it.

Kyle drained the rest of his beer and gestured with the bottle as he talked. "*I* didn't hire him. In fact, I said it was a bad idea, but . . ." He shrugged and rolled his eyes like nobody ever listened to him. "And it was obvious from the first day that it *was* a mistake, but . . . the mistake has been rectified."

Kelli looked over at Jim, eyes asking for an explanation he couldn't give. "Well, hopefully he'll get another shot somewhere else and everything will work out."

"Guys like that get so many chances, but every time they throw them away." Kyle elbowed Jim and pointed his empty beer across the table. "Perfect example . . . senior season. We were 5–0—*cruising*—and then somebody decides that Colton Reid's problems come from a lack of structure or belonging or something and he needs to be on the basketball team. Like that was gonna do anything. The guy'd never even played before."

"So how did it go?" Kelli was looking at Jim, but Kyle answered.

"Exactly as expected. He lasted a few weeks, and then they found beer in his truck, and he got kicked off the team." Kyle laughed. "Kid actually had a twelve-pack of Keystone Light in the back of his truck *at practice*. I mean . . . c'mon dude."

"It's too bad," Kelli said. "Sometimes you wonder if guys like that ever had a chance."

"Don't feel sorry for him," Kyle said. "When Coach Frederick told him, he went after him. Completely psycho."

"He attacked the coach?" Kelli looked over at Jim for confirmation, and he nodded. He could still hear the screaming from the office. They all ran in and saw a kid who was absolutely feral. Even with five inches and forty pounds on him, Jim could barely pull Colton away. His muscles felt like braided piano wire under his skin. Jim had never seen anger like that in someone's face.

"It was scary."

"So what happened after that?" Kelli said. "I assume he got suspended from school or something?"

Jim and Kyle exchanged an awkward look as if they were deciding who would tell the story, but it was Carrie who spoke. "Something happened out at his house with his dad. Nobody really knew the details, but they got in some kind of big fight, and the cops had to come out and break it up. His dad was arrested, and Colton ended up in the hospital. Never came back to school after that."

Kelli let the story settle over the table for a beat.

"That's terrible."

Jim glanced over at Kyle, but much to his relief, his friend didn't look like he was going to add anything.

"Yeah, it's too bad," Carrie said. "He certainly created a lot of his own troubles, but I remember him in elementary school being kinda smart. Now that I'm a teacher, I wonder what would've happened to him if he hadn't grown up how he did."

An uneasy silence fell, even with increasing Friday-night noise building in the bar.

"Anyway, that's enough of that." Kyle slid out of the booth and grabbed his empty off the table. "I'm getting another. Anybody need one?"

They all shook their heads, and Kyle turned into the crowd toward the bar. The three of them sat in awkward silence for a minute before Carrie spoke.

"Purple." Kelli looked over at her confused, and it took Jim a second to realize what Carrie was talking about. "Asymmetrical-cut skirt. Ruffles in the back."

Kelli busted out in laughter, and Jim felt the tension that had descended on them lift. Carrie said there were pictures somewhere in her parents' basement and promised to dig them up the next time she was over there. Jim figured there was probably a similar box down in the basement at his mom's house but chose not to volunteer that information.

Jim took a fleeting glance at the bar, hoping his friend hadn't gotten himself into trouble. Luckily, Kyle was waiting for the bartender, and the stool where Colton had been sitting was empty. Not that he thought Kyle would have started anything. Even with a beer too many, he wasn't that stupid. Colton probably had fifty pounds on him and spent his entire life fighting.

Jim thought back to that day in the park, and a chill hit him despite the warmth of the room.

Hopefully it was nothing they'd experience again.

Kelli's hand on his pulled Jim back to the present. "I think I'm going to call it a night."

"Oh . . . okay." Jim slid out of the booth as Kelli reached back for her purse.

As Jim stood there, Kyle came up behind him with four bottles in his hands. "What's going on?"

"We're gonna take off," Jim said.

Kyle was too buzzed to hide his disappointment. "Um . . . okay."

"You can stay if you want," Kelli said.

"No, it's fine . . ." Jim turned back to Kyle as Carrie got up behind them.

"Actually, I'm kind of tired too. Besides, it's really loud in here."

"Aw, come on . . ." Kyle said.

"You two stay and have fun," Kelli said. "I can give Carrie a ride home."

"Nah, that's okay." Jim stood up and nudged Kyle out of the way. "I'll walk you out."

He blazed a trail for Kelli through the Friday-night crowd. When they got to the door, Jim turned back before ducking out and saw Kyle having a quietly animated conversation with Carrie back at their booth.

The night air had a crispness to it he hadn't expected, and the glow of the streetlights seemed to put a haze around them as they headed down the block toward the parking lot.

"That was fun." Jim felt his stomach flip as he spoke, a feeling he hadn't experienced since middle school.

"We'll have to do it again sometime," Kelli said. "It's nice to hang out with someone and not be a third wheel, you know?"

They turned the corner into the parking lot and left most of the light from the street behind. Shadows weaved around the handful of cars back there, including Kyle and Carrie's SUV sitting in the first spot.

Kelli pulled her keys out, and the lights on her Outback flashed next to them. "Anyway, thanks again."

They stood facing each other in the dark of the parking lot, awkwardness descending on them like ash from a first-date volcano.

"So, maybe next week we can do something." As plans went, it was as vague and weak as could be, but considering the giddy fog Jim was pulling it from, it was good enough.

"Yeah, I'd like that."

Kelli stood there for another awkward few seconds, each of them waiting to see if something happened but not daring to initiate. Eventually she said goodbye with a sly smile and got in her car.

Jim stood there, swimming in self-consciousness, and gave one last wave as Kelli pulled out and disappeared down the street.

He relitigated everything he'd said as he got in his own car and followed her out of the parking lot. As soon as he hit the street, the car started to wobble. Before Jim could slow down, the front passenger side of his SUV slammed down to the pavement with a crunch of metal and asphalt. The steering wheel stiffened as his car lurched to the right. He jammed his foot on the brake before running into one of the cars parked along the curb.

Jim looked up and saw his front tire bounce off a white Suburban before spinning out to a stop in the middle of the street.

Chapter Six

Jim's SUV sat cockeyed on the road, right in front of the door to the North Star, where everyone who came in or out got a good look at their hometown hero rolling his right front tire back to his car.

He'd had flats before, but never in his life had the whole tire come off. *How does that happen?*

Jim leaned the tire up against his front bumper and looked down at the exposed rotor, resting on the pavement. He wasn't a car guy but knew enough to know the force of impact he'd felt wasn't good.

"Got a flat?" Kyle and Carrie came out of the North Star, and Jim stepped away so they could see the damage. "Damn . . . how the hell did that happen?"

"No idea," Jim said. "I was coming out of the lot, and it fell off."

Kyle gave him a dubious look that may have looked worse because of the streetlights or the number of beers he'd downed that night. "Tires don't just fall off."

Jim agreed, but before he could think of a response, the street was lit up in flashing red and blue lights. They turned and saw a Silent Creek police car pull up behind Jim's SUV.

The driver's side door opened up, and a cop stepped out.

"You can't park here."

Jim bit back a sarcastic response as the officer stepped around the front of his vehicle. He didn't recognize him, but he looked like all the cops Jim remembered from when he was a kid. Same navy blue uniform, same buzz cut. The belt had a few more things on it—pepper spray, flashlight, something that looked like a collapsible baton—alongside his radio and holster, while his chest had the bulk of body armor.

"Yeah, sorry, but my wheel fell off."

The cop gave him a suspicious look. "What do you mean?"

"I mean I pulled out of the lot, and when I turned down the street, my car started wobbling and then the wheel came off."

The cop came around the car and took a look at the wheel well as if he thought Jim was making the whole thing up. The flashing lights atop his police car attracted the attention of passersby, and an old pickup crept around them on the street.

Jim looked up and saw Colton Reid smirking at him from behind the wheel. Before he could say anything, the truck was past them. It rolled to a stop at the end of the block, then took a right and was gone.

Jim glanced back at Kyle, who'd seen the same thing he had.

"You need to get that back on and get going, 'cause I can't have you out here blocking traffic."

Jim looked up and down the now empty street. "Okay, but I'm a little concerned about how this happened. It's not like a flat tire or something. A front tire doesn't randomly fall off."

The cop looked up at him, and the still-flashing lights from his car highlighted the lack of interest or sympathy in his face. "What are you trying to say?"

He took another look back at Kyle, who gave him a little nod with his eyes.

"So, earlier this week we had to fire somebody . . . wait, sorry . . . my dad owns . . . I mean, used to own McCann LP out on 14? I guess I'm running it now. I'm Jim McCann."

Jim stuck his hand out to the cop, who waited a beat before shaking it.

"I know."

Jim kept a pleasant face throughout the cop's indifference and bullshit alpha-dog handshake.

"Anyway, we had to let someone go this week, and well, we saw him here at the bar earlier tonight. Guy's name is Colton Reid." Jim pointed down at the corner. "He literally just drove past."

"Uh huh . . ." The cop didn't appear to be connecting the dots Jim was trying to lay out.

"Well, it's a little suspicious that my tire fell off right after he left."

"You think he did it?"

Colton's smirk burned into Jim's thoughts.

"I mean . . ."

"You have any evidence that he did it?" There was no mistaking the impatience in the cop's voice. He spoke like a prosecutor who knew the answer to every question he asked.

"No, but, come on . . . this stuff doesn't just happen."

Jim was floundering, repeating himself, and they both knew it.

"You had those tires off anytime recently? Rotation done, anything like that?"

"No." Jim's voice was confident, but his memory second-guessed him from the back of his head. "I had my oil changed a month or so ago, and maybe they did a free tire rotation?"

The second the words were out of his mouth, the cop's expression changed from doubt to *I told you so.* "Get it done over at Kirby's?"

"No. At a Qwik Lube back in Boston before I drove here."

The cop looked at him like he was a kid. "If you don't tighten the lug nuts correctly, they can loosen over time and eventually fall off. Wouldn't be surprised if you've been dropping them along the road for a while now and were down to your last one. You check them regularly?"

Who checks their lug nuts regularly?

"No."

"Well, if you're gonna go to those cheap lube places, you probably should." The cop started back to his car. "Now that you're back home, I suggest getting your car serviced at a place that does real work like Kirby's. Those spots in the city don't do much more than cash your check."

Jim looked down at the cop as he passed by. "Okay, but . . . what about tonight?"

The cop paused, and Jim could see his annoyance turning into outright hostility. "You're gonna get that tire back on and move along so you stop blocking traffic out here. Can you handle that, or do you need me to call Kirby to come down with the tow truck?"

Jim's own frustration began to boil, but before he could respond, Kyle appeared beside him.

"We can handle it, Rob."

The cop's expression softened a bit, and he gave a curt nod, like he was glad someone he trusted had shown up to fix things.

"But could you do me a favor and keep an eye on Reid? You know how that guy is." Kyle put his hand on Jim's shoulder like he was trying to give him a stamp of approval. "Jimmy just moved back to town, and we want to keep him around this time."

Jim knew his friend was trying to help, but also knew it was the wrong thing to say to a local cop with a small-town-size chip on his shoulder.

"Get that wheel back on."

The cop got in his car, and for a minute Jim thought he was going to sit there, lights flashing, lording over them until they wrangled the tire on, but he drove off.

Jim pulled out the jack, and they started cranking the front axle off the ground.

"You remember him? Rob Ellison? Grew up over by Blue Earth. He was a grade ahead of us. Always been kind of a prick if you ask me." Kyle started chuckling. "He was the starting point guard on that Blue Earth team we rolled junior year. Remember that game? Oh man, that was awesome."

Kyle continued with the play-by-play as Jim tuned him out and tried to get his wheel back on.

Chapter Seven

A yellow leaf fluttered down and gently landed in the water. The lazy current carried it downstream and past where Jim stood in his old waders. He could feel the cold water through the neoprene and rubber around his legs, but the sun of that unseasonably warm early-November Saturday peeked through the remaining leaves above him and kept most of the chill away.

It was a perfect fall day on the creek.

Weather-wise, anyway. The actual fishing wasn't going well.

The fly rod bent back behind Jim's ear as he heard his father's voice counting the rhythm inside his head.

One-and-TWO-and-three-and-FOUR.

The line shot out in front of him on the final beat—more in the general direction of where he wanted as opposed to the spot on the water he'd picked out, but he was improving. Still, the fly floated back atop the water, uneaten.

Jim hauled in his line and waded up the stream. The farther he got from his car, the more the trees encroached on the left bank. Tall weeds came up against the water on the other side, putting him in a little corridor.

The water shallowed up as he crept around a bend, not coming much over the tops of his wading boots, which he'd been surprised to find in his parents' basement. They were the last pair his dad had bought for him, right after his final growth spurt that saw his feet jump four sizes between his freshman and sophomore years. By that point, their fishing trips had dried up almost completely. Basketball had become pretty much a year-round activity, and it gave Jim an excuse not to go fishing that his father actually accepted.

When he found the waders that morning, they were practically new, and after Friday night, he needed to get out.

Not because of the tire or the cop or Colton Reid or anything. That crap he could handle.

He needed to get out because, if he didn't, he wouldn't be able to resist calling Kelli. He'd dated a few women out in Boston, but nothing serious.

Not that Kelli was serious.

Yet.

But if he played it cool, maybe it could be. Bombarding her with text messages the day after their first date would probably scare her off, so he figured he'd get out to an area with bad cell service.

Jim cast out again, but his tempo was out of whack. The line bunched in the air and crumpled to the water in an unappetizing mess. His dad's impatient cadence echoed in his head, letting him know that even in the grave he could be disappointed. They'd stood in that very creek when Jim was a kid, his dad counting as Jim tried to cast. Slowly, Jim would get the hang of it. They'd net a few, and it would start to be fun. Just a dad and his son spending the afternoon fishing.

Until Jim would mess up a cast. Land his line on the water in a noisy heap that spooked every trout in the goddamn river, and what were they even doing out there if he wasn't going to listen?

One-and-TWO-and-three-and-FOUR.

Even by himself all these years later, he could still hear his dad's voice.

He took in a deep breath and tried to blow out the past, let the gentle babble of the creek scrub the tension and anxiety from him.

The sun snuck out from behind one of the three clouds above, and Jim squinted downstream. A long, lean shadow hovered on the far side of the creek. He froze, not wanting the shuffle of his boots to scare it away.

Jim watched for a minute, waiting to see what it was doing. He held his patience as it rose up and sipped something from the surface with a little *schlop*, then settled back to its spot.

He debated changing his fly but decided against it.

A good drift catches as many fish as the right fly.

Jim watched as it slipped up to the surface again. Hungry fella, and bigger than he'd realized. He picked out a spot about ten feet upstream from it, where a line of bubbles marked a seam in the current.

Get his fly in that, and it'd float right in front of that monster.

He'd probably get only one shot, because a bad cast would spook it. Jim adjusted his aim a bit more upstream to give a little more cushion but still waited. He'd been content to spend a perfect day on the water but was suddenly fixated on getting that fish in his net.

He couldn't screw this up.

The four-count casting cadence filtered into his head again, but no matter how many times his dad had preached it to him, it had never caught on. He remembered Coach Hutch, one of their assistants in college, always talked to him about simplicity.

Simplify.

Jim ignored his dad's counting and thought of his cast as a clock. Stop at ten o'clock going forward and two o'clock going back.

He hauled his line up off the water.

Ten and two.

Forward.

Ten and two.

Let out some line.

Ten and two.

Jim let the line go, and his fly shot out in a tight loop upstream. It was by far his best cast of the day. Too good, really, and he overshot his target by a good six feet.

But the little fly found its way into the seam and slowly floated downstream.

Jim hadn't realized he was holding his breath until the shadow of the trout flickered and the fish burst through the surface. An unconscious whoop broke from his lips as he jerked his rod up to set the hook.

The fish took off against the current and put a huge bend in Jim's rod. He let some line slip through his fingers but kept as much pressure on as he dared without snapping it off. The trout made two beer-commercial-worthy jumps before tiring and settling into Jim's net.

He worked the fly out of its mouth and admired his catch. Its bronze skin was covered in dark spots with silver haloes around them. Jim didn't have a tape measure, but he'd bet it was pushing twenty inches. Without a doubt the biggest he'd ever caught.

Its hooked jaw opened and closed a few times as Jim lowered the net back into the water. The trout recovered for a second, then bolted upstream away from him.

Jim stood in the knee-deep creek, basking in accomplishment. He felt the phone in his back pocket and regretted not getting a picture. His eyes searched the water for any sign of the fish, as if he could get it to come back and pose if he asked nicely.

"Well, look who's here."

The voice was sharp and devoid of compassion. It was loud enough to scatter fish more effectively than an errant cast ever could. Water splashed up as Jim spun around, almost losing his balance as the rocky bed shifted below him.

Colton Reid loomed on the bank to his right. He was wearing worn jeans and a T-shirt with the sleeves ripped off. His work boots were caked with mud from traipsing through the trees and weeds. Jim opened his mouth to say something, but Colton cut him off.

"Did you get my invitation?" The question bounced around Jim's head, a step ahead of comprehension.

"I . . . huh?"

Colton stared down at him—not a feeling Jim was used to. "I asked you if you got an invitation from me? Maybe a fancy one on that expensive paper with ribbons and whatnot? Some glitter in the envelope, perhaps? 'Cause, you see, this here's my property, and when I want somebody on it, I like to send them a pretty little invite so they feel welcome. Now, I don't do that a lot, so when I do, I remember, which is why I'm a little confused as to what the fuck you're doing here. Did I send you an invitation and then forget about it?"

Jim's mind sputtered as he tried to figure how far upstream he'd come. They'd fished this stream plenty of times when he was a kid, and there was always an easement that allowed public use. Either way, rivers and streams were public in Minnesota—even on private land. The rule was if your boots were in the water, you were allowed to be there.

Unfortunately, Colton didn't sound like he was interested in the finer points of Minnesota DNR rules.

"I guess I wandered too far upstream," Jim said. "I can leave if you want."

Colton smiled, wide enough that Jim could see the gap where his right incisor had once been.

"Well, if you never got an invitation, then I guess you better." Colton folded his arms across his chest and reached up to scratch his temple with the barrel of a well-worn silver Smith & Wesson.

Jim froze at the sight of the gun and felt sweat break out across his body. "Whoa, man. Take it easy."

Colton paused a beat like he was genuinely confused before looking over at his gun. "What, this? It's for protection. You know, in case I gotta deal with trespassers." His eyes narrowed a bit. "But you don't have to worry because you just wandered too far upstream, right? Besides, there aren't any of those stand-your-ground laws around here. If I shot you, I'd have to prove I had a legitimate fear of bodily harm, and no offense, but . . . guys like me aren't afraid of guys like you. You're a big dude, but you grew up comfortable. Everybody looking out for you. Never had to fight for nothing. You just played a game. Then when it's time to work, you come in and get your dad's job. Must be nice."

A single bead of sweat trickled between his shoulder blades, but Jim fought the shiver because he was scared any movement might provoke a response. Jim stared into Colton's dark eyes, which were a stark contrast to the playful nature of his voice.

"Look, man . . . I don't want any trouble." Jim held his hands out in front of him, trying hard to keep the tip of his fishing rod still as his hands trembled.

"Speaking of trouble, looked like you were having some car trouble last night."

The anger from outside the North Star sparked inside him, but the gun in Colton's hands kept it in check.

"Yeah."

"Well, hopefully that doesn't happen again, am I right?" Colton stayed rooted on the bank, arms crossed like a bouncer. His gun carelessly waving like a conductor's baton as he spoke. "But I will say, while I don't believe in a lot of things, I do believe in karma. You know, what goes around comes around?"

Jim opened his mouth to defend himself, then thought better of it.

"I'm gonna get going."

He made one step before his boot slipped on a grapefruit-size rock and pitched him forward. Jim splashed down into the creek and clamped his eyes shut, expecting a shot to crack through the air and blow out the back of his skull.

But nothing happened.

He pushed himself up from the forty-five-degree water and looked at Colton. His expression hadn't changed. Jim stood there, dripping, fifteen years of nerves cascading through his body.

But they were adults. It was time to act like it.

"Look, Colton." Jim started talking before he knew how to finish, and Colton's lack of reaction didn't tell him where to go with it. He sure as hell didn't want to make things worse. "My car troubles last night . . . well . . . I'm happy to think of that as an accident. Whatever. And hopefully that's the end of it, right? There's no reason this needs to go any further."

Colton didn't say anything but nonchalantly waved the barrel of his gun downstream.

When Jim realized that was the only answer he would get, he started walking, carefully shuffling his feet along the bottom so another rock wouldn't send him into the water again. He kept his eyes on Colton for as long as he could but eventually had to turn downstream to see where he was going. When he got to the bend in the creek, he looked back and Colton hadn't moved.

And he still had the gun in his hand.

Chapter Eight

When Jim got home, the kitchen was empty and the lights were off. The afternoon sun came in through the windows and gave everything a bit of a burnt orange tint. Jim could hear the television bleeding in from the living room.

He poked his head through the doorway and saw his mom sitting on the couch, watching *Wheel of Fortune*. That show had always been her favorite. As a kid, Jim would sit with her, and so often she would joke that he'd learned to read from watching Pat and Vanna with her. The older he got, the more competitive they'd become, but she was always a letter ahead of him.

Jim watched the television dance in her eyes but didn't see the same competitive fire. It was like she was watching out of habit as opposed to taking on the challenge.

"Hey, Mom, I'm back."

She looked up as if he'd startled her. "Oh. Hi." The clicking of the wheel filled the pause between words. "How was . . . how'd it go?"

He chose to ignore the run-in with Colton the same way he ignored the nonspecificity of her question. "I caught a twenty-incher."

"That's great." Her face lit up with genuine excitement—something Jim hadn't seen since he'd been back. "Your father would be so proud."

"I got it on one of those flies he'd tied up," Jim said. "There are boxes full of them in the basement. He must've spent a lot of time down there, huh?"

Gail looked back at the television as more letters were flipped. "Your father tied those things all winter."

"Well, there's enough left down there I probably won't have to learn how to do it myself."

He watched his mom's eyes gloss over again as the television pulled her in. A bell sounded to announce that only vowels remained, so Jim glanced over as the unsolved puzzle filled the screen. He looked back at his mom, waiting for her to say the answer, but she watched passively as the contestant did.

The doorbell rang.

"I'll get it," Jim said.

Usually, a visitor would have sent his mom into frantic hostess mode. At the very least she'd feverishly tidy up the living room, lest someone think real people actually lived in the house.

But she didn't move.

An opaque blob hovered on the other side of the frosted glass alongside the front door. Jim took one last look back at his mom before opening it.

"Hello there, Jimmy." Wayne Nelson stood on his parents' front porch. The short sleeves of his navy police uniform were tight around his arms, and the buttons strained to hold together across his stomach. He still had the same bushy mustache as he'd had when Jim was growing up, but now it was mostly gray.

"Chief Nelson." His police SUV was parked at the curb in front of their house, a thin bar of lights on the roof. Back when Jim was in high school, the cops had escorted them out of town on the way to the state tournament, lights blazing SCHS purple and white instead of the normal red and blue. "What can I do for you?"

The old police chief put his hands on his hips and glanced down the street with as much nonchalance as he could muster. "Oh, it's nothing much. Mind if I step inside a sec?"

Jim stepped back from the doorway and motioned him inside.

"Hello, Gail." Chief Nelson stood politely just inside the door, as if Jim inviting him in wasn't enough.

The sound of the police chief's voice snatched her attention, and she practically bolted off the couch. "Oh . . . officer." Jim's mom frantically folded the blanket that had been across her lap and hastily arranged the remote controls as Jim tried not to read into the fact that she hadn't used the chief's name.

"Don't get up, Gail," Nelson said. "Watch your show. I'm here to talk to Jimmy for a second."

Jim watched her face as she looked up at the cop she'd known for years, and for a second he swore she thought Chief Nelson was talking about her late husband. "Let me get you some coffee at least."

"That's nice, but I can't drink coffee this late in the day or I'll be up all night." But she was already in the kitchen.

The two men stood in awkward silence for a second as the sound of a filling pot came from the kitchen. Jim debated telling him about his run-in with Colton but figured he should wait and let him take the lead. "So, Chief . . . what can I do for you? I assume you're here to talk about last night."

Chief Nelson slid his thumbs into his belt and arched his back. "No, just wanted to let you know that we got a call from Colton Reid saying you were trespassing on his property this morning."

"*What?*" Jim's frustration lit like tinder at the suggestion.

"Were you out there?"

"I was fishing out on the creek, and he showed up out of nowhere with a gun."

Chief Nelson didn't seem at all moved that Jim had informed him Colton had a firearm. "You were out fly-fishing today? Season ended on the first of the month."

It had been so long since he'd gone fishing, Jim hadn't given any thought to when the season ended. With the unseasonably warm weather, it never crossed his mind. "I guess I didn't realize. But—"

"Doesn't start up again till January first, so people don't go tearing through the spawning beds."

"Okay, fine, but that's not really the point here." Jim saw the corner of the chief's mouth twitch at a local-born out-of-towner telling him his business.

"Were you on his property?"

Jim tried a steadying breath. Getting pissed wasn't going to help. "I parked by the bridge on Elkwood Road and got in the water there, then made my way upstream. I didn't even know the guy lived out there."

"Yeah, his place sits about a half mile from there," Chief Nelson said.

A clattering came in from the kitchen, reminding Jim to keep his voice down. He didn't want his mother to hear any of this.

"I didn't see any signs or anything posted, but even if there were, I was in the water. If your boots are wet, you're okay . . . isn't that right?"

Chief Nelson nodded. "That's what the DNR says, yes. Even if that part of the river isn't eased by the state, you can be in the water. But some people don't take those laws too serious when it comes to their personal property."

"But if it's the *law* . . ." Jim had to tamp down his voice again. "That's not the point. The point is I was perfectly within my rights to be there, and he showed up with a gun talking about invitations and stand-your-ground laws and whatever. If anybody was threatening anybody, it was the guy with the gun, not the guy with the fly rod."

The chief still looked nonplussed. "No law against carrying a gun on your own property, especially if you're checking out a trespasser."

"You've got to be kidding me." Jim couldn't hold it in any longer, and Chief Nelson looked at him as if he were still a high school kid giving him lip.

"Did he point this gun at you?"

"Yeah—well . . . not, like, directly, but he was waving it around as he talked careless as hell. I didn't know what he was going to do. You know what he's like."

Nelson held up his hand as Gail McCann came in from the kitchen with a mug full of coffee for the chief. "I couldn't find any cookies or anything," she said. "I know we have some, but I couldn't find where I put them."

Nelson took the mug he'd never asked for with a smile. "Oh, that's okay. Susie's got me on a diet, and if she found out you gave me some cookies, she'd be after me with her hair on fire."

The chief took a polite sip and smiled like it was the best coffee to hit his lips. "Thank you."

Gail drifted back into the kitchen as Nelson lowered the mug.

"I came here to let you know we got a call about you trespassing on Colton Reid's property. I don't need to get involved with a lot of he-said-she-said business, so I'm going to tell you it's probably best if you stay away from Mr. Reid's land and contain your fly-fishing to the designated season. I know it may not seem like a big deal to you, but the DNR makes those rules for a reason, and they don't take poaching lightly."

Frustration coursed through him, but Jim could tell anything he said would only make things worse.

"Fine."

Chief Nelson smiled and placed his mug on the table next to the door. "Thanks again for the coffee, Gail, but I've got to run."

She waved at him from the couch but didn't take her eyes off the television. The chief turned back toward the front door but motioned for Jim to follow him out.

Once they were on the front porch, the cop turned back. "How's your mom doing?"

He was speaking as Wayne Nelson, not the police chief, and Jim felt the gears of their conversation shift.

"It's hard to say."

"Susie's sister went through Alzheimer's a few years back," Nelson said. "Awful."

Jim felt seen for the first time in a while, and the weight of the conversation they'd just had on the other side of the door drifted away in the autumn breeze.

"Yeah, we're still not sure exactly what's going on. I think Dad covered for her for a lot of years, so I don't really know how long it's been. Or how bad it really is."

Chief Nelson turned to face Jim. "She's gonna need you to be there for her. Don't let this petty shit with Reid or anything else distract you from that."

Jim considered what he said and nodded.

Chief Nelson stuck his hand out to Jim, and they shook. "It's a good thing you're back for this. Keep a good eye on her."

"I will."

Jim stood on the front porch as Chief Nelson made his way to his SUV and drove off.

Chapter Nine

Jim's phone announced a new text message down in his pocket, but he ignored it. No texting while driving—although the traffic in Silent Creek was sparse enough one could probably pull out a quill and hand scribe a letter and not run into any problems. But with his luck he'd pass a local cop with nothing better to do than write him a ticket.

There was nothing that couldn't wait until he got to work, so he left the phone in the pocket of his khakis.

It pinged again.

He yawned and turned onto Lake Street and headed past the SCHS baseball and softball fields on his way out of town.

After he'd passed the city limits on Highway 14, the white tanks of McCann were visible ahead.

When he was a kid, he'd asked his father why they'd put the business out in the country, because when Kyle went to work with his dad, he could walk down to the Corner Stop and get Swiss Cake Rolls.

Because if there is an accident at Kyle's dad's office, it won't blow up half the town.

Jim had been afraid to go out there for months after that. He'd always enjoyed running around between the lines of tanks but hadn't seen them as military-grade bombs waiting for the wrong spark that would vaporize him like Sarah Connor clinging to that fence in *Terminator 2*.

When his mom realized what was behind her son's newfound reluctance, she made his dad explain all the safety systems they had out there to prevent such a disaster. The talk was delivered in the gruff, quasi-condescending manner that James McCann had honed over years of interactions with his son and had been only partially effective.

A sliver of unease remained in the back of Jimmy's mind throughout his childhood, and he could still feel the itch every now and then.

Gravel crunched under the tires as Jim turned off the blacktop into McCann and pulled into his dad's old parking spot. There was no sign designating it as such, but his old man had parked there every day for forty years.

Jim sat behind the wheel for a second, staring at the McCann LP logo on the glass door to his right. If Silent Creek were a black hole, that door would be the singularity. He'd thought he'd broken free from its gravitational pull when he went off to college and then moved out East, but he was starting to feel there was no escape. The pull and inertia were relentless in places like this, and the brighter your star burned, the more spectacular it was when it inevitably was torn apart and consumed.

Jim opened the door and stepped out of his car. The autumn breeze had a bite in it and served as a well-earned slap in the face. Jim took a deep breath and held the cold air in his lungs for a second before blowing it out, hoping it would take the doom and gloom with it.

He walked through the door and smiled at Theresa, who was already at her post behind the reception desk.

"Brent Halverson wants to talk to you."

"Okay." Jim shifted direction from his office to her desk. He reached over to the glass dish and plucked one of the same butter mints she'd been putting out since he was a kid. "Did he say why?"

"Just said to tell you as soon as you got in."

Jim popped the mint in his mouth and tasted his childhood as it melted over his tongue. He'd eaten these by the fistful back then,

Theresa smiling and slipping him a few more after his father had told him he'd had enough. "Let me drop my stuff off, and I'll head out there."

Theresa gave a little shrug and kept her focus on whatever paperwork she was shuffling around in front of her. She'd always been the friendly face of McCann LP and treated him like a prince whenever he'd been there, but since his first day in the big chair, Jim couldn't help but notice her cheery disposition felt more like forced politeness. Maybe she'd always been that way, but he had been too young to notice.

It was one of the many things he was seeing differently since he'd moved back, now that he was old enough to look behind the curtain.

Jim caught a glimpse of his breath as he stepped back outside and headed across the parking lot toward the massive garage that serviced their trucks. Three of the four doors were open but empty. Their fleet of tankers was always parked across the way, but a few were already out making deliveries. Another was over by one of the large white tanks getting filled.

Jim walked through the side door. Bright industrial light filled the inside of the garage, while the scent of motor oil and strong coffee from a pot that had never been cleaned filtered up into Jim's sinuses. All four repair bays were occupied by trucks with their hoods popped up.

Not a good sign, considering their first deliveries were usually on the road by now.

Brent Halverson was sitting at a cluttered metal desk pushed up against the wall. It was well worn and stained with decades of motor grime, but the few papers on it were pristine and organized.

"Theresa said you needed to talk to me."

Brent glanced up and nodded at Jim. "Problem with the trucks. Greeny and Blake were the first out this morning, and 'bout five minutes after they left, they called in dead on the side of the road."

It took Jim a second to realize he wasn't talking about the drivers.

"What happened?"

"Couple miles out both had lights come on and lost power. Got off the road and checked under the hood, found their serpentine belts gone."

Brent must have noticed Jim's blank expression. "Drive belt . . . runs the alternator, power steering, AC compressor . . ."

"Yeah." He tried to put whatever confidence he had into that word. "Same on both? That's a bit weird, isn't it?"

Brent nodded, then gestured at the trucks behind him. "Had the guys check out the rest, and it's the same story. Belts gone on all of them."

"Shit." Jim didn't need Brent's mechanical knowledge to know there was no way this was all a coincidence. "So, what's the plan? How long is this gonna keep us down? Do we need to start contacting customers about rescheduling?"

"Well, there weren't any belts in the shop, so I sent Pete and Charlie over to the AutoZone to buy some and drive them out to the trucks so they could get going again. They'll take a quick look when they install 'em, but as long as the pump's okay, the guys should be able to go on with their deliveries." Brent looked back at the trucks lined up in the garage bays. "When they get back, we'll replace these."

"Don't we usually have replacement belts and stuff here in the shop?"

Brent paused. "We're s'posed to."

Jim could see the hesitance in the mechanic's face. "But we don't?"

Brent leaned back in his chair, and Jim noticed him taking a quick look around to see who was listening. "Whenever I ask Kyle, he says it's problems with the vendor. That's fine, but I'd think if a vendor can't keep us supplied, maybe we need to find a new one."

Jim wanted to reassure him but realized he didn't know anything about their suppliers.

"I'll talk to Kyle. I know today was . . . abnormal . . . but we still should have enough stuff to maintain our deliveries if weird things happen, right?"

Brent nodded.

"Speaking of this . . . anyone else see anything strange this morning?"

"Nope."

Jim took a deep breath and rubbed the back of his neck. "I mean, there's no way this could be an accident, right?"

"All six trucks? Wouldn't think so."

"How hard is it to do this? I mean . . . who would know what to do?"

The mechanic shrugged. "Easy if you know what you're doing. Just need to get under the hood with a knife. Lucky the guys knew enough to pull over right away so the engines didn't overheat, or that would have been much more expensive. Gonna be more of an annoyance than anything."

Jim nodded. "Thanks for letting me know and for taking care of this. Have the guys give Theresa the receipts for the belts, and I'll make sure they're reimbursed right away. I'll talk to Kyle about fixing whatever is going on with the suppliers, make sure you guys are properly stocked up out here in case anything like this happens again. Speaking of, maybe tell the guys to keep an eye out for anything else out of the ordinary."

Brent agreed and headed over to one of the trucks. Jim watched for a second, then walked back to the office to call the cops. He wasn't sure what they were going to do, because it wasn't like they had any evidence or anything.

But Jim knew who'd done it. It was simply a matter of whether they could do anything about it.

Chapter Ten

"How are those ones?"

Jim pulled a wheeled rack of basketballs and a whole lot of memories out of the storage closet. It was his first time back in the SCHS gymnasium since he'd graduated, and he could feel the faded championship banners on the far side looming over him.

2008 Conference Champions
2008 District Champions
2008 1A State Tournament

Participant, that last one. Not champion.

He squeezed a few of the balls on the top row and felt plenty of give. "They're low."

Kelli knelt by the first rack of balls they'd pulled out of storage, the electric air pump rumbling next to her.

Needing to get out and get his mind off the hurricane his life had whipped into the past few weeks, Jim had finally called Kelli, who graciously offered him the opportunity to dig through the storage closet in preparation for the first practice of the season on Monday.

"Honestly, we may as well top them all off," Kelli said.

Jim palmed one off the rack and examined it. The orange leather was scuffed enough that it could have conceivably been one of the ones he'd dunked back in the day. "These are pretty beat up."

Kelli laughed. "We don't break out fresh balls for every practice, Mr. Big Ten. But if you want to donate some cash for new ones, be my guest."

Jim tried to hide the embarrassment that popped up on his ears and barely noticed Kelli pull the needle out of the ball she was working on and toss it his way. "How's this feel?"

It bounced off his chest, and Jim scrambled to catch it in some sort of coordinated way, but flailed and made Kelli laugh even harder. It bounced over to the free throw line, and he chased it down. Instinct and muscle memory took over as he scooped it up and sent it arcing toward the hoop.

Swish.

No matter how much he'd tried to get past his playing days, there was still no better sound in the world than the snapback of the net on a perfect shot. It sent the same surge of endorphins through him that it had back in high school.

Jim stared at the hoop as a second ball snapped through from behind him. He turned back to see Kelli smirking from behind the three-point line. The ball she'd shot bounced slowly toward him—the backspin of a shooter's touch at work. He let it roll onto his foot and kicked it up to himself, then passed it over to her again.

Swish.

"Somebody's been practicing."

"Natural talent never goes away."

Jim chuckled but didn't disagree. Kelli's form was effortless, and Jim would bet it had been that way from the first time she picked up a basketball. Hard work could get you far, but there had to be some natural talent at the core to make it in college basketball. Even at the Division II level.

Watching her shoot, Jim couldn't help but wonder if she could have made it in the Big Ten.

What if she'd been at Minnesota? Could I have met her years ago?

He tracked down the loose ball and tossed it over to her again, but instead of launching another, she stood rooted in her spot and held the ball out to him. It took a second to recognize the challenge on her face, but when he did, it brought a smile.

Only after Jim had walked over and took the ball from her did Kelli move from her spot. Jim planted his feet right where she'd shot from and sent the ball arcing toward the hoop.

CLANG

"That's *p*." Kelli jogged over to the wayward ball and set up her next shot from the corner.

Nothing but net.

Jim grabbed the ball and headed over to her spot.

His shot was short. So short it barely scraped iron. Embarrassment stoked the competitive fire that smoldered in his gut.

"*P-i*." Kelli put more mocking in those two letters than anyone ever had. "You ever lost a game of pig in three shots?" Jim opened his mouth to defend himself, but Kelli cut him off. "Because you're about to."

She dribbled over to the wing and launched another three-pointer. Jim watched it do a full 360 in the hoop before flying out.

"HA!" Jim hustled over and snatched the ball up from the floor. "Enough of this long-range crap. Now you gotta play my game."

He hit a turnaround jumper from the elbow, a hook shot from the block, and a pair of twelve-footers, but Kelli answered the call every time.

"That's the thing you bigs don't understand." She tossed the ball over to him at the free throw line. "We can hit your shots, but you can't hit ours."

Jim shrugged, then bounced the ball off the backboard, caught it midair, and dunked hard enough the backboard rattled.

"All right . . ." Kelli said. "Maybe not all of them."

Good God he hadn't done anything like that in a long time. His bad knee sent out a warning flare when he landed, but he barely noticed with the adrenaline coursing through his veins. The last time he'd done that in here, a thousand people shot to their feet, screaming. This time it was just the echo of a lone ball bouncing away from him.

But it still felt good.

"JIMMY BUCKETS WITH THE FLUSHHHHHH!" The words bounced around every corner of the empty gymnasium at least three times before fading out. Kyle was walking across the hardwood floor, clapping. "He's still got it, ladies and gentlemen."

A small bead of sweat dripped down Jim's temple, and he scooped up the ball at his feet. Kelli had already returned hers to the rack and pulled the pump over to her.

"So, you won't help your best friend coach your old team, but then I find you out here in the gym with *another woman* . . ." Kyle's fake outrage was well performed, but Jim could see the kernel of truth under all that bluster.

"I'm just helping get the balls out." He heard it before Kyle could even open his mouth. "Shut up."

Kyle put his hands up in mock surrender while Kelli giggled like a middle schooler behind him.

"You set yourself up for that one," she said.

Jim tried to wipe the sweat and embarrassment from his face and put that unfortunate turn of phrase behind them. "What're you doing here on a Sunday afternoon?"

"Carrie forgot some papers, and I told her I'd swing by when I was out and about," Kyle said.

"That's nice of you," Kelli said.

"I'm a real sweetheart," Kyle said. "Speaking of sweethearts, you hear anything more from the police?"

Jim had called the police station about the missing belts on their trucks, and Officer Ellison came out to take a look around. Once again, there wasn't any evidence pointing at Colton, and like that night in front of the North Star, Officer Ellison hadn't seemed very interested in actually looking for any.

"Police?" Kelli said. "What are you talking about?"

"Oh, nothing." Jim had been having such a good time, the last thing he wanted was to bring Colton Reid drama into the gym.

Unfortunately, Kyle wasn't exactly the let-it-go type. "Somebody cut the belts off all our trucks the other day."

"Really?" Kelli asked.

"Yeah." Jim chose to ignore the way Kyle had said the word *somebody*. "Ellison came out, talked to some of the guys, looked around but, you know . . . not a whole lot they can do."

"As isolated as we are out there, we really need cameras," Kyle said. "I talked to your dad about it a few years ago, but he said it was too expensive and I was being paranoid. *Who's gonna do anything out there? Well . . .*"

"Yeah, I know," Jim said. "We can look into it tomorrow. Until we can get something installed, I guess we gotta hope it's out of his system."

Kyle's eyebrows crinkled together like Jim had ripped a fart. "Good luck with that."

Kelli pulled a ball off the rack and tossed it over to Kyle. "I was just beating your boy here in pig. You want in? I win and we get the gym first through Christmas."

As changes of subject went, it wasn't the most subtle, but Jim appreciated the effort anyway. He'd forgotten that the boys' and girls' teams had to share the gym for practice time.

"As much as I'd love to, I gotta get these back to Carrie." Kyle folded the papers and stuffed them in his back pocket before launching a shot that clanged off the side of the rim.

Jim jabbed Kyle in the ribs. "Looks like you've still got your old shot too."

"I'm in street shoes." Kyle's voice reeked of defensiveness as he pointed to his feet.

"Probably for the best." Kelli grabbed a ball from the rack and drained a shot from a few feet beyond the three-point line. "We'd probably end up with first practice all season."

Jim let out a howl of laughter and gave Kyle a playful shove toward the door.

"You college studs always love to gang up on the little guy." Kyle pulled his wife's papers out of his pocket and pointed them at Jim. "But for real, though, we need to think about upping security out at McCann. Until we get a camera system installed, we gotta make sure everything is locked up. And I'd keep an eye in the back of your head, because as much as I hate to say it, I don't see this problem going away anytime soon. It'll probably get worse."

"Yeah, okay." Jim heard the dismissiveness in his own voice, so he knew Kyle did.

"I'm serious. You're the boss, and it's your business now, so if you want to let Colton Reid mess with that, there isn't anything I can do about it. But it does bother me to see someone like that messing with my best friend at a place where I've worked for my whole life. I don't want to say this, but I warned your dad about him, and he didn't take me seriously. I don't want you to make the same mistake." The comment landed hard and sucked all the playful banter out of the gym. The look on Kyle's face said he knew he'd stepped over the line, but he had probably done it on purpose for that exact effect. "I'm sorry, man, but it's true. We can talk about it tomorrow."

Jim watched him retreat across the gym and out the door, then glanced over to Kelli, who'd busied herself by putting the last of the balls back on the rack.

"You okay?"

Jim nodded.

She snatched a ball off the rack and put up a shot from a good six feet beyond the three-point line.

Swish.

"That's *g*."

Chapter Eleven

The North Star wasn't as full as Jim had expected. About half the tables were occupied and maybe a third of the stools along the bar. The TV over it broadcast the local news out into the dark room, but the sound was low enough it blended with the general din of a small-town watering hole.

Jim felt like it should have been a party, while Kelli was humbly suppressing the excitement of her first win as a head coach. Not just a win, but a full-blown ass kicking. She'd had her girls running circles around the sorry squad that New Ulm bussed over.

Jim felt the crackle of excitement radiating from Kelli as soon as she'd found him after the game. "That motion offense you ran tonight . . . whew. They were chasing you around all night. It was impressive."

They weaved through a few tables over to a booth along the far wall. The same one they'd sat in the last time they stopped for a beer.

And when they went out for burgers last week.

And when they met Kyle and Carrie for drinks the week before that.

Jim blushed at the realization that it had become "their" booth.

"At this level a simple offense that's executed well is better than anything," Kelli said. "So many coaches think they're in the NBA or something and bring in all these complex plays . . . these are high school kids. The more you give them, the more chance there is of them messing up, and it all falls apart from there. So, we keep it simple."

"That's smart." Jim thought back to the contorted mess he'd witnessed in the first half of the boys' game. It had been downright painful to watch. Players kept getting bunched up, passing lanes were almost nonexistent, and more often than not, the possession ended up in a contested shot as the shot clock expired. "You should mention it to Kyle."

Kelli chuckled to herself. "I'll let you tell him."

Kyle still hadn't stopped pressing him to join his coaching staff.

You don't even have to be on the bench—you can be like a consultant or something. Maybe show up to a few practices. The guys would love it. Show them how it's done at the Big Ten level.

But Jim begged off every time, waiting for his friend to get the hint that it wasn't happening.

Kelli slid back out of their booth. "I'll go get the first round."

"Let me." She waved Jim off, but he still dug for his wallet. "I should buy you a victory beer."

"That's what I'm going to get. Miller Lite, the Champagne of Beers."

"That's High Life you're thinking of."

Kelli ignored his outstretched ten-dollar bill and headed to the bar. Jim watched her go from the booth.

Their booth.

The thought made him blush again.

Kelli leaned up against the bar, politely chatting with the bartender as she pulled two bottles from the cooler. That swooping feeling spread through his chest like a swarm of butterflies, and he pulled his eyes away so nobody could catch him staring. The rest of the bar slowly blurred over in a haze of Friday night and a fog of giddy infatuation as Jim waited for Kelli to return.

But he couldn't resist for long, so he turned back to the bar, where Kelli was standing with a beer bottle in each hand.

Talking to Colton Reid.

An alarm sounded in the back of his head, but Jim tried to ignore it. They were in a public place. It wasn't like he was going to do anything to her. Most likely trying to get under his skin.

It was working.

He couldn't tell what they were saying, but Kelli's posture was open and she had a conversational look on her face. Colton looked as serene as a wild bison, the kind people try to take a picture with in Yellowstone before getting trampled.

Kelli said something seemingly polite and started back. Colton's gaze followed her, then quickly switched to Jim. The smirk on his lips matched the quick wink he gave him before turning back to the bar.

A bottle of Miller High Life appeared on the table in front of him, and Kelli slid into her spot across the booth and cut whatever sick tether Colton had him on. "Your champagne, sir."

Jim snapped his head back to her and forced what he hoped was a nonchalant smile.

"You okay?"

"Yeah, fine." He leaned back in the booth, because that's what somebody who was definitely relaxed and not worried about a guy across the bar would do. The pull was excruciating, and he held off as long as he could before looking back. "What did he want?"

"To buy our beer," Kelli said. "I said it was unnecessary, but he insisted."

Jim put the bottle down on the table like it had been spit in. He looked at the bar, fully expecting to see Colton staring at him but only saw the back of his head.

"What?" Kelli said.

"Nothing . . . just . . ." Jim turned toward Kelli. "What did he say?"

"I told you, he wanted to pay for our drinks."

"But that's Colton Reid." Jim spoke as if she didn't know.

Kelli looked over at Colton. "Maybe it's a peace offering. You said yourself you want all this to blow over. Well, that seems like a pretty good sign, doesn't it?"

It sure as hell did not.

"I guess so."

"Why does Kyle have such a problem with him?" Kelli took a drink of her beer. "I get it that the guy had some issues when he was a kid, but . . . I don't know. He seemed genuine."

Jim reached out for the bottle in front of him but still didn't drink. He tilted it on its edge and slowly rotated it on the table, making circles with the neck as he thought of how to answer Kelli's question.

"There's some history there," Jim said. "When Colton got put on the team our senior year, he took Kyle's spot in the lineup."

"That's it?" Kelli furrowed her brow in disbelief.

"There's more to it than that," Jim said. "Kyle's dad was a big basketball guy. Heck, he was the guy who taught me how to shoot free throws as a kid. Super-nice guy."

Jim got sidetracked by memories of the Eriksons' driveway, Kyle's dad showing them tips and tricks from his own playing days. Kyle would always get bored after fifteen minutes, but Jimmy ate it up. He'd stay out there with Mr. Erikson as long as he could.

"Anyway, right before sophomore year, he died. Pulmonary embolism. Just . . . *bang* . . . gone. After that, Kyle got *really* into basketball. I'm sure there's a whole psychology paper in that, but whatever. Problem was, he wasn't that good. He made varsity junior year but rode the bench. Senior year, he was finally gonna start. Then Colton showed up, and he was back on the bench."

Kelli gave a small nod, but her expression was still dubious. "Still seems like a long time to hold that grudge, though. Especially when you guys said he got kicked off within a month, right? There's gotta be something else to it."

Jim shrugged, even though he knew there certainly was more to it than a lost spot in the starting lineup. Jim didn't know how much more, but there was a day in fourth grade he'd always remembered.

He and Kyle decided to cut through the park on their way home from school. Joking about whatever kids joked about back then. Colton shouldn't have even been there, because he lived way out in the country and rode the bus home after school, but he was, and so were they. Kyle was yapping on about something, probably didn't even see Colton sitting in the picnic shelter.

For whatever reason, Colton told him to shut up, and Kyle's smart-ass comeback was out before either of them knew who he was talking to. Nothing more than a reflex, but intent didn't matter to Colton Reid, who, for whatever reason, was probably waiting for something to unleash on.

Unfortunately for Kyle, he'd been the one to spring the trap.

The two of them took off like a pair of gazelles when Colton exploded off that picnic table. Jimmy hadn't hit his growth spurt yet, but his legs had always been long. Too afraid to look back, he heard Kyle get taken to the ground and kept going. Didn't look back until he was out of the park, and by then Colton was finishing up.

Kyle had sworn Jim to secrecy, and although the statute of limitations on that promise had certainly passed long ago, he didn't feel right sharing that story.

Jim took a long swig from his beer and buried the memory. "So the boys' team sucks, eh?"

Kelli made a face like she'd taken a shot of Jameson. "No comment."

As the ice Jim found himself frozen in slowly melted, they fell back into a familiar conversational rhythm. The bar filled up as the night went on, putting more and more bodies between him and the bar, which helped keep Jim's mind off the man sitting over there.

They kept an eye out for Kyle and Carrie, but they never showed. Considering Kyle's demeanor on the bench earlier that night, it shouldn't have been a surprise.

They talked for another hour or so before Kelli caught herself in a yawn and figured it was time to call it a night. As they weaved through the densely packed throng of small-town drinkers, Jim finally stole another look at the end of the bar.

Two old men sat where Colton had been, and while it should have been a relief, a bit of the panic he'd suppressed earlier shot into his bloodstream. Jim scanned the crowd, suddenly convinced he'd see

Colton pushing his way across the room, but noticed nothing except loud conversations and alcohol-induced laughter.

Maybe he'd left.

Or maybe he was out messing with Jim's car again.

"What?"

Kelli looked back for some explanation as to why her date had stopped following her out.

He forced another smile and grabbed her hand.

"Nothing."

The air had a bite to it. They couldn't see their breath, but the faintest tint of haze seemed to hang around the streetlights like they were setting up for a late-autumn freeze.

Jim half expected to find his windshield shattered or his tires slashed, but when they got to the parking lot, everything seemed fine.

Cars buzzed up and down Main Street, but by the time Jim had driven them a block from downtown, the streets were empty.

Jim snuck a glance over at Kelli. She was staring out the passenger window, face glowing in the pale-blue light that came from the dashboard. They'd used up most of their conversation at the North Star, but it still didn't feel awkward. The fact that neither felt the urge to fill up every moment of silence with inane banter was oddly comforting.

They'd advanced past that. He could be happy simply existing in her presence.

The warmth that realization brought chased away whatever chill remained in the car.

Jim turned down Winnebago Street with a dorky smile in his heart and glanced in his rearview mirror.

A pair of headlights had followed them around the turn.

There was nothing abnormal about that. It was a Friday night after a basketball game. People were out and about.

So why had he noticed them?

You're paranoid.

The lights followed about half a block back as Jim kept his pace down the street. He couldn't tell what kind of car it was or who was driving. Back in high school, when one of the only things to do was cruise around with friends until something better came up or it was time to go home, Jim could identify almost every car on the road by the shape of its headlights, but that skill was long gone.

Which doesn't matter because it's literally just a car.

Their turn crept up on them, and Jim almost blew past. He cranked the wheel and felt the seat belt tighten across his chest.

"You asleep at the wheel or something?"

Her voice was easy and accompanied by a playful jab in the ribs.

"No, no . . ." He eased back off the brake and recovered in his lane. "I think I was on autopilot or something. I don't come down this way often."

"Well, this *is* the rough part of town." Kelli played it straight. "Pampered boys like you wouldn't last five minutes down here."

"Pampered, eh? You don't—"

The lights turned into his rearview mirror and settled behind them.

"What?" The tone of her voice told him he'd missed the first time she'd said it because he was too busy watching the headlights get closer. Only a few car lengths away.

There were a few porch lights on, the occasional TV flickering through a living room window, but the houses that lined the street were mostly dark. Jim kept his eyes in the rearview mirror, waiting for the car to pull into a driveway and cut them loose.

But it stayed back there.

"You okay?"

Jim pulled his eyes from the mirror and forced a smile. "Yeah."

He slowed down a bit, and the car got close enough Jim could tell it wasn't a car but a pickup truck, but he still couldn't get a good look at whoever was inside. Staring into the glare of headlights, he couldn't tell the model or color or anything.

You know who it is.

Kelli's turn was a block away, and he debated blowing past in case the truck was following them. But then he'd have to explain what he was doing, and there was no way to do that without sounding paranoid, so he slowed down and took the turn as casually as his nerves would allow.

Her house was in the middle of the block, and as he pulled into Kelli's driveway, the headlights turned down her street. They pulled alongside the curb and stopped two houses down. Jim waited for them to go dark and the driver's side door to pop open, proving it was just some dude coming home for the night and not Colton Reid stalking them from the bar.

But that didn't happen.

The truck sat there.

It took Jim a second to notice Kelli was sitting there, too, awkwardly waiting for whatever date-night goodbye was coming.

Before Jim could bring his focus back to her, Kelli got tired of waiting and pulled the door handle. The dome light washed through the car, casting them both in a harsh, unflattering light and preventing him from seeing through the windows with its glare.

"Thanks for the beers." Her voice had a self-conscious lilt that grabbed his attention.

"Yeah, it was a good time as always." Jim fumbled for something endearing but sounded awkward.

Kelli waited another beat before stepping out of the car. "Talk to you later this week?"

"Yeah, for sure." Jim looked out the open door and saw the truck was still parked down the block, mostly hidden in the shadow between streetlights. "Let me walk you in."

Kelli's expression instantly changed, and her smile went from genuine to forced. "That's okay."

It took a split second for Jim to recognize how his offer sounded. "No . . . not *that* . . . it's just . . ." He popped open the driver's side door and got out. Kelli took a step back toward her front door, her eyes hardening and smile evaporating. "I think that truck down there was following us." He nodded down the block at the still-glowing headlights. "I didn't mean . . . I'm staying right here. I wanted to be sure it's not . . . never mind. I'll wait here until you get inside. That's it."

Jim waited another awkward moment. "I'm sure it's fine."

Kelli gave him a smaller but genuine smile and thanked him before heading to her front door. The spillover from his car's headlights lit her path well enough that he could see she was watching the car down the street as she walked.

Still no movement from the driver.

She twisted her key in the lock and waved one last time before heading in. Jim bit back the urge to tell her to lock her doors tonight. He didn't want to seem overprotective, and no woman living by herself had to be reminded of that anyway.

Her living room window lit up through the blinds and offered a bit of relief.

But the truck still hadn't moved.

Jim didn't want to leave while it was still there but knew he couldn't sit in Kelli's driveway all night, so he slowly backed out. He got into the street and looked at the truck idling there only two houses down.

He couldn't stay there in the middle of the street, so Jim slowly crept ahead, his eyes in the rearview mirror looking for any movement. Nothing came before he got to the end of the block. Jim had a decision to make.

He wanted it to be nothing. To go home and know it was a neighbor, that his paranoia had morphed into something sinister.

But he couldn't.

When the truck still hadn't moved as he turned at the end of the block, Jim knew he couldn't go home. Colton had already approached

Kelli once that night, and he knew they were together. Being cautious and being paranoid were not the same thing. Worst case scenario, it wasn't him and Jim would apologize.

He stomped down on the accelerator and flew around the block, nerves firing all over under his skin like someone had dumped a packet of Pop Rocks into his bloodstream.

When he circled back onto Kelli's street, the truck was still sitting there. Jim pulled up behind it, his headlights lighting up an instantly recognizable head of rusty-red hair.

Jim jammed his SUV into park and jumped out.

Colton sat behind the wheel of his truck, elbow propped out the open driver's side window.

"What the hell are you doing?" Jim put as much behind his voice as he could without waking the neighbors.

"Nothing." Colton's voice was casual, like Jim had asked if he wanted fries at the drive-through.

"In that case, why don't you get out of here?"

Colton looked out the side of his eyes as the blue-green glow from the dashboard illuminated his face. "Actually, I choose not to."

"Come on, this isn't funny," Jim said.

"Ain't no one trying to be funny here," Colton said. "I'm just sitting in my own truck on a public street in the freest country on God's green earth. And if I'm being honest, I find it a little troubling that you seem to care so much. Maybe you were hoping to get up to some funny business with that little lady over there and didn't want anyone to see what yer doing?"

The cloying implication was like a squirt of lime juice in Jim's eye. "If you don't leave, I'm calling the police."

The threat bounced off him with a shrug.

"That's fine. I'll explain that I met a nice young woman at the bar tonight, then I saw her leave with somebody who seems awful nervous about anyone seeing what he plans to do with—"

Jim slammed his fist down on the roof of the truck. "Like hell you will."

Colton looked up at Jim from the dark cab, all playfulness gone from his eyes.

"I would advise you not to do that again."

The two held eyes long enough the anger started to seep from Jim's veins, laying bare the nerves in his gut.

"You know what . . . fine. You aren't the only one who can exercise their *freedoms*."

Jim stomped back to his car and settled in behind the wheel. Part of him knew Colton was probably trolling him, same as buying their beer at the North Star, but Jim didn't care. He'd rather stay out here all night than let Colton sit out in front of Kelli's house alone.

He stared at the back of Colton's head, a cauldron of emotions roiling inside him. Jim reached down and flipped his high beams on, bathing Colton's truck in even more crisp halogen light, but it didn't move him.

After a tense few minutes, Colton's taillights pumped red as he put his truck in gear and finally drove off.

Jim watched the truck disappear around the corner but waited another five minutes to make sure Colton didn't circle back the same way he had earlier.

The adrenaline seeped from his system, and Jim loosened his fingers from the steering wheel. He looked down the street at Kelli's house. It was dark. His head clearing, Jim was relieved she didn't know he was still out there. He debated texting her to let her know it had been Colton in the truck but thought better of it.

He'd most certainly done it to get under Jim's skin, and Kelli may look at the way he'd handled it differently.

Jim sat for a second, letting good judgment settle in. He reached down to put his car into gear as a pair of headlights pulled to the curb behind him.

He squinted against the light in his rearview mirror, his fight reflexes firing as he threw open his car door and flew out.

"Stop right there."

The voice froze him, not because of the command but because it didn't belong to Colton.

Neither did the vehicle. Out of his car, Jim could make out the shape of a Silent Creek police SUV.

―――

"Whoa, whoa . . ." Jim shot his hands up in front of him as Officer Ellison stepped away from his patrol vehicle. His eyes adjusted enough to the light that he could see the cop didn't have his gun out, but his right hand was close enough to his holster to add a lot of nerves to the conversation.

"You wanna keep your hands where I can see 'em?" Ellison said. "Then tell me what you're doing here?"

"Nothing, I'm . . ."

I'm just sitting in my own truck on a public street in the freest country on God's green earth.

"We got a call about a strange car parked out here with its lights on."

Jim kept his hands in front of him and took as unthreatening a step as he dared toward the cop.

"That's actually what I was doing . . . but it wasn't me." Even in the harsh glare of the headlights, he could see the impatience on Officer Ellison's face. "I had brought my . . ." Jim stumbled over the right title to give Kelli, as if that made any difference at all in that particular scenario. ". . . friend home. Kelli Alexander." Jim pointed back at her house. "We'd been at the North Star after the game tonight, and Colton Reid followed us back here. After I dropped her off, he was sitting here . . . I don't know . . . watching. It was creepy. So I told him to get lost or I'd call the cops, but he said he didn't have to, so I pulled up behind him because I didn't want to leave him out here alone not knowing what the hell he was going to do."

The words came out fast and felt jumbled in the cold night air around them.

"Seems like every time I see you, you bring up that man's name."

Maybe there's a reason for that? Jim bit his tongue. "It's not my plan, but unfortunately he continues to be a problem."

The cop looked up and down the empty street. "Doesn't seem to be much of a problem right now. All I know is I got a call about someone here that isn't supposed to be, and when I show up, I find you."

Another flare of anger shot up into Jim's chest, and he struggled to swallow it down before it flew out at the cop in front of him.

"I don't know what beef you still have with this guy, but I don't expect to be getting any more calls about this nonsense, you hear? We're not some weapon you can point at men you don't like."

"That's not—" Jim stopped himself before charging headfirst into another losing battle. "Never mind. I'm gonna head home."

"I think that's for the best." Officer Ellison stood on the curb and watched Jim get in his car and drive away.

He glanced at Kelli's house as he passed, even more thankful the lights remained out.

Jim stewed the short drive home, eyes locked in his rearview, scanning for both pickup trucks and police cruisers, but the ride was uneventful.

He pulled into his parents' driveway and saw a faint glow coming from the front windows. His mom would have been in bed long ago. Maybe she left a light on for him. Or simply forgot to turn them off. But a clanking from the kitchen greeted Jim when he finally got through the front door.

"Mom?"

He hustled over through the living room and found his mother digging through her cabinets, an aluminum baking sheet on the floor and an old mixing bowl in her hand. "What're you doing?"

She looked back at him with the same confusion Jim felt. Like she couldn't figure out what he was doing there.

"I've got to get the treats ready."

"What treats?"

"For the camp fundraiser. Helen asked me to bring brownies, although I don't see why I can't do cookies like I do every year. I think she doesn't want to do the work is what I think."

Jim tried to put as much caring in his voice as he could. "It's kinda late for baking, isn't it?"

"Helen needs these today."

When he was a kid, the church did a bake sale to send kids to Bible camp, but he had no idea if that was still a thing. He hoped so, because while finding his mother trying to bake at midnight wasn't ideal, it was much more concerning if the bake sale was twenty years ago.

Jim walked over and picked up the baking sheet from the kitchen tile. "Why don't we wait till the morning for this, okay? You'll have plenty of time then."

The confused look on her face worried him, but she allowed him to take the bowl from her and put them back in the cupboard alongside the baking sheet. His mom didn't say anything as Jim led her down the hall and back to her bedroom.

He hit the light and saw his father's clothes folded up in piles alongside the far wall. Jim didn't make it a habit to check out his parents' bedroom, but he was pretty sure they hadn't been there the last time he'd looked.

"Okay, Mom, get some sleep." Jim stood there and watched his mother climb into her side of the bed and pull the covers up around her. She laid her head on the pillow and closed her eyes like the scene in the kitchen hadn't even happened.

Jim snapped the light off and closed the door, praying it would remain that way the rest of the night.

Chapter Twelve

The torrent of students pouring out into the parking lot had slowed to a trickle in the few minutes Jim had sat there in his SUV. He hadn't considered the optics of an adult man loitering around a school parking lot until the first kid side-eyed him on their way by. Their parents may all know who he was, but this generation didn't know and didn't care. His instinct was to slide down out of view, but he'd never be able to hide his long frame and it would make him look even creepier.

So, he smiled back and tried to look as nonthreateningly boring as possible.

All worries of getting mistaken for a kidnapper aside, Jim wasn't sure being there was a good idea. He'd texted Kelli earlier but hadn't heard back. They hadn't talked since he'd dropped her off Friday night, and under normal circumstances, that wouldn't have been a thought in his mind, but after everything that had happened, he couldn't shake the feeling that it had left a bit of a stain.

And then there was the thing with his mom. He'd lain in bed listening for her door to open again, letting anxiety dance around in his skull. When he'd woken up the next morning, his worries had metastasized.

Or, more likely, he'd finally accepted that the situation with his mom wasn't something he could ignore like his father had.

He needed someone to talk to, and the only one in town willing to talk to him about anything but basketball was Kelli.

But she hadn't answered his text, so when he was driving past the school right around three o'clock, he figured he'd stop. He'd tried to convince himself it hadn't been his plan when he told Theresa he was running into town for a quick errand, but he knew better.

And now Jim sat in his old high school parking lot like a creep.

He let good judgment take the wheel and put his car into gear. He'd rolled barely six feet when someone stepped into his path, and Jim slammed the brakes. His seat belt kept his torso in check while his head slapped forward and sprang back into the seat.

He shook his head and saw Carrie standing in front of his SUV, her hands on the hood and eyes the size of coasters. "Oh my God, Carrie . . ." Jim shifted into park and jumped out. "I'm so sorry, I . . ."

She waved him off as the color returned to her face. "It's okay. I wasn't watching where I was going."

"No, I was spacing out—it's my fault." He looked her up and down, but she seemed fine. "Are you okay?"

A smile forced its way onto her face, and she nodded. "Yeah, fine." She took a deep breath to steady herself and flush out any remaining nerves. "What are you doing here?"

Jim wanted a second to gather himself but wasn't prepped to handle the awkwardness silence brought and plowed ahead. "I was hoping to catch Kelli after school."

Something might have flashed through Carrie's eyes, but it was gone before he could register it. It was the first time he'd talked to her without Kyle around since he'd come back to Silent Creek. And there was no reason that should be weird.

"She's at practice."

"Of course . . . duh!" Jim smacked himself on the forehead like he was in a cheap sitcom and was immediately embarrassed by the lameness of it, like he was walking through a field of rakes. "I guess I thought they had late practice this week."

Carrie either didn't pick up on his awkwardness or didn't care. "I can run back in and give her a message or something . . . have her call you when she's done?"

"No worries. It wasn't a big deal or anything, I . . ." Carrie smiled, and for the first time since high school, he saw the girl he'd dated. It didn't stir anything romantic inside him, but it reminded him of why he'd liked her in the first place. Had they been compatible in a happily-ever-after way? No, he'd known that back then. But she was always a good listener. A comfort whenever the pressures of being Jimmy Buckets threatened to overwhelm him. They both probably knew what they had wasn't a forever thing when he was fretting over official visits and scholarship offers, but she'd listened. "It's my mom. I don't know if you've heard much, but she's . . . she's having some memory problems."

Carrie nodded sympathetically. "Yeah, I've heard some stuff. Is it getting worse?"

Jim nodded and told her about finding his mom in the kitchen Friday night.

"It's hard, because I don't know what to do about it. A lot of the time she seems fine, but then . . ."

"They learn how to hide it," Carrie said. "You remember my Grandma Retta? She was diagnosed with Alzheimer's shortly after graduation. You notice a few things here and there, but you blow it off because you want to. She forgets her purse, no big deal. Everybody does. She says something odd, that's just Grandma. But eventually you know there's more to it, and you have to have some hard conversations because you want what's best for them. That's gonna be hard for you because you're doing it alone. You don't have any brothers or sisters to help. I was still pretty young, so I didn't have to really get involved, but Mom had her sisters, and they eventually sat down with my dad and had a long talk about what they needed to do."

"That's the thing," Jim said. "It had to be going on for years, and Dad never said *anything* to me about this. I had no clue until I came back and she's baking brownies in the middle of the night." His voice had risen to match the emotion he'd been swallowing, and Jim glanced around at the now deserted parking lot. Even while he complained about his dad hiding his mother's condition, he worried that others would hear him.

That's different.

Yes, not wanting the Silent Creek rumor mill to pick up on his mother's condition wasn't near the same as not telling your own son about it.

Jim blew out some anxiety and noticed the length of his shadow stretching across the parking lot. He'd been gone much longer than his excuse of an errand had any right to take.

"I should get back to work. Sorry to unload on you like this."

Carrie smiled again. "It's not a problem at all. It's a tough thing, I certainly know that. Especially if you are doing it alone."

"Yeah, well, you probably weren't ready for it on the way to your car," Jim said. "Thanks though."

"Anytime," Carrie said. "It was nice talking to you. We should go out Friday after we get back from the game . . . assuming it goes well."

"Sounds good." Jim pulled his car door open and slid behind the wheel. Carrie walked around the bumper to his door, so he rolled the window down.

"Hey . . . if you're planning on going and want to ride over to Stewartville together, let me know."

Jim considered it for a second. Might be nice to have someone to talk to on the drive over. "Sure. May as well save some gas."

He waved one last time and drove off toward McCann. It hadn't crossed Jim's mind, but there was no reason that should be weird. If they were going to be friends, there should be no second thought and no reason for them to both drive all the way to Stewartville.

Jim weaved through the streets of Silent Creek out to McCann LP and pulled into his dad's old parking spot.

The wind hit harder and colder outside town, and the sun was too busy retreating over the horizon to do anything about it as Jim took the dozen steps to the door.

Theresa was playing some late-afternoon solitaire on her computer and barely paid his return any attention. Jim said hi as Kyle popped out of his office.

"There you are," he said. "I've got some orders I need your signature on."

Kyle plopped a manila folder on Theresa's desk and pulled out a handful of papers. Jim grabbed a pen from a collection in an old Silent Creek Beavers mug and started scribbling. He no longer felt like he was actively drowning at work but was still leaning hard on his old friend to stay afloat. And while Kyle made a point to defer to Jim as the boss, it was obvious he was dolling out only the most mundane tasks for Jim while doing most of the heavy lifting himself.

Jim wondered if that's how it had been with his dad the last few years.

"I thought you were just running to the post office," Kyle said. "What took you so long?"

Jim opened his mouth for a second and paused. He didn't care what he said in front of Theresa—she probably knew more about his private family business than he did—but Jim wasn't comfortable bringing Kyle in yet. Not that it would be a problem or anything. Heck, Carrie would probably tell him everything that night anyway.

But he didn't want to.

"You know how the line is there."

Chapter Thirteen

The smell of fresh popcorn hung in the thick gymnasium air and combined with at least fifty years of sweat soaked into the hardwood to form the unmistakable smell of small-town high school basketball. Sneakers squeaked through gym doors into the foyer, where much of the late-arriving crowd lined up at the concession window or stood in little pods of parents, catching each other up on the latest gossip from around town.

A wave of memories crashed over Jim from the moment he and Carrie walked through the school doors, and it pulled a smile out of him. Two kids no more than five cut in front of them, chasing each other around the foyer like greyhounds, parents nowhere in sight. They'd be out there all night, joining up with others to form a feral pack of littles, roaming the deserted halls of the school in *Lord of the Flies*-style anarchy until their parents rounded them up after the game, never seeing so much as a second of basketball.

Another small-town basketball tradition.

Not for Jim, though. He hadn't been allowed to run around like a wild child. He sat between his parents, because they didn't come to a game to run around like a maniac. They came to watch basketball, so that was what they were going to do. Even though all his friends were out there, he knew better than to ask, so he watched the game.

Probably where he'd gotten his interest in the sport. He'd had no other choice.

Jim paid for Carrie's admission over her objection—five bucks was a small price to pay for a twenty-five-minute ride over. He'd been a little worried it would be awkward, but it was nice to have someone to talk to. They'd spent time together since he'd moved back, but always with Kyle and Kelli around. With only the two of them in the car, they found themselves reminiscing about high school days. Carrie told him about driving over here with her friends to watch Jim play, taking wrong turns and ending up on country roads in the middle of nowhere. It took so long to find their way they missed most of the first half.

She'd asked if he remembered that happening, and he'd lied and said he did.

He only had bus rides to look back on, and all those blurred together.

"You want a pop or anything?"

Carrie declined, and they headed over to the gymnasium doors on the visitors' side.

"Haven't seen you two together in a long time."

Jim turned around and took a second to recognize the lady walking in behind them. Patricia Harper. Her daughter was in their graduating class and one of Carrie's best friends growing up. He remembered Mrs. Harper being nice but wasn't a fan of the grin on her face.

Carrie chose to ignore it, so Jim did too. "Good to see you, Pattie. Heard from Sara lately? I always see her stuff on Facebook, and her kids are absolutely adorable."

An opportunity to brag about her grandkids wiped whatever implications Mrs. Harper had inferred off her face, and if Carrie had done it on purpose, Jim was impressed. They stood there in the doorway as the woman gushed. More and more people squeezed by them into the gym until Carrie used it as an excuse to cut the woman off and said goodbye.

Kelli's team was running through a layup drill on the near side, while the other team warmed up on their half of the court. Kelli was talking with two of the referees near the scorers' table, but Jim didn't want to bother her pregame, so he headed for the bleachers.

As if she could feel his presence, Kelli shot a quick wink over at Jim as he turned into the stands. He put his head down, trying to hide the flush in his cheeks.

Is this how Carrie used to feel at his games?

They climbed up the steps, and Jim could feel more than Kelli's eyes on him. As someone who towered over most people around him, he was used to drawing looks but couldn't deny the fact that some of the Stewartville crowd knew who he was. He'd already had two middle-aged men say hi—neither of whom he knew, so he just gave an awkward smile back.

The Silent Creek boys' team was clumped together in the top corner of the bleachers, where they'd watch the girls' game until heading down to the locker room around halftime. Kyle was sitting with his assistant coach—*their* old assistant coach—John Pederson.

"Look what the cat dragged in." It was a bit of a weird thing to say to your wife, so Jim assumed it was meant for him. "You guys roll up at the same time or something?"

"Carrie gave me a ride."

"Oh." There was an unmistakable flash of surprise across Kyle's face, but he did a good job of burying it before things could get awkward.

"It didn't make sense for both of us to drive over." Carrie sat down on the bleachers next to her husband and started digging through her purse for something. Jim had worried about the ride being awkward between the two of them but hadn't even thought about Kyle having a problem with it. They'd been married for six years or something, while Jim and Carrie had barely spoken since high school. Besides, Jim's stomach was still netting little butterflies from the wink that Kelli had given him down on the floor. There was nothing for Kyle to worry about.

"Sure," Kyle said.

Was it weird that Carrie hadn't told Kyle about their plan? An awkward silence hung in the crowd noise, so Jim chased it away by asking Kyle about the Stewartville team they were playing that night.

Kyle went into a needlessly detailed scouting report as the referees blew their whistles and herded the teams to their benches.

Kyle lowered his voice so his players behind him wouldn't overhear. "If we can execute, we'll be fine, but we'll see how *that* goes."

Jim nodded as the girls' starting lineups were announced. He remembered what Kelli had said about keeping things simple for her players but kept his mouth shut. Kyle was going to do what he was going to do and probably wouldn't appreciate any Monday-morning quarterbacking from the guy who'd repeatedly turned down his offers to be an actual coach.

Kyle was telling a story about one of their old games at Stewartville as Kelli's squad jumped out to an early lead. Jim wanted to tell him to pay attention to what was working down on the floor but bit his tongue.

Before long the horn blew to end the second quarter, and the Silent Creek Beavers were up 38–21.

"All right, fellas, head down and get dressed." Kyle's team filed down the bleacher steps in khaki pants and sweaters their moms had certainly bought with no input from the players. The Silent Creek Beavers' dress code for road games hadn't changed since he'd been in high school.

"Okay then, see you guys after the game." Kyle gave Jim a fist bump, then leaned down and gave Carrie a kiss. She seemed legitimately surprised as he headed down the bleachers. He stole a quick look back at them when he hit the floor, and Jim waved.

"Good luck, buddy."

The stands began filling up between games, which bummed Jim out. The girls worked just as hard as the boys and deserved to play in front of full bleachers too. If anything, Kelli's team deserved *more* fans that year. They were certainly treating them to a better product. The Beaver girls came out of the locker room after halftime on fire, scoring their first half-dozen trips down the floor and putting the game out of reach early.

As fun as the team was to watch, Jim couldn't take his eyes off Kelli. She was a natural, roaming in front of the bench in her purple Silent Creek polo, dark hair pulled back in a long ponytail like this was just another practice.

Maybe that was the point? Even if it wasn't, she projected such a controlled aura it was no wonder her team played loose.

A stark contrast to what happened on the court in front of them when the boys' game started.

Jim glanced up at the scoreboard. The Beaver boys were down 18–11 with the first quarter ticking away. Kyle's sports coat had already come off in a rather impressive fashion, and they could see the frustration creeping up his face from the stands.

A few members of the girls' team were coming back into the gym, easy to pick up with hair still wet from the showers, and Jim caught that little flutter in his stomach again because it meant Kelli would be out soon.

A referee's whistle bleated and brought a roar from the crowd. Jim hadn't seen the play, but by the shade of Kyle's face, he strongly disagreed with the ref's interpretation of events. He was three full steps out onto the court as the ref jogged over to the scorers' table to record the foul. The home crowd was loud enough he couldn't tell what Kyle was saying, but if he didn't cool down, he was going to draw a technical foul.

The referee gave him a second to have his say before heading down the court, but Kyle kept chirping. Carrie put her head in her hands as chants of "SIT DOWN, COACH!" started up in the Stewartville student section and quickly filled the gym.

Before Jim could wonder how long a leash the referee had, he blew his whistle and brought his hands together in a T. The crowd erupted in a cacophony that shook decades-old dust from the rafters. Kyle took another two steps toward the ref, his arms spread like he couldn't understand what he could have possibly done, and it only amped up the home fans more.

Coach Pederson finally got up from the bench and grabbed Kyle by the wrist to pull him off the court.

Even with his eardrums thrumming, Jim could feel the mortification radiating from Carrie. Not knowing what else to do, he put his arm on her shoulder and gave a supportive squeeze. She reached up and patted his hand, then held his fingers for long enough Jim pulled them away.

The crowd eventually died down when their guy stepped up to the free throw line, where—fortunately for the Beavers' dimming hopes and Jim's ears—he missed both, and it tamped down some of the rancor.

The game settled back in as the final minute of the first quarter ticked away.

"Well, let's hope the guys got the road jitters out of their system and can settle in now." Jim didn't believe it for a second but didn't know what else to say. Luckily Kelli had finished up in the locker room and was headed up to them. If she'd seen—there was no way she hadn't heard—Kyle's technical foul, she didn't mention it.

"Hey, guys." She slid into the spot beside Carrie as the ref blew the whistle to start the second quarter.

Jim couldn't help but smile. "Nice game, Coach."

"The girls played well." She looked almost embarrassed to take the compliment.

Jim leaned forward and shifted on the bench. "That's because you had them ready. They handled that full-court press really well."

"We worked—"

"Come on Beavers!" Carrie had her hands cupped around her mouth between them, cheering on her husband's team for the first time that night as Jim and Kelli talked over her like she wasn't there.

It was an effective message, if not the most subtle.

Jim made a quick cringy face and leaned back into his seat. Kelli was more polite. "Why don't I slip over there so we don't talk over you." She got up and gave her friend a squeeze as she sidestepped in front of her and sat down next to Jim.

She was closer than she needed to be, and it didn't bother Jim one bit.

They talked about the girls' game, what worked and what didn't, getting into the weeds on basketball strategy in a way only people who've spent their lives in and around the game do. The whole time, Carrie found a sudden intense interest in the boys' game she hadn't shown before.

Kelli picked up on it before Jim and leaned into his ear. *"We can talk later."*

She turned back to the court and tracked the ball down the floor. One of the Beaver guards hoisted a three-pointer that found the bottom of the net, and Kelli let out a whoop.

Jim followed her lead.

They watched the game for the rest of the quarter, Kelli showing her school spirit and making small talk with Carrie to ensure she wasn't feeling ignored. By the time the horn blew for halftime, Kyle's squad had climbed back into the game and were only down five.

"I'm going to head down to the locker room and make sure the girls didn't leave it a complete disaster." Kelli stood up and maneuvered her way down the bleachers among the throngs of people heading out for some halftime concessions.

Jim watched as people kept stopping her to offer congratulations on the win. Silent Creek had never had much success in its girls' basketball program, so it was refreshing to see what Kelli was building there.

"I think I'm gonna get a pop." He wasn't really thirsty but needed to get up and stretch his legs. The cramped bleachers were doing his knee no favors. Jim looked down at Carrie as he stood up. "You want anything?"

"I'm good." Jim analyzed her voice for any awkwardness, but whatever had bothered her earlier seemed to have passed.

He followed the path Kelli had blazed earlier down the bleachers but turned the opposite way when he got to the floor and headed back out into the foyer. He got a few more nods from strangers who recognized him as he got in line at the concession stand.

"Hey, boss."

Jim looked up and saw Brent Halverson standing with his two daughters, both of whom played for Kelli. Jim shook his hand and smiled at Brent's kids. "You guys played well tonight."

The girls gave a pair of bashful smiles, while their dad beamed. "Yeah, they hit their shots. It was fun."

"Must've learned it from their old man," Jim said. Brent had been five or six years ahead of him in high school, but he remembered seeing him play for the Beavers.

"Shoot, I never filled it up like that." Halverson pulled the battered Twins cap off his head and ran a hand through his thinning hair. "I tell you what, though, Coach Alexander's got something going here. The girls really like playing for her."

Pride filled Jim's chest, and his face matched Halverson's.

"I was telling some of the guys at work that Kyle should get a few tips from her."

Jim chuckled but cut it off when he remembered Kyle was Brent Halverson's supervisor and it was probably bad form for the boss to be cutting him down. "Hopefully they can turn it around in the second half."

The conversation dried up as Halverson's kids got to the front of the line, bought their candy, and handed the change to their dad.

"Good seeing you, boss," Halverson said.

"Yeah, see you Monday." Even though he'd been there for over a month, it weirded Jim out to be called *boss* since he still felt like the new guy. "You know I'm still getting up to speed on things out there, so if there's anything you need or anything I can do for you guys, let me know."

Halverson nodded as his girls disappeared back into the gym. "I think we're good. I mean, running shorthanded isn't ideal, but we can make do until we get back to full strength."

Jim stepped out of line and let the people behind him step up to the counter. "You guys are shorthanded out there?"

Halverson suddenly looked sheepish, like he suddenly realized he'd said too much to the man in charge. "It's nothing. We're still adjusting to Reid being gone, that's all. It's all good."

The news blindsided Jim. Kyle hadn't said a thing about them running shorthanded. If anything, he'd made it seem like Reid was dead weight and getting rid of him was trimming the fat.

Before he could ask a follow-up, a voice called out from behind them.

"C'mon, move."

Jim realized they'd hit the front of the line and the people behind were getting impatient.

"Ope, better let you go," Halverson said and headed back to the gym.

Still flustered by what his head mechanic had told him, Jim quickly scanned the concession offerings. He ordered a popcorn and soda but got a blank look when he dug out his credit card to pay.

"Um . . . we can't take that."

Jim forced a smile and put the card back in his wallet. "Sorry about that, I—"

The same voice from before cut him off, with some aggression added to the impatience.

"Hey, McCann, some of us want to see the second half."

Jim spun around and locked eyes with a pair of middle-aged men in Stewartville Tigers caps about three groups back. He'd never seen them before, but they obviously remembered him. He opened his mouth to tell them off but realized that if they recognized him, there was a good chance others did, too, and the last thing he needed was stories spreading about him fighting with basketball parents from another town.

He held eye contact for another second before turning back to his popcorn. The people in line between them had quieted enough that he heard the words "overrated bust" from his new fan club.

Jim took a frustrated breath and pulled a twenty-dollar bill out of his wallet and handed it to the kid behind the counter.

"You see those two guys in the hats back there? Tell them their popcorn is on me."

He grabbed his stuff and headed back into the gym, feeling a dozen sets of eyes on him the entire way.

Chapter Fourteen

They'd sat in the SCHS parking lot so long that the windows on Carrie's car had started to fog up. Jim wiped the condensation off the passenger window so he could see if the team bus was coming down the street.

"Been a while since we steamed up the windows in this parking lot," Carrie said.

It was not what anyone wanted to hear from their best friend's wife, which was probably why it brought such a laugh from Jim.

"You think they stopped to get something to eat or something?"

"Not after that game," Carrie said. "Not a chance."

Yeah, if his sideline demeanor was any indication, Kyle wouldn't be in the mood to stop for ice cream after a fifteen-point loss. It hadn't happened often, but Jim remembered the black cloud that filled the bus after a loss back when they played. Coach Frederick would barely let them talk because they were supposed to be thinking about their game and what they planned on doing to make sure they didn't feel this way again.

He hoped Kyle had evolved from that medieval thinking but wasn't confident.

That said, his team wasn't the only one on the bus. The girls had done their jobs that night, stomping the crap out of Stewartville, so why should they have to ride home like they were headed back from a funeral?

"There they are." Carrie popped open her driver's side door, and a blast of cold air flooded the car as she got out to meet the bus. Jim stayed in his seat, figuring it was better to wait inside with heat and the 2000s channel on satellite radio than standing in a frosty night.

The bus pulled into the parking lot and started spilling out teenage basketballers and their bags. Jim climbed out of the car in time to see Kyle crossing the parking lot. He looked past him but saw no sign of Kelli.

Kyle had reached the car before Jim had a chance to think of something supportive to say, so he stuck with the basics.

"Hey, man."

Kyle nodded in his direction and tossed his bag in the back seat. Carrie hadn't said anything yet—she probably knew how to handle him after a loss better than Jim did.

Carrie gave him a half hug as he shut the back door. Jim saw Kelli haul a few bags out of the bus, then quick wave before turning back to talk with the driver.

"So . . . you guys want to pop over to the North Star for a beer?"

Kyle shook his head. "I just want to go home."

"Come on, man," Jim said. "I'll get the first round."

"Thanks, but I've got to send a few emails tonight."

Carrie got into the driver's seat as Kyle walked around the front of the car toward the seat Jim had recently occupied. He stepped aside so Kyle could get at the door handle. "Emails?"

"To the MSHSL. Those officials have no business reffing a high school game. Ever."

Granted, Jim hadn't been paying full attention to the boys' game that night, but he didn't remember any particularly egregious calls. Maybe the ref let the crowd get to him on Kyle's technical foul, but his friend had certainly put himself out on that ledge. To be honest, Jim wouldn't have been shocked had they given him a second one after his reaction.

"It was a tough game," Jim said. "But can I give you some advice—"

"*Now* you want to give me advice?" Kyle's shoes crunched on the salty concrete as he spun back at Jim, and his voice echoed through the parking lot. Over his shoulder, Jim saw Kelli stop and give him a concerned look.

"Whoa, take it easy," Jim said. "It was a bad loss, man. I get it. Losing sucks. But what I'm saying is don't do anything you're going to regret later. You start making complaints to the MSHSL and word's going to get out. You're going to have a long career in this league, and you don't want to be battling the refs every night, do you?"

"Did you even watch the game? They were hand checking *literally* all night, nothing called. How the hell are we expected to compete when our guys are getting held every time down the court? Then we *breathe* on someone . . ."

Some things never change. The two of them had sat in this very parking lot fifteen years ago, Kyle complaining about some kid from Fairmont who traveled every time he touched the ball or a guy from Albert Lea who practically knocked him to the ground on a shot that didn't go in. There had never been a failure Kyle couldn't find a scapegoat for.

"It's basketball, man." Jim glanced up and saw Kelli had resumed her walk across the parking lot—albeit slower than before. "Let's go get a drink. We can bitch about the refs, then flush it down and move on. Sound good?"

Kyle sucked in a deep breath of night air and blew it out in a cloud as Kelli stepped up behind them.

"Hey, guys." She bent down and waved at Carrie through the windshield. "You guys want to hang out a bit?"

Jim smacked Kyle on the shoulder as if he could knock loose the black cloud that surrounded him. "Come on, whaddya say?"

He reached out and opened the car door. "Sorry, man, I'm beat." He started toward the seat, then stopped. "And I know you're right about the MSHSL and the refs and stuff. I'm only blowing off steam. Didn't mean to snap at you, it's just . . ."

"Fair enough." Jim thought back to the conversation he'd had with Brent Halverson in the concession line before those Stewartville jerks interrupted. "But there is something I want to ask you about. Work related, not basketball."

Kyle dropped down in the passenger seat and rubbed his temples. "Can it wait till Monday?"

Kelli gave him a cautious look and Jim decided to let it go.

"Sure." Jim saw the weariness in Kyle's face. "It can wait."

Kyle thanked him and shut the door. Jim and Kelli stood there in the cold parking lot, watching them go.

When they disappeared around the corner, Jim turned to Kelli. "How was the bus home?"

"Pretty much like that."

Jim gave a little laugh. "He never was a good loser."

"Neither am I." A smirk slid across Kelli's face. "That's why we choose not to."

A laugh burst out of Jim and bounced around the now empty parking lot. He grabbed her icy fingers, and the two walked over to his car, sitting cold and alone across the way. "In that case, I better buy you a victory drink."

Chapter Fifteen

Jim and Kelli stayed out long enough the streets of Silent Creek were the kind of deserted reserved for school nights, not the weekend. Streetlights glowed above with a frosty haze, while porch lights were more sporadic as the town buttoned up for the night.

If it were up to him, Jim would have stayed out all night. The North Star had been packed, and there was a steady stream of people stopping by their booth to talk basketball.

And for the first time since he'd moved back, the majority of them weren't talking to him.

Everyone wanted to congratulate Coach Kelli on another big win—and Jim loved sitting there watching people pop over to heap praise on her and her team.

Eventually the crowd dwindled enough they could talk, but shortly thereafter it was last call. They stayed as long as they could, but when chairs started going up on tables around them, it was time to admit defeat and end the night.

As Jim pulled into the driveway of his parents' house, the tires below him crunched on the combination of sand and rock salt that caked the streets from November to March. He sat in his car, staring at the garage door in front of him, letting his thoughts and emotions swirl around inside.

When he'd first moved back, he could feel the town's tentacles wrapping around him, holding him down, waiting for him to stop struggling and accept the fact that he was not going anywhere.

But whenever he was with Kelli, the negativity he'd allowed himself to wallow in disappeared. The constriction felt more like a warm hug.

Maybe things are finally starting to turn around?

He chuckled at the memory of something she'd said that night. He didn't remember what it was, just the laugh it had brought, and he let that memory wash through him.

He thought about the two of them elsewhere. They could move into his old South End neighborhood in Boston. Walk out and get coffee on Saturday mornings. Go catch a decent band at the Orpheum or maybe even the Paradise. They wouldn't have to hang out at the North Star, but could drive out to Tree House Brewing, where the haze wasn't in the air but in the beer, where it belonged.

Maybe someday.

Jim cut the ignition and stepped out into the night.

The house was dark, which was a relief after coming home to find his mom in the kitchen the other night.

From the front, everything looked normal. But once Jim hit the right angle, he could see the front door was cracked open a few inches. Alarm bells blared through his head as he cut around his SUV and tore off toward the front steps.

He knocked the door open and flew inside. The living room was dark and still, the little light bleeding in from the street behind barely enough to give everything a blurry shadow.

"Mom?"

The word bounced around the dark before fading away unanswered.

Jim raced over to the kitchen and threw on the light. Pristine counters and a sink full of dirty dishes popped into view, but no sign of his mother.

Panic bubbled up his throat like bile, and he tried his hardest to swallow. The kitchen light spilled through the doorway and stretched down the hall. His mom's bedroom was back there, where she most certainly lay sleeping—if he hadn't woken her up with his panicked arrival.

Jim started down there, slowly because he told himself he didn't want to wake her up but more because he was afraid of what he'd find.

Or wouldn't.

The door was closed, while his bedroom was still open across from it. Jim squeezed the handle, waiting, scared to twist, but finally did. Something inside clicked, and the hinges squeaked loudly as he eased the door open.

The lights were off, but his eyes had adjusted enough he could tell the bed was empty.

"Mom?" As if she were hiding in a closet or something. Playing hide-and-seek and Jim could simply call off the game.

Jim flipped on the light to confirm what he knew. The bed was made, an annoying number of decorative pillows arranged precisely along the headboard.

He ran over to check his room on the opposite side for some reason. Empty. The bathroom at the end of the hallway was dark and unoccupied.

His phone itched in his pocket, telling him to call the police immediately. Jim ran down to the basement instead. He flipped on every light he could find as if that would make his mom appear. He checked the back porch, then the backyard, then back inside again.

"Mom?" If she were still there, she'd have heard him tearing around the house by then. The realization sent a bolt of fear through him. He'd heard stories of people suffering from dementia wandering off. Sometimes found miles away, standing in traffic or in the middle of the woods, their skin scratched up and burrs covering their legs.

Sometimes not found at all.

Jim ran out the front door, and the cold air outside slapped him in the face. He fumbled the phone out of his pocket as he ran down the path to the street. He didn't wait to look down the block before dialing 911.

"My name is Jim McCann. I just came home, and my mother is missing. She has . . . she has some memory problems, and I'm afraid she wandered off somewhere."

The operator offered practiced assurances and asked the requisite questions. She'd contact the Silent Creek Police Department, and they would be right over, but Jim was already in his SUV.

"Tell them I'm out looking for her."

As he pulled out of the driveway, she asked him to stay home so he could give the responding officers the information they needed.

"I'm giving *you* the information now so I can go out and find her."

Jim ignored her protests.

"Chief Nelson knows me. You've got my number, right? Tell him I'm out looking for my mom and if he needs anything to call, but I'm not sitting around while she's out there." Jim looked at the ring of frost creeping at the corners of his windows and wondered if there was any way his mom was properly dressed. "If I find her, I'll call back."

He didn't even notice he'd used the word *if.*

Jim's SUV slowly rolled down the street, his window down despite the cold because the damn thing kept fogging up and he needed to look into the yards and behind the bushes and down the side streets. His foot kept slowly pressing down on the accelerator, but he forced himself to pull back. Haste wasn't worth anything if he missed something because he'd flown by. He blew a frosty breath out the window as he craned his neck back toward the Batemans' house.

Maybe he should get out and walk. There's a lot of backyard space he couldn't see from the car.

But that would slow him down, and who knew how long she'd been out here? She could be freezing to death halfway across town while he's dinking around his neighborhood.

He smacked the steering wheel and accidentally let out a blast from the horn.

Maybe that was it. He should drive around hitting the horn, hollering out the window and hoping to catch her attention.

Anyone who didn't like the noise could get dressed and help look.

Jim got to the end of the block and was faced with his first decision. Like that stupid dungeon crawler computer game he and Kyle had been obsessed with in elementary school.

OBVIOUS ROUTES ARE (L)eft, (R)ight, and (F)orward

Not knowing what to do, Jim turned left onto Mill Street because it headed back toward downtown and going straight felt like doing nothing. Last week she'd tried to make brownies in the middle of the night; maybe this time she thought she was going to the grocery store or something.

He scanned up and down the street as he crept along, his foot still itching to stomp down and send him flying through every street in town.

Movement caught his eye to his right, and Jim slammed on the brakes. He popped out the driver's side door and looked over the hood. A pair of feline eyes glowed back from the bushes.

Jim slammed his fist on the roof of his SUV. The headlights showed nothing else ahead of him, but the red glow of the taillights showed the faint outline of someone walking back the way he'd come.

He threw himself behind the wheel and whipped his car around. Now basked in harsh halogen light, it was obvious it wasn't his mom—just some old guy giving the dog one last bathroom break before turning in.

Jim pulled into the guy's driveway and jumped out.

"Hey . . . Mr. Carlson." It took Jim a second to recognize the old man, and even then couldn't find his first name right away. He had on a puffy down jacket above a pair of fleece pajama pants and slip-on winter boots. Jim's headlights reflected off his glasses, kind of like the cat's eyes he'd seen earlier, and the man didn't seem too concerned about a car whipping into his driveway after midnight. "You haven't seen my mom out here, have you? Gail McCann?"

He didn't need to give her name, but his nerves added that detail. "Tonight? Can't say that I have."

Jim thanked him as he got back behind the wheel. He'd already put the SUV into reverse when the old man stepped up to the passenger side, motioning for Jim to roll his window down.

"Saw you at the game tonight. How about that girls' team, huh? We haven't had a team like that since . . ."

He couldn't believe the old man wanted to talk basketball when Jim's mom was missing, and he didn't have time to think of a polite way to tell him that.

"If you see her, let me know, okay?" How he would do that without Jim's cell number he didn't know. "I've got—"

A police cruiser passed behind them and headed down the street, then turned and disappeared toward his parents' house. "If you see her, bring her home, please?"

He didn't wait for a response before backing out and tearing off.

He'd told the operator to send them out looking. Had they found her already? Jim hadn't seen how many people were in the car, but they didn't have the lights on or anything. They wouldn't be in a hurry if they were bringing his mom home.

She'd die over all that fuss.

Jim flew around the corner in time to see the squad car pull into his parents' driveway. An officer got out of the driver's seat and headed to the front door as he pulled in behind them, bathing the cop in his headlights.

He was alone, and there were no heads sticking up from the back seat of the cop car.

"Mr. McCann." Officer Ellison walked back to the driveway as Jim choked down the disappointment that he'd been the cop to show up. "We got a call that your mother was missing?"

Jim shook his hand and used every ounce of patience he could muster while silently cursing the fact that this guy was going to make him waste time going through all this stuff again when they should be out looking. "Yes. I came home, and the front door was open. Went inside and she was gone."

"Can you show me?"

A wave of impatience flashed behind Jim's eyes. "I can, but can we please do it later? We need to find her first."

"We've got guys out looking right now," Ellison said. "But we need to go inside and take a look around to see if anything in there—"

"I know you're trying to help, but this isn't a mystery that needs to be solved," Jim said. "My mom has been struggling with dementia. She . . . she gets confused. Gets up in the middle of the night sometimes. We need to go find her right now."

"You seem a little stressed, Mr. McCann. Let's go inside for a minute and take a look around." Ellison's face was calm and helpful, like the police academy had trained it to be, and Jim fought the irrational feeling that the cop was being intentionally obtuse. "Unless there is a reason you don't want to go inside?"

Frustration boiled over.

"Because my fucking mother is out there in the cold somewhere!" Jim half expected some neighborhood porch lights to pop on as his voice echoed down the street. At the very least he expected Ellison's eyes to narrow, interrogating him without a word like he was some TV cop. "I'm sorry, I know you're doing your job, but she didn't get kidnapped or anything. If you need to, we can go in and you can look at whatever you want, but can it please be quick? We need to get out there and find her."

Officer Ellison nodded and motioned Jim toward the house. He hustled down the path and pushed inside without bothering to wipe his feet.

Gail would die if she'd seen it.

Jim flipped the lights on so Ellison could see everything he'd already said for himself—his mother was gone, and there were no signs of foul play.

"So, walk me through it." The cop scraped his shoes across the doormat about a half dozen times before stepping inside. "You came home . . . when?"

"I don't know . . . twenty minutes ago by now?"

"And everything looked normal? Nothing out of place or messed up or anything?"

"No . . . I mean, yes, it all looked normal. The lights were out when I pulled up, and I assumed Mom was in bed. But I noticed the front door was open, so I hurried in and looked around, hoping she had . . . I don't know . . . left it open by accident or something."

"And she wasn't here."

"No. I called 911 right away and went out looking." Jim looked out the front window at the empty street, mind reeling with all the places his mom could be. It'd been a long time—longer than he probably knew since there was no telling when she actually left. Anxiety boiled in his stomach. "I was talking to Bruce Carlson, when I saw you drive by and came back to meet you here."

"Is there anywhere you think she—" Ellison's cell phone pinged. He dug under his gun belt and pulled it from his pocket. "Chief Nelson is up and out looking right now as well."

That calmed Jim a little. Something about the chief getting out of bed on a cold night made him feel like they were at least taking things seriously.

"So, is there anywhere you think she may have gone? An old job? A friend's house? Sometimes people who get confused go to a familiar place."

"Nothing more than anything else." Jim leaned over and looked out the window again, somehow hoping to see his mom coming up the walkway in boots and a coat. The whole thing an embarrassing misunderstanding she'd passive-aggressively give him shit about for years. "I mean, she has friends . . . maybe the church? The grocery store?"

It hit Jim that he didn't really know as much about his mother as he'd assumed. Was there somewhere that would draw her in? Could he name more than one of her friends, let alone know where they lived?

Or was she nothing more than an old woman in the kitchen to him, prepping the same lasagna as thirty years ago because it had been his favorite as a kid?

Officer Ellison popped his head in the kitchen, then glanced down the hallway. "If you would like, Mr. McCann, I can stay with you until we hear something, or I can head out and join the search."

"I can't just sit here while she's out in the cold," Jim said.

Ellison put his hand up in a reassuring gesture. "We need someone here in case she comes home. If I leave, can I trust you're going to do that for us?"

The cop was right. The realization felt like swallowing a thumbtack, but he got it down. Silent Creek wasn't that big, and three cops driving around could cover most of the town.

He'd sit and wait.

Officer Ellison handed over his card with his cell number written on the back. "If she shows up, or if something pops into your head about where she may be, give me a call." He assured Jim they would find her and headed out to his car.

Jim watched from the front window as Ellison got behind the wheel of his police cruiser and said something into his radio. Jim scanned the street in front of their house as the car pulled away, blindly hoping his mom would appear.

Chapter Sixteen

After thirty minutes that felt like ninety once Officer Ellison drove away, the house phone rang. Chief Nelson was with his mother. He had called Dr. Berglund and was taking her down to the clinic to get checked out. The tone of his voice said it was more than precautionary, but Wayne Nelson wasn't one to worry someone over the phone, so he said Jim could meet them down there.

A single light above the glass door lit the parking lot of the tiny clinic, where Chief Nelson's police SUV sat next to a new-looking black Ford Expedition. Jim parked and hustled inside.

It was surreal being in the doctor's office after hours. Waiting room empty, registration desk abandoned, nobody to stop someone from walking back and digging through whatever medical file they plucked off the shelf.

"Hello?" The hallway to his right was dark, but light spilled out from somewhere around the corner. He heard muffled voices coming from down the corridor, so he followed them.

The clinic had been bought and rebranded by one of the big-city hospital chains, but it still smelled the same as when Jim had had to go for his yearly drop your shorts and cough in high school.

An oversize door stood open to Silent Creek's attempt at an emergency room. Nothing more than an exam room with a back door to the parking lot, where an ambulance could load and unload—usually load, because if someone was already in an ambulance, they'd most likely skip the clinic and go straight to the hospital up in Rochester. It's where they'd end up anyway if it was at all serious.

Gail McCann lay on a vinyl exam table, the harsh fluorescent light highlighting the red splotches that had blossomed across her face. Dr. Berglund sat on a stool by the end of the bed, while Chief Nelson leaned against the counter on the far side.

"Jimmy, it's good to see you." Dean Berglund had aged since Jim last saw him. He'd moved to Silent Creek as the new young doc to replace Dr. Hansen, who retired after serving the community for almost fifty years. Jim remembered his father saying it was pointless to hire him, that he'd be gone in a year. Had there been another option, James McCann would have sent his kid there, but Dr. Berglund was the only game in town, so they'd had to suck it up until Silent Creek got a permanent doctor—someone committed to the community like Hansen was. Not a young outsider. Jim's dad was probably surprised when Dr. Berglund met and married a young Silent Creek woman during his first year and settled into the community. He would have probably still refused to go there out of spite, but James McCann never felt the need to go to the doctor, so it was a moot point.

Had he done so, maybe he'd still be running his business and Jim would be in Boston.

Jim stayed rooted in the entryway, unsure of what to do. The anxiety that had coursed through his veins while his mom was missing needed to go somewhere, and it morphed into awkward nervousness. He should go over to his mom. Check on her, give her a hug, but that wasn't how they did things. Gail would probably shoo him away, scold him for making such a fuss.

"How is she?" He spoke like she wasn't there.

"She's going to be fine." Dr. Berglund scooted his stool up and patted Gail on the hand. "She was out without proper clothes for a bit, though."

Jim looked up at his mother. Her face was disturbingly passive. Gail McCann would normally be restless. Embarrassed that such a fuss had been made over what was obviously a misunderstanding and fretting that anyone see her in such a state. She was wearing an old cotton housecoat, its faded pink turned a wet dark color below the knee from the snow and slush she'd been walking through.

It was then Jim saw her feet for the first time. The skin looked tight and was the pallid, waxy color of an old bar of soap. Cotton balls were stuck between each of her toes, and Jim could see pale scrapes of red along the bottoms.

"I'm a little concerned about her feet, though." Dr. Berglund kept his voice low, as if he didn't want Gail to hear. Or was trying not to upset her.

Jim leaned back up and grabbed the front of his hair.

Chief Nelson motioned over at the counter next to him. "She was wearing these."

A pair of his mom's knit slippers lay in a soggy clump next to him.

"How long was she out there?"

The chief shook his head. "I don't know. She wasn't talking much when I found her, and I mostly wanted to get her out of the cold."

Water dripped from the counter onto the floor and the cop's boots. Jim looked back at his mom's waxy feet.

"What were you doing out there, Mom?"

She waved off the question like it was ridiculous. Jim walked over to her and knelt down by the bed.

"Mom." He gently grabbed her hand, then again when she pulled it away. "It's pretty late. And cold outside. Where were you going?"

"I know it was late." Her eyes sharpened, and her tone of voice was confident, whatever confusion had caused her to wander gone. "I was headed home."

Jim looked up at Chief Nelson and gave a half shrug. "You were at home, Mom. Where were you going?"

Her eyes darkened. "I *told* you, I was going home."

Dr. Berglund got up from his stool and nodded toward the doorway. "Can we have a quick talk?"

Jim followed him back into the dark hallway. Chief Nelson followed but leaned against the doorway so he could keep an eye on Gail in the bed behind them.

"I'd like to get her over to Rochester and have them take a look at her feet." The doctor's face was backlit in the hallway, so it was hard to get a read on how concerned he actually was. "It's probably just some superficial frostbite, but I want to get her checked out and make sure there isn't much permanent damage."

"*Permanent?*"

"I don't think it's too bad, but frostbite can be nasty," Dr. Berglund said. "They can check her out at Mayo and get her whatever treatment she needs."

Jim inhaled deeply and turned to take a few steps down the hall. How had it gotten this bad? Sure, his mom had been forgetting things, but he never imagined anything like this. It was twenty degrees at most outside, and she was out with nothing more than a robe and those ratty old slippers? How was that even possible?

Guilt hit him. If he'd been home, this wouldn't have happened.

"Where did you find her?" Jim didn't know why it mattered at that point, but he asked anyway.

"You know where Harold Powell lives?"

The Powells had lived in the area for years but were at best casual acquaintances of his parents.

"She was all the way out there?" The Powells had a farm a mile or so west of town, the opposite direction of where Jim had been looking.

Chief Nelson shook his head. "No, but she was headed that way. I found her out where Lake Street becomes Highway 115."

"What was she doing?"

"Walking," Chief Nelson said. "I was lucky. She happened to catch my eye as I was turning back toward downtown. I pulled up, and she said she was headed home, so I offered a ride, and she got right in. Could tell by what she was wearing that something wasn't right, so I had Doc meet me down here."

"Did she say anything else?"

"Didn't ask," the chief said. "I figured whatever reason got in her head was what it was. My priority was getting her to safety."

As much as Jim yearned to understand how this could have happened, it was hard to argue with that logic. He looked over at Dr. Berglund. "You want her to go to Mayo tonight?"

He nodded. "I've already called their emergency department. If you can drive her over, they said they have a bed ready for her. Hopefully it won't be anything that keeps her there more than tonight, but those feet really need to be looked at."

Jim sighed and nodded. He glanced at his watch and saw it was after midnight.

"Can you help me get her in my car?"

Dr. Berglund was able to get Jim's mom coaxed into a wheelchair, and Chief Nelson pushed her out the back door as Jim pulled his SUV around. Gail had perked up by that point and kept insisting she could walk just fine.

Considering what her feet looked like, Jim wondered how much awareness she actually had.

It was a good forty-minute drive to Rochester, and an awkward silence hung in the car for the first ten. Jim had a million questions, but if he couldn't trust the accuracy of the answers, what was the point?

His mom fidgeted in the passenger seat, looking out the window as if expecting to see something as they blew down the interstate.

Jim flipped through his satellite radio stations, looking for something she would be familiar with, and ended up on some soft '60s. "The Sound of Silence" floated from the speakers as his mom kept staring out at the darkened blur along the road.

"How soon till we're home?"

"What's that?" Jim heard her but didn't know how to answer. Given a second to think, maybe she'd remember where they were going. If anything, her feet should be a reminder.

"I've got to get up to make breakfast."

"Don't worry about that, Mom. You don't need to cook for me." But Jim knew she wasn't talking about him. She'd been up to cook breakfast for his dad every day of their thirty-six-year marriage. What was he supposed to do? Was it better to correct her or go along and hope the right synapses clicked together at some point?

If anything, this proved Jim was woefully unqualified to handle this on his own. Had he truly appreciated how complicated the situation was from the beginning, he wouldn't be driving his mother to the hospital at 1:00 a.m.

Denial must run in the family.

The Mamas & the Papas came on, singing about a place where the weather wasn't near as cold. Would they have to move somewhere warm so this didn't happen again? Gail would never agree to leave Silent Creek. She'd spent her entire life there. Even if they did, would she wake up some night and try to walk home?

Jim briefly closed his eyes against the blur of the empty highway in front of him.

"Did your friend find you?"

He let out another breath of exasperation. "What do you mean, Mom?"

"He was out front."

Jim wanted to dismiss it as another fantasy, but her voice was clearer than before, less distant.

"Who was out front?"

"Your friend." Again with the hand wave. Her frustration was evident. "The guy you played basketball with. You know who I'm talking about."

She was right; Jim did know who she was talking about. "What was he doing?"

His mom stared out the window long enough Jim thought she'd left the memory behind. "He said he was looking for you, but then he drove away."

"That's why you went outside? To go see . . . that guy?" It sparked a fire inside him where the nerves and anxiety that had built up over the last few hours went up like kindling. Jim had mostly ignored what Colton had been doing, giving the benefit of the doubt and hoping it would go away. Petty shit at work was one thing, but showing up at his parents' house was a whole other level. Whatever he'd thought he was doing, it ended up with his mom wandering off in the middle of a cold night. Hell, maybe that had been his plan all along? Make some noise to lure a poor woman outside, where maybe she'd get confused and wander off.

The fire inside burned into rage as he drove down the highway.

Chapter Seventeen

By the time they got to the Mayo Clinic, it was past 2:00 a.m., but the emergency department never sleeps. The waiting room was half full of people in various stages of coughing or drunkenness, toting Kleenex or bags of ice held against their faces or ankles. Luckily the desk was expecting his mother's arrival, and she was wheeled back into a glass bay that felt more like a cubicle than a hospital room.

After a few minutes, a woman in blue scrubs under a long white coat came in and introduced herself as Dr. Christine Russi. She gave Jim a nod and Gail a reassuring smile before starting her examination.

Jim stayed as out of the way as he could, but seeing the doctor's dark-brown fingers gently holding his mom's feet really revealed the pallid-white coloring of her toes. The doctor finished her examination and was relatively confident there would be no lasting damage, which should have calmed Jim some. But while the news was welcome, he wasn't ready to douse the fire inside him. He sat and stewed in a hard plastic chair as nurses soaked his mom's feet in tepid water, slowly turning them from chalk white to rosy pink as the skin thawed.

They made small talk with his mom as they worked, sticking to benign topics, and if you didn't know how Gail had come to be in the emergency room with frostbitten feet, you'd never have thought there was any impairment.

But they knew. Not long after the nurses had started working on her, a social worker pulled Jim out to ask him questions about what had happened. The questions felt pointed, but he answered as nondefensively as possible.

Yes, he suspected his mother suffered from dementia.

No, she hadn't been seen by a neurologist.

No, she hadn't had other episodes of wandering—he neglected to mention the incident in the kitchen because he was afraid of how that may look.

Yes, he understood that he needed to take more precautions to make sure this wouldn't happen again.

In the end, she gave him some colorful pamphlets and suggested he make an appointment in neurology as soon as possible.

And he would. He'd known he'd have to eventually, and this was a wake-up call.

About a couple of things, actually, but the doctors couldn't help with that.

When he got back into his mom's room, she had fallen asleep. Her feet had finished their soak, and the nurse was lightly wrapping them in gauze. Dr. Russi returned and went over home care instructions with Jim. She'd have to keep off her feet as much as possible for the next few days, while Jim would need to change the bandages every twelve hours. Any blisters were not to be popped, and he was to keep an eye out for darkness and discoloration in the skin.

Other than that, she should make a complete recovery.

Before discharging them, she asked if Jim had spoken with the social worker. Her long dark braids were twisted up under a scrub cap, and she was tall enough not to have to crane her neck to make eye contact with Jim. He nodded and held up the pamphlets.

"We got a little lucky tonight that things didn't turn out worse." Dr. Russi explained that dementia was something that didn't get better on its own, or at all, really. It was a steady slide downward, and while they could slow it down with treatment, they couldn't stop or reverse it. He needed to be prepared for that. "It's your job to make sure something like this doesn't happen again."

He agreed, and she reassured him that while this would be challenging, he'd be able to handle it with some help.

Shortly after, the nurses helped his mom into a wheelchair, and Jim pushed her out to the car.

Gail slept the whole ride home as Jim watched the sun creep up behind them. He'd thought a caffeine boost might be necessary to keep them on the road, but the anger in his gut was more than enough to chase away the drowsiness that tried to poke through.

He would make an appointment for his mother when they got home. If nothing else, that night had proven the need for action. He wasn't going to be like his dad.

But there was another phone call he needed to make first.

Jim called as soon as they got home, but Chief Nelson waited until after lunch to stop over so Gail could get some rest. It was a good idea for Jim, too, but sleep wasn't an option.

Jim felt a little guilty for not having taken Kyle seriously earlier. It's not like the signs weren't there. Hell, they've been there since high school. But Jim hadn't wanted to admit it.

Some things run in the family.

As mad as he'd been at his father for ignoring all the signs of his mom's decline, was it really any different from what he'd done? He'd let Colton keep messing with him and was just as responsible for what happened last night as his dad was.

Jim walked down and poked his head in his mom's bedroom. She was sound asleep.

He glanced at his watch and paced around the house for the next few hours. At some point he picked up one of the booklets on *Living with Dementia* and leafed through it. Most of it was stuff he already knew, but he found a section about how to prevent wandering.

Sometimes it can be caused by disrupted sleep cycles, and limiting daytime or evening naps can help. He glanced at his watch and went down to get his mom up immediately.

There was no television in their bedroom—James McCann would never allow it—but she needed to keep off her feet, so Jim decided to set her up on the living room couch. It took a decent amount of convincing and repeated assurances he would be careful not to scuff the walls, but he eventually got her in the wheelchair they'd brought home from the hospital and pushed her out to the living room.

The nurse had asked if they already had one at home, or knew of one they could borrow, but Jim took the one they'd had there. He couldn't imagine how much the bill would be, because he assumed whatever bare-bones policy his dad had found wouldn't cover it. Since he considered doctors for the weak, why invest in an insurance policy they'd never use?

It was another log on the fire, but that was fine. In fact, he didn't need to calm down. He needed to keep that fire burning to break the cycle and actually do something.

With Gail comfortable and her bandaged feet propped up on a pillow in front of her, Jim pulled their gigantic coffee table a little closer to her so she could reach the remote, phone, and glass of water he'd brought over.

It would also serve as a barrier to keep her from getting up without his help.

"Are you hungry?" Jim asked. "I could heat up some soup for lunch if you'd like?"

"Oh, I'm fine. You don't have to worry about me." She may be stuck on the couch, but Gail McCann would go hungry before allowing her son to cook for her.

"It's not a problem at all," Jim said. "Remember when I had that last knee surgery junior year? You came up to my apartment and took care of me when I was stuck on the couch, remember? It's my turn to do the same for you."

His mom's eyes drifted away from the television, and Jim worried he was losing her, but her vision cleared, and she looked up at him. "That apartment was so small."

The words brought a wave of relief. He didn't care that older memories often remained, while new experiences flittered away like gossamer butterflies. "It sure was." Reminiscing with his mom felt normal for the first time in a while, so he cast again. "You remember trying to cook in the kitchen?"

She chuckled. "You boys didn't even have a pot to boil water."

Jim sat down on the end of the couch and talked about that apartment for ten minutes. His mom remembered everything about it, even things Jim didn't recall. The cream-colored linoleum that was probably white at some point, the oven that smelled of burnt frozen pizza whenever she turned it on, the entire set of plastic cups from McDonald's. It was like they'd been looking at each other through a frost-covered window, then the sun popped out and melted it all away.

The doorbell rang, but Jim didn't want to answer it. He wanted to stay in this moment because, if he disrupted it, who knew if they'd ever get it back? Walk away and he risked knocking down whatever precariously piled-up blocks his mom was standing on that allowed her to break the surface of the murk inside her head.

Jim wanted to ask more questions while he was getting real answers, but the doorbell rang again.

"Can you get that?"

He nodded. "Sure, Mom."

Jim looked back at her once more before opening the door for Chief Nelson, who was zipped up in a fleece jacket with the Silent Creek Police Department logo and carried a paper plate covered in aluminum foil. He kicked the doorjamb with both his feet to dislodge as much slush as he could before coming inside.

"Good afternoon." He wiped his feet on the rug and stepped into the living room. "How are you feeling today, Gail?"

The light of clarity Jim had been so careful not to chase away was already gone as she offered a polite smile and started to get up from the couch. Jim ran over to stop her, but Chief Nelson held up his hand. "Oh, please don't get up on my account." He stepped over and placed the plate on the coffee table. "Susie wanted me to bring you some kringla, in case you needed a little treat."

"I should get some plates."

"No, ma'am." The chief's voice was friendly but stern. "If Susie found out you let me have anything sweet, I'd be sleeping on the couch for a week." He patted the stomach currently testing the zipper on his fleece. "She's got me on a strict diet. Besides I can't stay long. Just wanted to check in on you after last night."

He let that last sentence hang as if it were a test.

"You remember me giving you a ride last night?"

Gail's eyes darkened and found the television again. "Of course I do."

"Well, that's good." Chief Nelson stole a quick look at Jim before continuing. "It was pretty late. You remember what you were doing out there?"

She kept watching whatever game show was dancing across the screen, either upset or embarrassed by the question.

"I'd like to talk to you about that, actually," Jim said, but Chief Nelson brushed him off.

"Gail . . ."

She continued to ignore him.

"We talked about that earlier," Jim said. "Colton Reid was sitting outside in his truck."

That got the chief's attention.

"That's why she went outside. She said he was parked out front and said he was looking for me." The words rolled off his tongue like he was a lawyer giving his closing statement, but it didn't get the aha moment he'd wanted. Instead, the chief looked dubious.

"She told you that?"

Jim nodded. "Last night, on the drive to the hospital."

Chief Nelson chewed that over as Jim waited for something. If not an apology, at least an admission that he'd been right.

"I'd kind of hoped whatever problems you have with him would be over by now."

Maybe if you'd done something about it.

"Yeah, me too. Unfortunately, ever since I moved back to town, he's been causing problems for me, my business, and now my family. I've told you every time, but you don't seem to want to do anything about it."

It was the wrong thing to say, and Jim knew it before it left his mouth. But at that point he didn't know if he cared. Wayne Nelson was the chief of police, and he had to do his job even if his feelings got hurt by someone who had the audacity to call him out on it.

"Maybe we should talk in the other room." His voice was cold, and he'd turned to the kitchen before Jim had a chance to answer.

The chief had already turned around, thumbs stuck in his belt, waiting for Jim when he came in. "I heard what you had to say, and I looked into it every time. Unfortunately, just because you want to blame someone for every bad thing that happens to you doesn't make it true."

"I had to take my mom to the hospital last night," Jim said. "What else has to happen for you to take this serious?"

Chief Nelson held him in a stony glare across the kitchen. It was like he still saw Jim as a kid, and he didn't like getting lip from a kid. "I think if you were taking things serious, it would have never come to that."

Jim swallowed a hearty *fuck you* and kept his lips clamped together so it couldn't shoot back out like rancid potato salad. "What are you talking about?"

"I know you went up to Minneapolis for college, then moved out East when that was done, so you may not remember how things work in small towns like this, but you're back home now and this is a place where family is pretty darn important. Your mother needs someone to watch over her, and with your dad gone, that makes it your job, whether you want it or not."

Jim could taste the steaming bile bubbling up in the back of his throat. "Maybe if you did *your* job and did something about Colton Reid, he wouldn't have been stalking outside my mom's house?"

The chief's expression didn't change. "And maybe if you spent less time taking out that cute new coach, you'd be here to keep your mom from wandering out after him."

A million comebacks rushed for Jim's mouth like a swollen river, but he bit them back. It was like taking a hard foul under the basket. Retaliation would get him a whistle of his own. Coach had always said take it and move on. Pay them back with your play. Jim couldn't do that here, but he wasn't going to give Chief Nelson the satisfaction of striking back.

"Thank you for coming by, Chief."

The cop held his gaze for a second before turning out of the kitchen without another word.

Gail was still on the couch, watching whatever soap opera that came on after the game shows were done. Chief Nelson walked over to the couch and put his hand on her shoulder. "I'm going to take off now, Gail. Thank you for letting me stop by and talk to you."

She pushed the blanket off her lap and started to swing her bandaged feet to the floor. "No, no. I can show myself out. You rest up and let those feet heal, okay? Your son's going to be right here if you need anything. It's his turn to take care of you for once, right?" He winked down at her, but Jim caught the steel in his eye as he glanced up. "Susie's going to bring something over later, so you don't have to worry about dinner."

The chief patted Gail on the shoulder again and headed for the front door. Jim followed him out, still roiling over what to say but choosing nothing. Chief Nelson had made his feelings and priorities clear. Jim couldn't expect any help from him, so he'd have to find it somewhere else.

Colton Reid was a problem that had to be dealt with, and if the cops weren't going to do anything about it, he'd have to take matters into his own hands.

He pulled the phone out of his back pocket and fired off a text to Kyle.

Need 2 talk. You around?

Chapter Eighteen

Kyle didn't get back to Jim that weekend, so he pulled him aside first thing Monday morning. Unfortunately, it wasn't a conversation they could have at the office, so they had to wait until after practice. Since the girls' team had the gym first that week, Kyle wasn't able to get to Jim's place until nine or so.

The kitchen windows reflected the dark night back at them as they huddled around the kitchen table. Jim's mom was in the living room watching television, so they kept their voices low.

"We've got to do something," Jim said. "I mean . . . my car, the trucks, that's one thing, but . . . this is over the line."

"There's no line with guys like that. You ever hear what he did to get thrown in jail?"

"Wasn't it a bar fight over in Albert Lea?"

Kyle shook his head ominously. "It started there. Some guy said something to him or something, but Colton left and waited outside. When the guy came out, he followed him all the way to Twin Lakes and beat the shit out of him in the guy's own driveway. I heard he had a length of chain with a huge padlock on it. If the guy's wife hadn't come out, he'd have killed him. She's lucky he didn't go after her too."

Jim stared at him across the table, unable to picture the damage a weapon like that could cause in the hands of a guy the size of Colton. "So why isn't he in prison?"

"The guy he went after was a piece of shit too. Drugs, assault . . . birds of a feather, right? I figure the cops thought he deserved it, so they didn't push for anything more than assault. They were probably happy he did it for them." Kyle leaned forward on his elbows and lowered his voice even more. "Guys like that don't have a line, man. He's gonna keep coming and coming until one of you is gone."

Jim looked across the table at his childhood friend.

"So what do we do?"

The question hung over the kitchen table like the haze of smoke that used to permeate the North Star back when you could smoke indoors.

"Like I said, they let him off fairly light, but when he came on at McCann, I know there were a lot of conditions on his release." Kyle's voice was quieter and calmer than Jim was used to. The brash obnoxious undertones were gone, which at least told Jim his friend was taking this seriously. "That's the reason your dad gave for hiring him in the first place—if he did anything wrong, he'd be taken care of." Kyle shook his head.

"With conditions on his parole like that, you'd think he wouldn't be stirring shit up like this." Jim swirled the water around the glass in front of him. "It's like he has no fear."

"Guys like Colton Reid don't subscribe to logic. Besides, he's been getting away with this kind of stuff his whole life because nobody around here wants to do anything about it, as you're finding out." Kyle's frustration trailed off. "But if we could tie him to something with real evidence . . . something they can't ignore . . ."

A bubble of nerves popped up in Jim's gut. Kyle was right—the cops didn't care about petty harassment or whatever. It would have to be something major, and that brought a lot of risk on them. Anything big enough to get Colton's probation revoked would be big enough to get them in serious trouble if it went sideways and ended up pointing back at them.

"We've seen him at the North Star a few times," Jim said. "What if we wait until he leaves, then call the cops and say he's driving under the influence? It's a ways out to his place, so there's probably time for them to catch up to him."

Kyle leaned forward on the table, his own glass of water clasped between his hands, and shook out a dismissal. "First off, I don't know how anonymous a call can be in a town this size—especially from you. But even if you could do it anonymously, there's really no way for us to tell if he's over the limit or not. Even if they do catch up and pull him over, it doesn't do any good if he passes a field test."

"Could you slip something in his drink?"

Kyle gave him a look across the table. "If you can't make a phone call anonymously, how do you think you're gonna get near his drink without him or anyone noticing you?"

Jim could see all the people packed into the North Star, all their eyes that tended to follow him around even to this day. Former sports star or not, a six-foot-nine guy tends to draw looks.

"You're right. Besides, if he was out driving, he could end up crashing on the way home."

Kyle tilted his head at Jim and spread his hands across the table, like a blackjack dealer showing the table his hole card. "Problem solved."

"Jesus, I'm not looking to kill anyone," Jim said. "Besides, you never know what would happen. He could plow into someone else or something."

"No, I know." Kyle leaned back, and the old wooden kitchen chair squeaked the same threat to break it always did when it tilted back on two legs. He chewed on an idea for a minute before speaking again. "Maybe if they found some drugs on him?"

"When they pulled him over?"

"Maybe," Kyle said. "But it'll be tough to get anything into his truck. And you can't just toss something in the bed like when he got caught in high school. Nobody's that stupid. But maybe we could plant something out at his place?"

Jim leaned back in his own chair and tossed the suggestion around.

It could work.

"Okay, but how—" The realization hit like a fork in the toaster, and Jim bolted back to the bathroom with barely more than a mumbled explanation. He had been thinking about street drugs, forgetting that prescription drugs were the poison du jour nowadays. With the opioid epidemic still raging across the country, doctors were hesitant about giving out prescriptions for anything stronger than ibuprofen, and when they did, it's for an exact number of pills. But things had been different back when Jim wrecked his knee. Through ignorance or apathy, doctors used to toss around hardcore painkillers like they were parade candy.

He pulled open the cabinet door under his bathroom sink and dug out an old shoebox.

Right there, sitting alongside half-empty bottles of cold medicine, nasal spray, and a box of Band-Aids, was a trio of giant orange bottles.

The label said *OxyContin* and that they had expired years ago. But that shouldn't matter for their purposes.

Jim carried the bottles back to the kitchen and plopped them down in front of Kyle.

"Whoa." Kyle picked up one of the bottles and scanned the label. "Where the hell did you get these?"

"They gave me some every time I had knee surgery, but I never liked them, so I stopped taking them."

It wasn't that Jim hadn't liked how they made him feel—they knocked out pain even better than advertised—but they destroyed his digestive system. After his initial surgery, he got so constipated his mom went out and got him some extra-strength laxative. It had worked—unfortunately a little too well—while Jim was sleeping. He never took another. If anything would embarrass a college-age kid off taking his meds, it's watching his mother pull shit-stained sheets off his bed.

But he wasn't about to tell Kyle that.

"You think that would work?"

"I don't know." Kyle popped the top off one and spilled a palmful of pills out on the table. "I'd like to think so, but possession may not be enough for a judge. Again, it *should* be, but you know how things are nowadays."

Kyle pushed the little white discs around with his index finger, doing math in his head.

"Although with a little creativity, we should be able to put something together that sends that psycho away for good."

Chapter Nineteen

Jim sat in the dark car, engine slowly ticking down, staring out into the night. His stomach roiled with nerves, his heartbeat thrumming in his ears. The moon had ducked behind some thick low-hanging clouds that had blanketed the area all day, leaving nothing to light up the rural countryside.

An old Nike duffel bag sat on the passenger seat. Something he'd picked up at a tournament or something during his basketball days. He'd given or thrown away most of that stuff over the years, but this one survived for some reason. The pills were in there. Not only his, but a big bag of tramadol he'd found in his parents' medicine cabinet. The bottle said it was prescribed to his father in the year before he died. The label listed twenty-four pills with no refills, and Jim was not surprised that every pill was accounted for, as James McCann was not one for medicines.

Kyle had come up with a bunch of small plastic baggies, then had the idea to crush up a couple of pills and put some residue in a few of the bags to make them appear used. He'd also added a couple of hundred dollars in cash, wadded up and crumpled, figuring it was worth it to add some realism.

"He'll say somebody planted it, but nobody would give away that much cash."

As nervous as Jim was about this, Kyle seemed completely calm. More excited than anything. He'd been warning people about Colton for years, so it must've felt good to finally be proven right.

It also helped that he wasn't the one who had to do it.

Jim took a deep breath and got out of his car. The night wind was brisk and smelled like it was barely holding back a flurry of snow. It was dark enough Jim could only hear the rushing babble of Winnebago Creek. He'd parked in the pull-off below the bridge where he'd parked all those weeks ago. Back when all this was just starting. There was little worry about anyone driving past at this time of night, and even if the moon had been out and full, nobody would see his car down there.

The snow had melted and refrozen enough times the ground below his feet wasn't much more than dirty ice, so tire tracks and footprints wouldn't be an issue. The walk along the stream to Colton's house would be a different story, but there were enough old guys who came out on warmer winter days to toss a line in that any footprints he left wouldn't be out of the ordinary.

Not wanting to leave anything to chance, he brought his father's old fishing boots and jammed his size-fourteen feet inside so any prints he might leave weren't former-collegiate-basketball-player size. His mashed toes complained as Jim started for the creek, but snipping away any potential dangling thread was worth it.

The rushing current kept the creek from freezing over most of the winter, but it didn't keep snow and ice from encroaching on the sides. Jim kept a safe distance from the edge, not wanting to unknowingly step on an ice shelf and break through into the water. Not only could he injure his leg that way, but while the water didn't freeze, it was certainly bitter cold. He could just imagine lying there in the snow with a broken ankle as frostbite quickly set in.

The thought reminded him of what his mother had gone through when she wandered out, and the shot of adrenaline washed away his nerves.

It was time to stop this.

He slung the duffel bag's strap around his neck and pressed on through the muted midnight blue blur ahead of him. Colton's place was at least a mile upstream, but Jim had figured this route was the safest. Kyle had said he could drive right down Colton's driveway, insisting that his property was isolated enough that nobody would see him. Besides, Kyle was at the North Star keeping an eye on Colton and would text the second he made a move for the door.

Nervous that if something went wrong they'd be able to trace his phone out to Colton's property, Jim had left his at home and brought his mom's. Kyle said he was being paranoid, but Jim figured it was better to be extra cautious. His mom was at home asleep, so she'd never miss it. Not that she used it much. It mostly sat on the kitchen counter anyway.

Speaking of paranoid, Jim dug it out of his back pocket and lit up the home screen. A picture of his parents at a cabin up north appeared, and he tried not to make eye contact with his dad.

Battery, 94 percent.

Three bars of reception.

No messages.

He put the phone away and let his eyes adjust to the dark again.

That stretch of Winnebago Creek was picturesque during the trout season. Gin-clear water snaking through the countryside. Tall grass lining the near bank, dense thickets of trees stretched along the far side.

The terrain was different once it got cold. The tall grass had all died back, making walking along the creek easier. The crunch of old snow under his father's boots carried in the cold night air, pierced by the distant hoot of an owl. Alone at night, the sound wasn't as cute as it was in nature shows. It was foreboding, almost a warning.

Nothing but trouble up here.

He thought about the last time he'd been out there, Colton showing up out of nowhere, waving the gun around as he spoke. Casual. Almost indifferent as he threatened Jim.

He shivered and pressed on.

He'd trekked a half mile or so to the spot the creek bent to the right and jogged east. They'd searched some satellite images online and figured this was the spot to head up through the woods toward Colton's place. A couple of hundred yards uphill through the trees was Buckthorn Road, a little ribbon of gravel that jutted off Highway 14. He could follow that right up to Colton's house. It was an open stretch of road, so he should be able to see any cars coming in time to find some cover in a patch of trees or slip down into the shallow ditch that ran alongside Buckthorn.

Jim stared at the trees across the running water, and a realization hit him like a snowball in the back of his head.

He had to get across the creek.

Every other time he'd been out here, that was no problem—he'd been wearing his fishing waders and boots and could trudge right through the water as dry as a Sunday sermon. While he had his dad's boots on, his legs were covered in nothing but an old pair of jeans.

Trout-stream water is cold during the warmest months—that's what makes them trout streams—but during the winter the creek was probably in the 30s. Certainly not something you wanted soaking your pants before a hike through the woods.

The only dry crossing would be all the way back at the bridge where he'd left the car, but that wouldn't work either. The trees were thick on that side of the creek, and there were a few spots that came to mind where the extended bluff ate up the entire shoreline.

With all the planning they'd done, how the hell had he not thought of this?

The spot in front of him was out of the question. He'd fished that bend plenty of times. The water cut deep, and fish stacked up at the bottom. It was at least waist deep and not an option without waders.

Jim walked upstream a bit more, stretching his brain to remember how deep it was up ahead. Water levels went down during the winter months, so that should help. If he could find a spot where it was ankle deep, his waterproof boots should keep him dry enough. Or maybe there was a spot where the current slowed enough the whole thing iced over?

Even if it did, he couldn't imagine it being thick enough to trust with his weight. The current would keep that ice pretty thin.

He kept walking, scanning the water the whole time.

About fifty yards upstream Jim found something that might work.

The stream narrowed to about fifteen feet, although the snowpack along the water's edge probably made it look a little closer than it actually was, but a pair of small boulders sat in the middle, spaced out just enough that Jim could maybe *Frogger* himself across.

He stepped up to the edge and judged the distance between the rocks. Five, maybe six feet. His long legs shouldn't have much of a problem bridging that gap. And if he got on the second boulder, the far bank was within leaping distance.

The problem would be getting to the first one.

Even with his long legs, it was out of stepping range, and jumping from shore would be risky for a lot of reasons. It was too dark to get a good look at the top of the boulder. No way to tell if there were any bumps that would make for an uneven landing or maybe a shallow dent that had filled with water, now frozen into a little patch of ice waiting to send him careening into the stream with a broken ankle.

But it wasn't too far.

Jim turned away from the water and looked around for a branch or something he could use to brace himself, but there wasn't much. He kicked through the crunchy snow, looking for anything useful, but it was mostly dead prairie grass. Most of the trees were on the other side. There was a cluster of them about a hundred yards away, but Jim didn't want to walk that far if he didn't have to.

Off to his left a brushy bush sat weighed down under the snow and ice that had accumulated over the winter. It was hard to tell, but the branches were maybe five feet long. He trudged over and tugged at one. It was only a half-inch wide and not near sturdy enough to hold his weight, but he snapped it off and took it over to the bank anyway.

Jim poked at the snowpack at the edge of the stream. The little shelf collapsed into the water and was whisked away. He kept prodding and knocked away as much as he could, until he was sure what remained was solid. By the end the stream had expanded about six inches, which wasn't too much, but it was still six more inches over freezing water he'd have to navigate.

He probed into the current to find the bottom and was pleased to see it was roughly ankle deep between the bank and the first rock. It would be deeper in the middle, certainly, but probably not more than two feet.

Hopefully he wouldn't find out.

Jim stretched out and poked at the boulder with his stick. As much as it weighed and with the current pushing against it as long as it had, it should be wedged into the bottom of the stream. Tight and unmovable.

But he had to be sure. His dad's voice echoed in his head. He'd always warned him about stepping on loose boulders.

Couldn't have his son's basketball career derailed by a random rock.

It felt as if it were set in concrete. He flipped his stick around and used the few dead leaves and little branches to try and sweep any loose sand or gravel off the top. Before he could think of all the reasons this was a bad idea, Jim tightened the duffel bag's strap across his chest and stepped out into the abyss.

His boot found a grip on the top of the rock, and he brought his full weight onto it. It held, but there was little room out there, and Jim felt himself wobble. Instead of pausing to collect his balance, he stepped out for the second rock. He found the top of the boulder and stepped across.

Maybe it was snow that had landed and melted or the little bit of mist that floated up from the current washing against it, but something had frozen across the top of that boulder. As soon as Jim put his weight on it, his foot slipped off the side and into the water below. He flew forward, arms windmilling as his foot slammed into the creek bed.

Water rushed over the top of his boot, slipped around his ankle and down inside as his momentum continued forward.

Working on nothing more than instinct, Jim pushed off from the creek bed and lunged for the far bank. He landed on the frozen ground and felt all the air forced out of him. His feet splashed in the shallow water alongside the bank, but he pulled them out as he rolled into the fetal position.

He lay on the side of the creek like a trout tossed to the bank, rolling atop the frozen snow with lips gulping for oxygen.

As his breath returned, the panic subsided and Jim was able to push himself away from the water. He sat up and let the relief that he'd avoided a major catastrophe flood through his system.

His ankle was cold and wet, but his father's fishing boots were waterproof and the fact they were so tight on him probably kept a lot of water from squeezing in over the top. He reached down and rubbed his leg, trying to squeeze some of the water out of his pants and sock.

Jim was shocked that he hadn't broken his ankle. This far away from his car, something like that would be a catastrophe.

His duffel bag had twisted around his left shoulder, so he adjusted that and pushed himself up off the ground.

He looked back at the boulder he'd just slid off, as if he'd find a banana peel there. He'd have to be much more careful on the way back, but there was a lot to do before he had to worry about that.

Jim took a last steadying breath and started up the hill into the trees, trying to convince himself that was the last of the bad luck he'd experience that night.

Chapter Twenty

The darkness was impressive. Clouds had continued to roll in, blocking out the moon and anything else that might reflect a bit of light down to guide him along. He pulled out his phone a few times to get a look where he was going, but even in this isolated spot of southern Minnesota, he was paranoid someone would see the light from his screen, so he made his way slowly and carefully until he found Buckthorn Road. Colton's driveway was roughly a quarter mile ahead.

Jim didn't know where the property lines were, but he wasn't surprised to see the No Trespassing signs nailed haphazardly to the trees that lined the gravel road as he walked.

The woods alongside funneled the wind down the little gravel road as if it were trying to push Jim back. A warning.

Don't come this way.

If that was too subtle, the metal gate across Colton's driveway was much more explicit. It looked like one of those thick metal bars that came down across the on-ramp when a blizzard closed the interstate. Another no trespassing sign hung from the center of it. Chain-link fencing extended in each direction and disappeared into the woods along the road. Jim figured it made a perimeter around the grounds, so it was probably good he'd come via the road.

Luckily, the gate only seemed designed to keep vehicles from accidentally turning down the driveway. Jim lifted a latch on the far side and pushed it open, then closed it behind him. The sound of metal locking into metal did everything it could to call attention to the intruder. But it wasn't only the sound; everything seemed to be amplified on the other side of the fence. The air Jim pulled into his lungs seemed colder than it had only a few feet away. The frozen smell of dirt and foliage was more intense, and the dark was thicker because even though he was still outside, he'd stepped into Colton's domain.

Jim hustled down the driveway before the panicking voice inside him convinced him to hightail it out of there. Parallel tracks of iced-down snow showed where Colton had come and gone without bothering to plow it. Jim stayed in the tire's ruts, not wanting to leave any tracks of his own. It was slick, but enough gravel stuck up through the ice to give some traction. The trees were thick on both sides, turning the driveway into a canyon and funneling anyone stupid enough to ignore the clear warnings into a choke point at the front of Colton Reid's property.

No lights shined up ahead, but Jim could already tell the overhead images they'd pulled up on the internet were woefully out of date. The shadows of multiple structures loomed as the trees faded and opened up to a clear expanse where Colton lived.

A small two-story house stood in the center of the property. Even in the dark, Jim could tell it was in no condition for anyone to call it home. The first-floor windows were cracked, broken, or boarded up, while the front porch sagged to the right where the rotten wood had finally collapsed. Peeling paint that had once been white softly glowed in the dark and gave way to water-stained wood underneath. The top floor may or may not have been intact. It was impossible to tell from there.

Opposite was a trailer home that looked to be two winters away from joining the collapsing house. A single light bulb, burned out or broken, stuck out next to the door. The metal sides were streaked with dirt and dust and whatever the rain had left over the years. An old couch sat along the front, a chunk of stuffing pulled out of a tear in the fabric, its cushions long gone.

About twenty steps from the trailer, a corrugated metal shed stood. It looked newer and in better shape than the other buildings, but that wasn't much of a compliment. It seemed homemade, not one of those fancy prefab ones, and a smaller wooden shack stood around the side. A pair of rusted-out cars sat next to it, a scraggly shrub growing between them.

Jim shrugged his duffel bag's strap up on his shoulder and started toward the trailer home.

The woods surrounding the clearing were thicker than those he'd walked through coming up from the creek, and Jim couldn't see the fence through them. He assumed it circled the property at some point but had no idea how far back that was. If Colton showed up, he could probably hide there until the coast was clear.

But that wouldn't be necessary because Kyle would give him plenty of warning if Colton left the North Star.

The thought made Jim pull his phone out to check again.

No messages, but his reception had gone down to a single bar.

He ignored the warning siren that popped off in his brain. A bar was a bar, and that was enough. That said, there was no point in dawdling around.

Get it done and get out so it's not an issue.

He moved toward the trailer again. When they'd hashed out the plan, Jim worried about where he could plant the drugs, but Kyle kept pushing back that it wouldn't be a problem. Even if they were stashed under the front porch or in a shed, that would be fine; when his probation officer got word he was dealing, they'd look everywhere. Besides, as old as the trailer looked, there was at least a fifty-fifty chance the door would pop open and he'd be able to plant them inside.

Jim would try, but considering the amount of fencing around the property, he fully expected it to be dead bolted. If so, the skirt around the trailer looked like it was nothing more than a thin wooden lattice, and there were plenty of holes in it already.

Mid-step, Jim blinked as the yard suddenly flooded with light. His heart leaped into his throat, and he froze, still at least fifteen yards from the trailer. There was no cover nearby; he was exposed in the middle of the yard.

Colton couldn't be home—he'd just checked his phone, and there was no word from Kyle. Also, if he were here, Jim figured he'd be on his back, blood oozing from a quarter-size hole in his forehead as Colton's shadow stretched over him.

I told you trouble was gonna find you.

Jim squinted at the glowing light atop a pole to his left, looming over the gravel patch by the trailer. He couldn't see through the glare, but it had to be a motion sensor set to pop on whenever Colton came home. Jim looked below and saw a dark stain in the packed snow where Colton probably parked his truck every night.

Jim stood still long enough for the light to cut out, then started around to the right, trying to keep out of range. He made it a dozen steps when a paralyzing string of barks tore through the silence. Jim turned in time to see a massive dog come flying around the side of the shed. Jim didn't have time to process what he was seeing, let alone run or piss his pants, as the enraged ball of muscle and teeth bore down on him. It launched off the ground, not at his neck but his midsection, and the sound of its teeth snapping together barely inches from his crotch pushed Jim back.

A taut length of chain stretched back around the corner of the shed and tugged against the leather collar around the dog's neck.

Sweat broke out across Jim's entire body as he watched the dog struggle against the leash, not even thinking to pray that whatever it was tied to would hold. Angry spittle shook off the dog's muzzle as it kept straining with zombielike intensity, pawing at the frozen ground below.

Adrenaline slowly seeped from his veins as Jim realized he wasn't going to be mauled to death. The cold air took the sweat from his brow and raised goose bumps across his skin.

At some point the dog tired enough to realize the futility of fighting its chain and stopped. Its eyes remained locked on the intruder, glowing in rage and the scant amount of moonlight that seeped through the clouds above, muscles tight like piano wire.

Jim shuffled backward and brought out another series of barks that stopped him cold. He let his brain spin for a second before reorganizing his thoughts into something resembling comprehension. Another half step toward the trailer brought out a low growl, letting him know in no uncertain terms that it was off limits.

But as long as that chain was as heavy duty as it looked, there wasn't much the vicious mutt could do about it.

Jim glanced at the mobile home. He needed to stash the pills over there and get the hell out. The dog could bark all it wanted.

He turned for the trailer, and the dog went nuts again, canine fury echoing all through the property, but Jim did his best to ignore it.

But he wasn't barking at Jim this time.

Out of the corner of his eye, he saw a pair of headlights approaching up the driveway.

Every bit of residual fear that remained inside him went nuclear, splitting, and resplitting like an out-of-control fission reaction that mushroom clouded into one thought.

RUN.

Chapter Twenty-One

Jim took off as the lights bounced closer on the rough driveway, the sound of tires crunching on the frozen gravel sneaking into the yard. He'd never make the tree line, so he cut over toward the dilapidated house Colton had grown up in. If he got inside, he could hide out until Colton got into his trailer, then sneak to the woods and find his way back to the car. Hell, maybe there was even a back door or something.

You aren't that lucky.

Shadows gradually stretched across the ground in front of him as the headlights bounded closer.

If Colton couldn't see him yet, it was simply a matter of time. Jim pushed his legs faster than he'd run in years. He could hear his coach's voice, which sounded suspiciously like his father's, yelling at him to go faster. Jim didn't dare turn to look. He ignored the pain of toes smashed against the end of too-small boots and the jostling of the bag slung around his neck, desperate for refuge against whatever was coming behind him.

The porch steps were a few feet away, and the front door hung half open on rusty hinges. Jim leaped up on the stairs, and the rotten wood gave way under his weight. His foot busted through to the ground, and momentum pitched him forward before he could get his hands up and keep the side of his head from bouncing off the porch landing. His brain exploded in a static of fireworks and pinwheels, but he was still able to recognize a familiar pop inside his left knee.

Survival instinct pulled rank over conscious thought and started barking out orders. He rolled over on his back and pulled his foot from the broken step. The headlights were almost to the end of the driveway, lighting up the trailer on the other side of the yard. He reached up for the doorknob and saw the whole thing was boarded up before he even tried to twist.

Jim flipped over on his stomach, not daring to stand up and risk being seen, and crawled for the far side of the porch, ignoring the pain metastasizing in his left knee.

He pulled himself over the edge and landed in a heap on the frozen ground below as the truck ground to a halt somewhere out in the yard. A car door slammed shut.

"Shut the fuck up."

Colton's voice echoed into every space of the property, and his dog immediately stopped barking as if it knew something violent would happen if it didn't.

The same thing that would happen to Jim if Colton found him. He swung the duffel bag around to his chest and pushed back against the side of the porch, trying to stay hidden.

"You still here?"

The words paralyzed Jim. Colton's voice was loud, but there was no anger. It was cold. Controlled.

The dog started up again as if it were telling its owner about the trespasser hiding a few yards away.

"I already saw you, you know. Got an alert on my phone. I'm sitting there having a beer and buzz . . . *buzzzzzzzz*." Colton let the sound leak out all over the yard. "Used to think maybe I was paranoid setting up those trail cams around. Ain't nobody stupid enough to come creeping around out here. At least there weren't till you showed up."

Jim pressed back harder against the side of the porch, as if it would open up and absorb him so he could hide out until Colton figured he'd left and went away.

But that wasn't going to happen. Colton wasn't going anywhere, and sooner or later he'd find him cowering in the shadows.

Panic built in Jim's chest.

How the fuck did this happen?

He shifted the duffel bag out of the way and pulled his mom's phone out of his pocket. The screen lit up, and Jim pressed it against his chest to hide the light, but there were no messages.

A single bar of service showed in the corner.

"Where you at, boss man?" Jim tossed the phone into the duffel bag and shifted forward. Colton's voice seemed farther away, so Jim took the chance to push himself up and peek around the corner of the porch.

Colton was heading over to the shed.

Jim watched for a second before ducking back behind the house. His heart pumped like it was bailing water from a leaky lifeboat, and he could feel the swelling rushing into his injured knee, turning his formerly intact joint into a water balloon. A salt dome halfway up the topography of his leg.

He tried his best, but there was no denying what he'd felt when that board gave way.

Pop.

Banging your knee hurts but doesn't feel like that. Neither does a sprain. But twist it just right—sudden and violent, like when a floorboard breaks underneath you or you land wrong because some shit-heel from Ohio State fouls you on a breakaway—and you get that familiar pop. Like snapping a rubber band.

Ligament tissue stretched beyond its capability.

"May as well come out, Jimmy Buckets, 'cause I'm gonna fiiiind you." Colton sounded like a kid on the playground, calling out *Olly, olly oxen free.*

Jim realized he couldn't stay huddled on the far side of the house. As soon as Colton checked the sheds, he'd come over here and find him. Or maybe he'd let his dog loose to track him down.

He crawled back alongside the house and pushed himself up onto his feet. Jim braced himself against the wall and tried a step. He felt fairly stable, and it gave him a flash of hope before he took another and felt a familiar wobble in his leg. He fell into the side of the house, all weight on the weather-beaten siding and his good leg.

Shit.

Jim's brain started flying back over the route he'd taken to get there but quickly shook the thought out of his head. It didn't matter how far it was; staying there wasn't an option. Fear was keeping the worst of the pain in his knee at bay, but that wasn't going to last forever, and he had a long way back to his car. Even if he got out, he'd be easy to track down. He was no better than a wounded deer, only able to get so far before his hunter found him and delivered the kill shot.

Hand on the wall, he took another step, then two more before his knee shifted and jabbed him with a fresh bolt of pain.

There was no way this was going to work.

Jim stood frozen for a second before he remembered the bag slung around his neck. He yanked it open and pulled out one of the ziplock bags they'd loaded inside. Jim didn't know what was Oxy and what was tramadol, but he shook two into his hand and popped them in his mouth. Bitterness caked his tongue as he chewed them up, hoping that would kick-start their effectiveness. Swallowing was almost impossible, so he reached down for a mouthful of old snow to help.

Even with the cold of the melted snow, warmth spread through his chest as the pills went down. He tried another step and felt a stab of pain. Determination and adrenaline would have to be enough until the pills kicked in, because he couldn't wait any longer.

Jim kept as much weight as he could on his right foot and hopped toward the back corner of the house, practically dragging his left leg behind. He looked around the corner and saw the shed. Colton was nowhere to be seen, but the dog was still patrolling at the end of his chain.

He looked over at the woods ahead of him, a good twenty yards of exposed ground away. With only one functioning leg, it may as well be a hundred. And while Colton may not see him, the dog surely would, and it wouldn't be shy about ratting him out.

Jim scanned the ground below him until he found a decent-size rock in the snow. He snatched it up and snuck around the corner.

He didn't see Colton, which probably meant he was headed for the front of the house. With it boarded up, he'd probably come right around the corner and find Jim if he didn't get the hell out of there.

Jim took a step away, braced his left hand against the corner of the house, kept his weight firmly on his right foot and chucked the rock as far as he could.

It quickly disappeared in the dark, so Jim had to hope his aim was decent. Right when he was about to panic that he'd messed up, he heard a metallic clang as it hit the roof of the shed.

More importantly, the dog heard it and went absolutely nuts. It flew after the sound, hopefully taking Colton's attention with it.

Jim couldn't afford to wait and find out, instead limping as fast as he could across the yard to the woods. The drugs weren't working yet, but the adrenaline rocketing through his veins blocked out the pain along with Colton's voice behind him, shouting at his dog.

He waited for the crack of a gunshot, for a bullet to tear through his shoulder and knock him to the ground, where he'd lie bleeding until Colton casually walked up behind him and put another through the back of his skull.

Found you.

Jim pushed harder for the trees, sweat already dripping down his forehead, the heat of his face the only thing keeping it from freezing.

Before he knew it, Jim pushed through the underbrush and collapsed to the ground. A dull throb reached up from his knee, along with the knowledge that Colton was still out there, but he couldn't push himself up, so he crawled farther into the woods. The snow was thin under the trees, and he could feel every twig and rock underneath him as he dragged himself across the ground.

A huge oak was rooted in his path, and Jim reached for it like it was a life preserver. He pulled himself over by an exposed root and then propped his body up against the trunk. The drumbeat of his heart thudded in his ears, but he couldn't hear anything beyond. The dog had stopped barking, and Colton had stopped yelling.

Jim fought to get his breath under control and wanted nothing more than to lie there on the frozen ground, but he couldn't.

If he stayed there, Colton would eventually find him, but his car was at least a mile away through thick woods and uneven terrain, and he was moving on one leg.

Before he could figure out how the hell he was going to get away, the dog started barking again.

Chapter Twenty-Two

The barking out in the yard kept going, and Colton wasn't yelling to stop it like before.

Jim's leg didn't want to cooperate, but staying put wasn't an option.

He pushed himself up from the ground and took a cautious step away from the tree. His knee worked okay, so he took another. It felt weird. The pain was still there but distant. Like it was yelling at him from underwater.

The pills must be doing their job.

The dog going wild provided all the motivation he needed to push through the underbrush. Jim limped from tree to tree, going as fast as he dared on his knee. It would shift ever so slightly whenever he put too much weight on it, but there was no choice but to keep going.

The barking built into a frenzy beyond the trees, then suddenly cut off. It took Jim a second to realize what that meant, and a fresh surge of adrenaline hit when he did.

Colton let it loose.

Jim hobbled between two trees and saw the chain-link fence he knew would be there but delusion had allowed him to ignore. But there was no ignoring it now. Nor could he ignore the ball of fury that was surely rocketing across the yard toward the woods.

Coming for him.

There was no plan, only action as Jim lurched for the fence. He was tall, but it was taller. At least seven feet. He grabbed the top of the fence with both hands and found a foothold about halfway up with his good leg.

A breathy snarling burst into the woods somewhere behind him as Jim hoisted himself up, dragging his bad leg behind, waiting for a set of canines to sink into his flesh and rip his Achilles tendon clean off.

Jim saw the dog burst through the underbrush as he swung his body over the fence. In a panic, he let go and fell toward the ground. The duffel bag he had slung around his neck caught something on the top of the fence and jerked him around. He hung there for a second before something ripped and he fell into the snow on the far side.

The dog hit the fence at the same time Jim hit the ground, spittle flying and jaws snapping in a frenzy. Jim didn't even try standing up but scrambled away as fast as he could on his belly.

After ten feet the ground disappeared beneath him, and for a second Jim was falling. He slammed into an exposed patch of frozen dirt, then rolled down. He reached out for branches, exposed roots, anything to control his descent, but found nothing. He flopped past trees and over the plants that grew between them while snow mashed its way into every seam and cranny on his body.

Jim eventually rolled into a fallen log at the bottom of the hill and stopped, his frozen breath like whiskey clouds puffing up from the earth. He stared up at the black sky above, not knowing if those were real stars he saw or if he was seeing stars.

The barking continued, but from far above and hopefully still behind a fence, so he had time to lie there for a second.

Or maybe he didn't, but he did anyway because he had to catch his breath. It took a moment to realize that sometime in the distraction of escape, the pills he'd downed had kicked in, and all he wanted to do was lie there because it wasn't even cold in the snow.

The dog's barking petered out somewhere above him, but a voice cut through the fog that had rolled up inside his brain.

It was his voice, and it begged him to get up.

You gotta go.

Jim rolled over and pushed himself up onto all fours. His head was heavy and hung below him. He tried to lift it but couldn't, so he looked around for something to help him get up the best he could. The log he'd run into was right there, and he was able to use it to push himself back on his feet.

He tried a step. It didn't hurt—nothing did—but it wasn't steady. He tried another. It was the same. Jim still *felt*, but kind of on the margins. He was floating in a sensory-deprivation tank of pharmaceuticals. Senses came and went—some dulled, some enhanced, some on a five-second tape delay.

He was a marionette, someone awkwardly controlling his limbs from above.

You gotta go.

No way he'd make it back to his car like that. He saw a stick on the ground and picked it up. About five feet long, maybe two inches in diameter, even had a little handle kinda thing where a branch jutted out from the side.

The snow and underbrush made for tough going, but it was manageable. He left the dog behind and was making real progress until he got to the creek.

Somehow in his fear- and drug-addled brain he'd completely forgotten about the creek of icy water between him and his car. The one he'd barely made it across an hour earlier, back when he had two good legs and a brain unencumbered by medical-grade narcotics.

Jim was farther upstream this time, a spot he was unfamiliar with. The water was still gin clear, but it was too dark to tell how deep it was or what was strewn across the creek bed—loose gravel, giant rocks, sinkholes could all be waiting for him down there, ready to pitch him into the freezing water. This far from his car, as cold as it was, that baptism could be deadly.

But the pills dulled his judgment enough that he went for it.

It wasn't so bad, really. The current kept trying to knock him down, sweep him away, but Jim had his stick-cane and that steadied him against the water and alerted him to anything that might be in his path.

He was Moses, if instead of parting the Red Sea he had limped right through it.

Once across, he followed the stream all the way back to his car. Jim fumbled with the door, then collapsed into the front seat like a fifty-pound bag of mulch that someone tossed into the back of a pickup.

He lay his head back against the seat in disbelief that he'd made it. Wasn't even so bad once he'd gotten going. He was surprised that it wasn't colder, to be honest, although that voice broke through the fog again to remind him that probably wasn't a good thing.

Jim reached down and felt his knee. He wanted to believe it wasn't so bad. If he could walk all this way on it, it couldn't be too terrible. Last time he hadn't been able to walk at all. They had to carry him off the court in front of all those people. They'd been quiet when he fell, but when they carried him, they all cheered. That was weird, he remembered. It's not like he was all better suddenly, simply getting out of the way so they could keep playing.

He grabbed the frozen denim and pulled his leg inside the car. A breakthrough of pain chased away whatever misguided and drug-addled optimism he'd been farming.

The pills hadn't fixed anything. They only put the pain on a credit card he'd have to pay off later.

Most likely with considerable interest.

Jim closed the driver's side door and realized he was shivering, which was weird because he wasn't cold. The voice cut through the haze again and asked how the hell he expected to drive home. A busted knee and a foggy brain did not make for good—or in any way legal—driving acumen.

Fear hit hard.

He looked out the window, expecting to see the dog flying at him like Cujo. Keeping him trapped inside until Colton showed up.

His panicked breath started fogging up the windows. Sweat beaded on Jim's forehead and popped up behind his neck.

He reached over and turned the heater off, even though the car wasn't on yet.

Jim clamped his eyes shut against everything, tried to even out his breathing. The silence of his frozen car rang in his ears, drumming out everything else around him.

You can do this.

He didn't need his left leg to do anything while he drove, so that's good. And he'd driven this stretch of road plenty of times. It was old hat. Probably wouldn't see another car the whole way.

While it wasn't something he was proud of, Jim had driven under a chemical influence before. Hell, probably on these same backroads when he was in high school and had had more than he should've.

Concentrate, take it slow, and everything would be fine.

Jim reached forward and hit the ignition. The engine roared through the silence outside, and his fear almost made him cut it off. His headlights lit up the ribbon of dirt ahead of him that led up to the road back to town.

Deep breath.

You can do this.

Fresh air would help.

He pressed the button, and the window slid down next to him. A puff of cold air came in alongside a hand that clasped Jim's neck and pinned him back against the seat.

"Looks like you got lost again." Colton's voice was eerily calm. "Out doing some late-night fishing?"

Jim clawed at the hand around his neck, his body bucking in the driver's seat like a trout trying to shake a hook. His left knee slammed into the underside of the steering console and exploded in pain.

Without anything close to conscious thought, he slammed the SUV into gear and thrust his right foot down on the accelerator.

The tires spun for a second before grinding down to solid ground and finding grip. Gravel shot out behind him as the SUV rocketed forward and tore Jim's throat from Colton's fingers.

Finally free, Jim scrambled to grab the wheel and jerk it away from the bushes in front of him.

The SUV bounced up to the county road above and fishtailed south toward town.

Every nerve in his body shot fire as Jim fought to remember how to breathe. He looked in the rearview mirror, expecting to see Colton chasing him down like Robert Patrick in that *Terminator* movie.

He saw nothing but red dust in his taillights.

Jim focused through the windshield again in time to jerk the wheel into a sharp turn back onto the old county road and avoid flying into a cornfield. Dust and snow fantailed behind him as the tires screeched onto the asphalt.

His heart thudded in his chest and echoed in his ears as Jim fought for control of his body. He had to breathe.

Jim checked the rearview again and saw nothing.

He forced himself to slow down. To inhale. To keep both hands on the wheel.

You can do this.

Sweat dripped down his temple, and Jim wiped it away on his sleeve. His neck hurt where Colton's fingers had tried to claw him back as he drove away.

Jim eased off the accelerator even more as the road in front of him curved back to town. He made it through the turn and saw the glowing haze of Silent Creek on the horizon.

He was going to make it.

Flashing red and blue lights in his rearview mirror disagreed.

Chapter Twenty-Three

Jim's heart thudded against his ribs like it was trying to bang out the drum intro to Van Halen's "Hot for Teacher."

He looked at the speedometer.

43

He wasn't speeding . . . then. He'd slowed down for the curves. Had he been speeding before? Hard to say.

Jim looked through the rearview mirror again, and the lights were still there. The cop was right on his bumper, matching his slow, legal speed.

The lizard part of his brain told him to hit the gas. Luckily fear had cleared his head enough to recognize what an epic disaster of an idea that was.

He pulled his eyes back to the road and realized he was still driving. Jim pulled his foot off the gas and drifted over to the shoulder of the road. Bees buzzed inside his skull, each whispering its own advice. It was too much, and he ignored it all.

He double-checked that he'd put his SUV in park and stared into the rearview mirror. The cop car was behind him, headlights beaming through his back window and flashers still going on the roof.

Why wasn't he getting out of the car? What was he waiting for?

Jim turned in his seat to look out the back window but didn't see anything new. He quickly turned back, not wanting to look suspicious.

Play it cool, and you'll get through this.

He pried his fingers away from the steering wheel and flexed them a few times, then wiped his brow again.

Deep breath.

The squad car door closed with a bang behind him and gave Jim a fresh wave of panic. Had his heart not been running at maximum velocity, it would have sped up.

Well before he was ready, a knuckle rapped on the window next to him. Jim fumbled for the switch and finally lowered the window.

"Hello, Mr. McCann." It was Officer Ellison.

"Yes . . . I mean, hello."

It wasn't good, but Ellison didn't seem to care. Maybe Jim was fine and just being paranoid.

"What brings you out this way tonight?"

Jim had no answer. He should have had one ready. A perfectly plausible excuse as to why he was driving on Highway 14 that night, headed back into Silent Creek a little before midnight on a Saturday. It wasn't hard, but Jim had nothing.

"Out for a drive." He knew it was bad as it left his mouth, and the cop's next question confirmed it. "Heading home, I mean."

"Have you been drinking tonight, Jim?"

He looked up at the cop's face with whatever innocent look he could put together on the spot. "No, no . . . nope. Not a drop." It was true, but Officer Ellison wasn't convinced.

"Could you step out of the car for me?"

Jim's nerves all fired electricity at the thought. Would one of those Breathalyzers pick up the pills? Would it matter if he couldn't walk the line?

Shit, his knee.

"I can, sure, but I tweaked my knee earlier tonight, and it's swelled up pretty good. Honestly, I'm afraid I may have torn something again.

It's the same one I tore up in college, but, like, hopefully not as bad?" He could tell he was rambling, but he couldn't stop. "I played basketball at Minnesota . . . and here, obviously, but you know that."

"If you could step out of the car, sir."

Sir. Now he was *sir*. That was a bad sign. "Yes, sir . . ." Now Jim was saying it. "I mean, yes, Officer."

Ellison took a step back as Jim opened the door. He gently swung his left leg out and could tell right away his knee had swelled considerably since he'd gotten in the car. The pain was there but still had a dull edge from the drugs. Hopefully it was enough for him to pass whatever tests Officer Ellison wanted to put him through.

Jim stood up and felt his knee buckle immediately. He fell forward, grabbing the car door with one hand and Ellison's uniform with the other.

"WHOA . . . okay." Ellison grabbed Jim under the left arm and pushed him back against the car. His hand stayed there until he was apparently convinced Jim was stable enough to remain upright.

"You sure you haven't had anything to drink tonight?"

Throbbing radiated up Jim's leg as he leaned against his SUV, trying to take the pressure off it but keep standing. "Nope . . . I swear. It's my knee, like I was saying. It's—"

"If I'm being honest, Jim, it's a little hard to believe. You were weaving in and out of your lane, and I'm looking at your eyes right now, and I gotta say they don't look too clear."

"No, I swear . . ." Jim studied the cop's face as he spoke, and saw absolutely nothing resembling belief in his expression, because of course he didn't believe him. Ellison wasn't stupid. Jim sucked in as much cold air as he could, hoping it would act like a bucket of ice water. "Like I said, I hurt my knee today, and it's swelled up pretty good. I was actually over at the emergency room—that's where I was coming from—but they couldn't do anything tonight. I'm really sorry, but, you know, all I'm doing is heading home."

Jim stared at the cop out of pupils the size of pinpricks, desperate for anything resembling leniency. His story was good, although it would have probably gone over better had he told it right away. But he wasn't thinking straight before the cold air and fear chased away enough of the fog for him to come up with that.

Officer Ellison studied his face, then looked down at Jim's leg. Hopefully the shadows hid his wet denim, because Jim had no explanation for that.

"Wait here."

Jim watched Officer Ellison head back to his squad car. He stood there on the side of the road, no noise but the gentle idle of the two engines, red and blue lights swirling around them in a surreal disco. A car approached from behind, slowed, and gave them a wide berth as it passed on its way back to town. Jim didn't recognize the driver and prayed they didn't recognize him.

By the time the car was gone, Ellison was back.

"Blow into this." He held his hand out toward Jim, a white tube pointed at his face like the barrel of a gun. A dozen pieces of two-bit legal advice, most gleaned from television and movies, jostled around his head. Jim considered refusing, but would that make things worse? Those things only detected alcohol, right? If he passed, Ellison would have to let him go.

Right?

He reached for the little contraption, but Ellison pulled it away. "Just blow."

Jim leaned forward and put his lips around the tube. He fought to hold his balance as he pushed whatever air he had in his lungs into the Breathalyzer.

Officer Ellison pulled it away, and Jim studied his face enough to detect a bit of disappointment when the cop saw the results. He didn't say anything before heading back to his squad car again.

A wave of dizziness hit, and Jim closed his eyes in an effort to keep from swaying. He opened them again, squinted through the headlights and flashers, and saw Ellison behind the wheel, talking on his cell phone.

The longer he stood there, the more paranoia seeped back in.

The drugs weren't helping.

Jim's eyes drifted to the sky. He'd always loved the way the stars exploded out when you got away from the lights of town. He'd been too nervous to notice on the way out to Colton's place and way too distracted on the way back. And there, on the side of the road, only the brightest and most determined were visible through the headlights of Ellison's car.

The slam of the squad car door jerked Jim back to reality. Officer Ellison walked around his front fender and through the cone of light that spread out from his headlights.

"Come with me."

The gossamer haze that had been draped over Jim's vision for the past few hours was gone, so the fluorescent lights above turned everything around him into a mess of harsh shadows and washed-out colors. It wasn't only his senses that had transitioned back into high definition, but whatever those pills had wrapped around his leg had dissolved as well, laying bare the thorny shard of pain his knee had become.

Jail sobers you up in a hurry.

Jim shifted his weight on the metal bench, and another squall of pain burst from his knee. He sat with it propped up on the bench, but it didn't seem to do much for the swelling. He couldn't think about what kind of damage he'd done to it when he had to consider how much damage he'd done to his life.

Ellison hadn't said anything on the ride in. Jim asked if he was under arrest but got no answer. He didn't know if that was legal, but if the guy enforcing the law didn't seem to care, there wasn't much that could be done.

Without knowing what else he could do—and it wasn't like he was thinking clearly—Jim had complied.

Could they keep him here if he got up and said he wanted to leave? His car was still out on 14, sitting on the side of the road. How would he get out there?

Jim scooted to the end of the bench and gently lowered his leg to the floor. He could feel the stiffness setting up shop and slowly bent his knee against the warm throb radiating from inside. He had no idea how long it had been since Ellison closed the heavy steel doors behind him, a sound that would haunt Jim for the rest of his life. It was final, like the last strike of a coffin's nail, which maybe it was.

It was said there was nothing to do in a cell but think, and Jim could confirm that. If he'd been worried that the only thing people in this town would remember were his days on the court, a DWI arrest would solve that because the only thing people in this town liked talking about more than the past was a scandal. This would supply gossip for the coffee shop and church basement for weeks.

"Ugh." Jim thudded his head against the wall behind him. At some point Ellison would have to come back, and he needed to have his story straight when it happened. He tried to remember what he'd said out on the side of the road, but it was like trying to remember a movie he'd seen twenty years ago and didn't enjoy.

Did the Breathalyzer have any sort of record to prove that he'd passed, or would Ellison use his instability as an excuse to arrest him? His knee should account for the wobbliness and erratic driving for sure, but he sure as shit couldn't tell them how he'd gotten hurt.

Before Jim could square that story, the hallway door outside the holding cell opened and Chief Nelson walked through. He wasn't in uniform but wore jeans and a polo shirt. It was jarring, not only because he'd expected Ellison but because Jim couldn't remember ever seeing the chief of police in civilian clothes. It felt like when you were a kid and saw your teacher at the grocery store.

Chief Nelson didn't say anything. He stuck his key in the lock and pulled the door open. He stared down at Jim, still rooted on the bench.

Silence of anticipation hung between them, but Jim was afraid to break it before he knew what to say.

"Come on." Chief Nelson nodded toward the door. His voice was flat, and he didn't wait for Jim to figure it out before heading back the way he'd come.

Jim sat with his nerves for a second, then got his good leg underneath him and stood up. A warm rush swarmed his head, either the remnants of the drugs or a result of however long he'd been on the bench, so he paused a second before limping out of the cell.

Chief Nelson waited at the end of the short hall, holding the door to the outer offices open. Jim held on to the cell bars as he made his way out.

The chief nodded down at Jim's leg. "What did you do?"

"Tripped on the basement stairs and landed weird." The story came without thought, which probably made it better. Jim wanted to keep it vague, but a detail he thought would work quickly followed. "Dish towel. The washing machine is down there so it probably fell out of the basket when Mom was bringing a load down or something."

Jim limped through the open door, and Chief Nelson pointed to his office. The Silent Creek police station wasn't that different from the offices at McCann. Reception desk out front, boss's office to the side. They had a watercooler instead of a mini fridge, though, and they didn't bother with magazines in the waiting area. Officer Ellison came out of a workroom on the other side of the reception desk, acknowledging his boss with a nod and ignoring Jim. Apparently, his job was over. He'd caught the fish and given him to the chief of police, who would choose to fillet or release.

The chief's office was small, but the walls were covered in plaques, pictures, and the accumulation of trinkets from a forty-year career in small-town law enforcement.

"Have a seat."

Jim eased into one of the two chairs facing Chief Nelson's desk. He quickly sorted through the pieces of story he'd already laid out, desperate to come up with something that could link them together in a satisfactory enough way he could wriggle out of there.

"Officer Ellison saw you swerving and pulled you over on a suspected DWI." Chief Nelson's voice was formal, like he was reading charges into the record, but Jim was still confused as to what his actual status was. He didn't know anything about how this worked beyond what he'd seen on TV but knew enough to keep his mouth shut as long as possible. "You passed a Breathalyzer but couldn't walk a line."

"That's because of my knee." Jim stretched his left leg out in front of him like he was presenting it into evidence. "I tried to explain it to Officer Ellison, but he wouldn't listen. I was afraid I reinjured it, so I drove over to the emergency room to get it checked out, but it was a waste of time because they can't really do anything until the swelling goes down. So I headed—"

"You don't listen, do you?" The disappointment in his voice was enough to knock Jim back twenty years. Listening to his father lecture him about missed chances from bad choices. What would happen if he didn't work hard, take advantage of the gifts that God had given him—and by genetic implication—gifts *he'd* given him. Jim hated Chief Nelson for bringing those feelings up almost as much as he hated himself for having them. "You're supposed to be taking care of your mother, and we pick you up after midnight swerving all over the road."

It took Jim a second to respond because Chief Nelson had awoken something in him. "I explained that. In fact, the reason I was out so late was because I waited until Mom was asleep to leave. To go to the *emergency room*." Jim hit those words hard, and his voice didn't soften as he continued. "I waited while my knee swelled up, knowing I'd probably retorn my ACL, to make sure my mother was okay. Isn't that what you wanted? Or should I have skipped the hospital and walked it off?"

If Chief Nelson was surprised at his tone, he hid it well. But even if Jim made a point, the cop wasn't going to concede it.

"You need to understand—"

"I understand perfectly fine," Jim said. "In fact, I think it's time I get back to my mother's house. Don't you agree?"

Chief Nelson didn't like the taste of defiance, and Jim saw it in his eyes. But he also smelled the frustration of defeat. If they were planning on arresting him, they would have done it already.

"I passed a Breathalyzer test, and it's obvious why I couldn't walk a line. So unless you have some other thing to charge me with, I'd like a ride back to my car so I can get home and take care of my mother."

Chapter Twenty-Four

His car was still on the side of the road when Officer Ellison dropped him off. Neither one had said a word on the ride out, which was for the best, considering both of them were probably sitting on a lot of anger. By then, Jim's head had cleared completely, which also meant paying the price for the trek away from Colton's house.

It was almost surreal that had been only a few hours before.

He watched the cop car's taillights fade into the night before following them back into town.

His parents' house was dark and locked up, which was more of a relief than he'd expected. Part of him worried the front door would be hanging open again, his mother out wandering in the cold.

Or even worse, left open by someone else.

Jim looked up and down the street for any strange vehicles, but nothing stood out. It didn't mean Colton wasn't hiding in a bush or lurking around the backyard, but Jim was crashing too hard to care. He went inside and limped down the hall to his bedroom, making a quick stop to poke his head in and check on his mom.

Thankfully, she was fast asleep.

He made his way across the hall to his own room and grabbed his phone from the bedside table. There were a half-dozen messages from

Kyle, each carefully worded, that had started around midnight. Jim tapped out a quick response before collapsing into bed.

Got home. Talk to you tomorrow.

Jim hadn't realized he'd fallen asleep until his mom's knock on the door woke him up like it had every Sunday morning as a kid.

Time for church.

Still fully dressed from the night before, Jim gingerly swung his legs off the side of his bed and felt a surge in the dull ache radiating from his knee. He sat there trying to figure out what he was going to do about it as the clatter of breakfast preparation filtered back from the kitchen.

Jim dug through his closet and found an old knee brace. Part of him had assumed his dad would have gotten rid of it but wasn't surprised his mom had stashed it in here, just in case he needed it one day. It was as clunky and heavy as Jim remembered but held things in place and made walking easier.

Not comfortable by any means, but doable. Unfortunately, it didn't do anything for the pain.

He managed to pull a pair of khakis over the brace so it wouldn't draw too much attention, but anyone who took a closer look couldn't miss the bulk underneath.

The smell of sizzling bacon wafted down the hallway and drew Jim to the kitchen, where his mom was cooking breakfast in her Sunday best. The walker that Helen had brought over for her earlier that week stood abandoned by the table. Once she'd healed enough to get off the couch, it had been almost impossible to get her to use it.

"Hey, Mom."

She smiled what looked like a genuine smile, then quickly replaced it with concern.

"What's wrong with your leg?"

Jim hadn't considered what he'd tell her but figured the story he'd told Chief Nelson last night would work. Especially if he had to elaborate on it at some point. "I slipped on the steps last night, remember?"

She didn't waver as she took in the lie and volleyed it right back. "Oh yeah. I guess I didn't realize it was still bothering you. Did you take some ibuprofen?"

Guilt smacked Jim right in the heart. Lying to your mother was one thing, but gaslighting her in a way that took advantage of her memory problems was a whole other level of shitty.

He didn't have any options.

"Yeah, but what about you?" Jim limped across the kitchen and held out a paper-towel-covered plate for his mom to place the bacon on. "You don't need to be out here cooking breakfast. Especially if you're not using your walker."

It was more to change the subject than anything. Jim knew that was a battle he wouldn't win.

They ate and left for church, where Jim gritted his teeth as he helped his mom down the aisle. He'd insisted his mom bring her walker, partly so he had something to lean on as he settled her in the same pew they'd sat in when he was a kid.

Jim looked around for Kyle as casually has he could before Pastor Mader started, eventually spotting him and Carrie a half dozen rows back. Kyle's eyes had a million questions, but Jim could only give a nod.

Pastor Mader hadn't added any new material since Jim's parents dragged him there every Sunday, and his knee wasn't helping. The hard wooden pews were never comfortable, but Jim's knee begged to be stretched out. Elevated. Iced.

Maybe he should have taken another one of those pills.

He tried to keep his discomfort under wraps until Pastor Mader finally told them all to go in peace and the crowd funneled out the back of the sanctuary toward the fellowship hall downstairs.

Jim hung back in the narthex, not ready to trust his knee on a crowded stairwell.

"How you doing?"

He turned and saw Kyle had sidled up behind him. Carrie was behind Kyle, talking with someone Jim vaguely recognized. She smiled at Jim and told her husband she'd meet him downstairs. They watched her leave, and Jim saw his mother heading to the elevator with a group of her friends.

The crowd thinned out quickly as Jim leaned against the wall, trying to keep as much pressure off his leg as possible.

"What the hell happened last night?" Kyle's voice was low but still carried in the nearly empty room at the front of the church.

"He showed up."

"You were still out there?" Kyle looked around to make sure they were alone. "I texted you."

"I never got it."

"Well, I sent it. Service is probably spotty out there." Kyle looked down at Jim's left leg. "What happened?"

Jim shifted his weight and felt a flare of pain in his knee. He told Kyle about the hike in, the fences, the dog, and the headlights that had come down the driveway before he could stash the drugs in Colton's trailer.

"I was gonna hide inside the old house, but the porch steps broke away under me and my foot went straight through to the ground. I could barely crawl over the side of the porch before he showed up."

A long breath whistled between Kyle's teeth. "Is it . . ."

Jim nodded. "I felt it."

"Damn, man," Kyle said. "How the hell did you get out?"

"I was hiding on the other side of the house, and he's, like, taunting me. And he had his dog that he's gonna let go, so I waited until he looked the other way and chucked a rock across the yard. The dog heard it and went nuts. I took off while they were distracted."

Kyle looked at him wide eyed, then checked behind them to make sure nobody was around to hear. "How did you do it with your leg?"

"I took a couple of the—" A thought Jim had conveniently ignored poked its head through the mess of memories from the night before. "*Shit*. The bag . . ."

"What about it?"

"I lost it when I was climbing over that freaking fence." Fear pushed all the quiet from Jim's voice. "It's still out there."

"Maybe he didn't find it?" Kyle said. "We can sneak back out—"

"No way. We couldn't get there undetected last time, and now he's going to be on the lookout. *Shit*."

Kyle glanced around them and tried to push back against the panic building in Jim. "The bag doesn't have any ID or anything on it, right? Your name or anything?"

Jim thought for a second. "No, but it was team-issued stuff from back in the U."

"Nobody's gonna know that. Every kid's got a Nike bag like that now."

"Yeah, it's pretty . . ." Jim paused as the realization hit him. "My mom's phone. I stuffed it in the bag after I checked to see if you sent any messages."

"Is she gonna notice?"

"Probably not." They still had a landline back at his parents' house, and his mom used that whenever she needed to call her friends. Her cell lay on the kitchen counter, plugged in next to the radio, most days. "I can get her another and say I wanted to get her an upgrade or something."

Kyle nodded. "So, besides the bag, you were able to get away okay?"

Jim told Kyle about Ellison pulling him over and the whole thing at the police station. "I passed a Breathalyzer, but if they find drugs in a bag they can trace back to me, out from where I was coming from, I'm screwed."

A pair of old guys who'd been picking up the church bulletins and candy wrappers left behind in the pews passed by them with a nod and headed downstairs to the fellowship hall.

"Colton Reid isn't the type of guy who calls the cops, so you should be okay there," Kyle said. "But you know there's no way he lets this go."

"I know." Anxiety bubbled up inside Jim's gut and threatened to boil over. He leaned back and thudded his head on the wall behind him. "What the hell am I going to do?"

"Maybe you should blow town for a bit," Kyle said. "Head back to Boston or up to Minneapolis for a week or so until we can figure something out. Hell, maybe he'll do something stupid while you're gone and the problem will fix itself."

It was tempting, but he couldn't abandon his mother, and she'd never agree to go with him, even for a week. She'd always been a homebody, but with her deteriorating condition, familiar surroundings were imperative.

On top of that, Jim couldn't get past seeing Colton sitting outside Kelli's house that night.

"I can't leave." Jim shook his head in resignation, despair radiating from the center of his chest like a chunk of uranium, poisoning his entire body. "Ugh . . . maybe this was all a terrible idea. You know CHS made an offer right after Dad died? I should have taken that and never come back."

Kyle let him stew a second before speaking. "You know you weren't going to do that. Your dad would've rolled over in his grave if you'd sold out to them."

"Yeah, well he can come back and deal with all this shit if he wants. It's mostly his mess anyway."

"Maybe, but it's your mess now." Kyle jabbed him in the shoulder. "You hear me? You did the only thing you could coming back to take care of your family, and you may not like it, but McCann LP is part of that. That place is important to a lot of people in this town, including me, so the last thing I'm going to do is let you sell out to CHS. I'd buy it myself before I let that happen."

Jim looked over at Kyle, never taking his head from the wall behind him.

"I'm serious, you know," Kyle said. "If you really think this is all too much and you want out, we can figure something out."

Jim scoffed. He didn't want to belittle his friend, but there was no way Kyle had the funds for something like that. Before he could figure out a diplomatic way to tell him, Carrie came up the steps next to them. "What's going on? I've been trying to find you guys. You ready to go?" She looked from her husband over to Jim. "Your mom is sitting with Helen and Marcia."

"Thanks. I should get down there."

Carrie motioned for Kyle to leave and turned to the front doors as a few more people came up behind her. He nodded and looked back at Jim before leaving.

"We can talk more tomorrow."

Paranoia followed Jim during the ride home from church and set up camp in his head. He could barely keep his eyes on the street in front of him, constantly checking the rearview mirror, expecting the top of every car behind them to explode into a swirl of red and blue lights. Sirens that would call out to everyone in town *COME WATCH US ARREST JIMMY MCCANN!*

But he couldn't simply keep an eye on the traffic behind him, because the shadows were worse than the roads.

That's where Colton was.

Lurking around every corner, peeking around every tree, waiting to bust out of the bushes, his dog pulling against the chain around his neck.

Unfortunately, Colton wasn't so constrained.

The cops had laws they were supposed to follow and some sort of oversight, but there wasn't a leash strong enough to hold Colton back if he decided to come after Jim.

And no part of him thought he'd make any other decision. Like Kyle had said, it was simply a matter of when.

Somehow, Jim got them home without incident.

He helped his mom make lunch, something she'd done every Sunday since he was a kid and could complete with muscle memory alone.

Whatever relief the ibuprofen had given him that morning had worn off, so he popped another three without considering what the label said about dosage. He didn't know if it mattered, but he also didn't know how much the pills helped. It felt like he was bailing water from a boat with a soup ladle.

There are more effective tools.

The Oxy would work. If the ibuprofen was a spoon, an Oxy was a bucket. Unfortunately, they were all outside Colton's fence.

Hopefully.

At some point, they'd have to go out there and get the bag. It was a loose thread that needed clipping. Something that tied Jim to Colton's place.

Jim leaned back and tried not to think about how much of a mess he'd made as a shot of pain went up his leg.

Maybe this whole thing had been a huge mistake.

Back at the church, Kyle had mentioned something about buying him out, but Jim hadn't taken him seriously because there was no way he'd have the capital for something like that, even if Jim gave him a huge friends-and-family discount.

But what if he did? Maybe he'd made some savvy investments over the years?

Honestly, half of Jim wouldn't care if he'd been robbing banks on the side if it got him out of this dumpster fire.

As if on cue, his phone buzzed in his pocket.

What happened?

It was Kelli, and Jim had no idea how much she knew. Luckily, a second message popped up before he had to figure out a response.

Carrie told me you hurt ur knee

It was a relief, but only temporary. Gaslighting his mother was one thing. Lying to Kelli was completely different. The stakes were higher, and the difficulty was a completely different level.

Yeah

He knew that wouldn't suffice but figured it would give him a little time while she typed.

Whatd u do?

If she was asking, Carrie must not have told her anything, which meant Kyle hadn't made up a story for his wife. It was little relief.

Tripped on the steps and landed bad.

He debated saying something about going to the ER but figured the fewer lies he had to keep track of the better.

Need anything?

More than she knew. He wanted to ask her to come over, to sit on the couch with him and put on a dumb movie, but until he got a handle on everything that was happening, it was better to keep her away.

Jim politely declined and said they'd catch up later in the week.

She tagged his response with a heart, and it sent a jolt of warmth into his.

And that's when he realized that he couldn't leave Silent Creek. He couldn't leave her.

He'd have to put away the delusions of sales and escapes and find a way to fix this.

Chapter Twenty-Five

Heading into McCann Monday morning was surreal. Jim had spent the rest of the day Sunday at home with his mother, and getting out made him feel exposed. Everything looked normal, but that made him more nervous than anything. He'd seen a police car pull in behind him on the way to work, and it had stopped his heart, but he couldn't see who was behind the wheel, and it turned away after a few blocks.

After what happened over the weekend, Jim couldn't fathom things going back to normal so quickly. He felt like something was looming beyond the horizon. A storm churning, building strength before it rolled through town.

He had to figure how to ride it out.

"Morning, Theresa." The secretary gave him an obligatory polite smile and went back to the stack of mail in front of her. Jim headed past her desk into his office, his gait improved but still not normal. Either she hadn't noticed or hadn't cared to ask why he was limping.

The swelling had gone down some. Finally getting off it yesterday afternoon probably helped. He'd put a compression sleeve on under his brace and brought a supply of ibuprofen to supplement what he'd taken that morning, so as long as he didn't do anything stupid, he should be able to get through the day without trouble.

He'd barely sat down and maneuvered his leg under the desk when Kyle popped in.

"How you doing?"

Jim reached under the Post-it note with his log-in that Theresa had stuck to his computer monitor and switched it on. The McCann LP logo his dad had used as his desktop wallpaper came into focus.

"Fine."

Kyle glanced back into the outer office, then stepped inside. He slid into the chair across from Jim's desk, his voice coated in the low tone of conspiracy. "Any fallout from Saturday? You hear any more from the police or . . ."

Jim shook his head.

"That's good." Kyle shifted around in the chair. "If they let you go, I can't imagine there's anything they can do at this point. If they had anything on you, they'd have arrested you then."

Jim thought about the bag of drugs lying at the base of that chain-link fence around Colton's property. "Hopefully, but it's not the cops I'm worried about."

Kyle's eyes darkened for a second, and he glanced behind him again, as if Colton were sneaking up on them. "Yeah, we've still gotta figure that part out."

The silence hung for a second. "Okay, what if—"

Kyle cut himself off when Theresa came in with a package. "This was outside when I got here."

Jim eyed the package she'd put on his desk, and a flare went up in the back of his head. It was a small USPS box, roughly the size of an old VHS tape. The white cardboard was creased and worn in a few spots, and the whole thing was wrapped in clear packing tape. It wasn't addressed to McCann LP, but the blocky print was scrawled out for him.

It took a second for Jim to notice there was no postage on it.

He picked it up and felt whatever was inside slide around a bit.

He looked up at Kyle, who shrugged.

"Open it."

Jim dug through his desk drawer for something to cut through the tape and settled on an old key that probably fit one of the short file cabinets behind him. Whoever sent it had used enough that Jim had to work for it, but he eventually peeled enough back to get the flap along the end open.

Jim reached in and knew what was inside before pulling his hand out.

He looked out his office door and saw Theresa at her desk once more, most likely absorbed in a game of *Candy Crush*, so he rolled back in his chair and emptied the box into his lap.

The pills he'd hoped to stash in Colton's trailer, the ones he'd left behind during his frantic escape two days before, lay across his legs. A small note fluttered out behind them.

Thought you'd want these back.

Kyle reached back and closed Jim's office door quickly and without subtlety.

"Jesus Christ."

Jim dropped the bag of pills on his desk and showed the note to Kyle. "What the hell's he doing?"

"Sending a message," Kyle said.

"And what's the message?"

"No clue," Kyle said.

"That's what scares me the most." Jim grabbed the bag and stashed it in his desk drawer. He lowered his voice and nodded at the closed door. "I'll flush these when Theresa leaves for lunch."

Kyle reached for the door, then paused and spoke more to himself than anything. "We're gonna have to figure something out because, one way or another, Colton Reid is coming."

Chapter Twenty-Six

The buzz coming from the Silent Creek High School gymnasium was as intense as it had been in the days Jimmy Buckets was running up and down the court. But even then, it hadn't been like this at 6:00 p.m. for the start of the girls' game.

Jim marveled at what Kelli had done for a program that had almost exclusively resided at the bottom of the South Minnesota Athletic Conference. Her squad was undefeated and sitting alone atop the conference standings, and the community was filling the stands for them.

He'd wanted to get here early enough to get a good seat but didn't want to leave without someone at home to hang out with his mom. Jim hadn't seen Kelli all week and didn't want to miss the game, so he was thrilled when Helen Anderson agreed to come over and spend the evening with Gail.

By the time he made his way through the foyer to the gym doors, the home side was packed.

Kyle was sitting behind his team in the far corner of the visitors' side, above the doors to the locker room, in the same spot Coach Frederick had had them sit for every home game.

Jim scanned the home side for a good spot, then quickly realized he'd have to settle for any open spot he could find.

Carrie caught his eye from the back row and waved him up. His knee wasn't crazy about that many steps, but he didn't have an option. Jim nodded to a few familiar faces on the way up the bleacher steps as she made room for him next to her.

"It's really packed tonight," Carrie said.

Jim squeezed in next to her and looked down at the crowd. "It's crazy."

"I hope they stay for the boys' game," Carrie said. "Kyle said he noticed people leaving early the Tuesday night in Waseca."

The fact that Kyle had noticed what was going on with the crowd in the middle of a game might give a clue as to why the boys' team was under .500 for the season, but Jim bit his tongue. "Probably needed to get home because it was a school night."

The crowd cut off any response Carrie had as the Beavers ran onto the court. Kelli stood at the baseline, high-fiving each player as she jogged past. It was hard to tell from the back row, but he thought Kelli spotted him and gave a quick smile as she turned back to the bench.

He and Carrie made small talk as the teams warmed up. They were forced to squish together a little closer than was comfortable as more fans squeezed their way into the bleachers. By the time the ball was in the air, they were close enough that Jim was sure Carrie could feel the knee brace under his pants.

If the overflow crowd came for a show, Kelli's team wasted no time. Brent Halverson's daughters each hit a three-pointer on the team's first two possessions, and the visitors from Blue Earth had no answer for the Beavers' full-court press. A steal and a layup that made the score 8–0 whipped the crowd into a frenzy and forced a time-out.

Jim was whooping it up with the fans, giving out high fives to total strangers, when a lone figure caught his eye on the visitors' side. The fans gradually sat back down as the game started again, but Jim's attention wasn't on basketball anymore. He could see Colton's smirking face from across the court, and it gave Jim a shiver despite the heat of the packed gym.

Before he knew what he was doing, Jim had stood up and headed for the aisle.

"Where are you going?" Carrie said.

He didn't have an answer, partly because he wasn't sure, but he knew he couldn't stay there with Colton staring at him like that. "Got to head out for a sec." The lady he'd stepped in front of grunted and leaned to the side so she could see the game. "Sorry."

He sidestepped down the stairs. With no rail, heading down to the floor was much harder on his knee than climbing up had been, and he almost went tumbling about halfway down. Luckily, one of the Beavers hit a ten-footer at the same time, so nobody noticed.

By the time Jim got to the floor, he was sweaty and breathing heavy. The steamy heat of the gym was pressing down on him like never before.

He needed air.

A whistle blew behind him, stopping play and bringing the cheerleaders out on the floor as the teams went back to their benches. Jim took the opportunity to head for the door.

Compared to before the game, the SCHS foyer was a ghost town. A couple of people stood talking with a woman working the concession stand, and about five kids were running around playing tag, but everyone else was in the gym.

Not knowing what else to do, Jim turned toward the men's room.

He walked over to the sink and splashed a handful of cold water on his face, then took a few deep breaths. The crowd's roar filtered through the concrete bricks around him, and his breathing returned to normal. Whatever urinal cakes the school now used were incredibly potent, and the familiar smell flipped a switch in his bladder.

Jim walked over to a urinal and unzipped his pants.

"Did you get my package?"

Colton's voice echoed through the bathroom and made Jim jump. Luckily, he hadn't started peeing yet, or the mess would have been considerable. He stared at the wall in front of him, mind racing. "You'd think after all these years you would've thought up some new tricks, but I guess you gotta stick with what works."

Jim zipped his pants and turned around. Colton was leaning against one of the three sinks behind him. The casual nature with which he stood lit something inside Jim. This guy was turning his life upside down but put off the attitude of an affable prankster. An aw-shucks, shit-eating grin on his face, daring him to do something about it.

"What do you want?"

Colton put his hand to his chest. "Me? I don't want nothing from you. I'm simply gonna fuck you the same way you been fucking me. That's fair, isn't it?"

"You don't think you've done enough?" Jim's voice had an edge he didn't expect, and it bounced around the concrete walls of the bathroom.

Colton laughed. "I haven't even gotten started on my payback."

Another roar from the crowd seeped into the bathroom, and Jim wondered how long they had before someone came through the door.

"You know, I never even liked basketball much," Colton said. "But after I got busted for some dumb thing or another, they said I had two choices—basketball or suspension. Personally, I wouldn't have minded the time off, but my old man said he couldn't have me hanging around the house all day, so they threw me a uniform and said to knock around any kid who came near you, so I did. You never did thank me, by the way."

Jim rolled his eyes.

"Your old man did," Colton said. "Came up to me after my first game and said I did a good job. Must be nice to have that kind of support."

Every critical word his father had ever said fought for space in Jim's memory. "Yeah, James McCann was real supportive."

Colton leaned back farther against the sink. "You know, my old man used to play ball back in his day. Apparently he was halfway decent but was too much of a fuckup to do anything with it. He never talked about it, and he never went to any of my games, but I will say the only time he didn't raise a hand to me was while I was playing. That was *his* support. His way of saying he was proud of me—not punching me."

Colton's eyes darkened, and he pushed himself off the sink. "You know what happened when he found out I got kicked off? He threw me through the kitchen table, then came after me with one of the legs that popped off. I got in a few good ones myself, but it's hard when the other guy's swinging a table leg. Fucker had a nail in it too."

Colton lifted his shirt to show a jagged scar down his right side. A pale river cutting through his rib cage. Jim took a step back. He'd always heard rumors about what had happened before Colton got sent away, but seeing the results standing in front of him was a shot between the eyes.

"That's what *my* old man did. *Yours* gave me a job when nobody else would." Colton dropped his shirt and pointed across the bathroom. "And then you came along and took that job away. Just like you got me kicked off the team."

"Hey, man, I'm sorry for what happened with your dad. That's messed up, but I didn't put a twelve-pack of beer in your truck, Colton. You did that, so as much as you want to blame me for everything shitty in your life, maybe turn around and look in that mirror there."

Colton laughed loud enough to fill the restroom. "Yeah, you're a real saint. Wasn't enough to shitcan me, but you gotta blackball me with every other spot in the area. It's like you're pissed Daddy gave me a shot and are determined to make sure I don't get another one anywhere else."

"I haven't said a thing about you to anyone," Jim said. "You ever think people may not want to hire someone with your history?"

Colton smirked like he was considering it. "Speaking of that, I got a phone call today you might be interested in. It was from some guy who works with an organization that pays people like your old man to give ex-cons like me jobs. Wanted to know how things were going. I thought that was funny, 'cause I don't work for you no more."

The confused look on Jim's face fed Colton's grin.

"Seems he thinks I'm still driving trucks for you, which I'm gonna bet means he's still paying you for that."

"I don't know what you're talking about."

"Oh, I'm sure you do, but don't worry. I told him things were just peachy." Colton stood up from the sink and walked over to Jim, close enough he could smell the hostility on his breath. "I wonder what would happen if I told him first thing you did when you showed up was fire my ass. You still cashing those checks, Jimmy?"

Jim tried not to shrink back from him.

"Whatever you're trying—"

The door swung open, and an old man in a flannel shirt walked in. He nodded at them and walked up to a urinal.

Before Jim could look back, Colton had slammed his fist into his midsection. Every molecule of breath in Jim's lungs exploded out of him as he folded in half. As he fought to breathe and to stay on his feet, Jim felt Colton grab his shirt and pull him forward. He jammed something in the back pocket of Jim's jeans before letting go.

"See you 'round . . . *boss man*."

Jim stumbled forward and grabbed on to one of the sinks along the wall as a rack of coughs shook him. He was vaguely aware of the old man who'd walked in on them hustling back out without even looking his way.

By the time he got his breathing under control, the bathroom was empty.

Jim leaned on the sink and drank a handful of water from the spigot. He looked in the mirror, watching the water drip down his chin, and tried to pull his thoughts together.

The door opened again, and two kids ran in, then ran back out at the sight of him.

Jim had spit in the sink and gone to follow them out when he felt the bump in his back pocket.

He stopped and pulled out a crumpled piece of paper.

It was the letter Kyle had put in front of him his first day in the office. The one that told Colton Reid they were letting him go.

The one that had started this whole thing.

It was exactly as he remembered, except for a handwritten note alongside his signature.

Have a 12-pack of Keystone on me

It was in the same color pen as his signature, but not in his handwriting. Although it was close enough to think it was if you weren't familiar.

But Jim was familiar with that handwriting. He'd seen it plenty of times on all kinds of papers around the office.

It was Kyle's.

Chapter Twenty-Seven

Jim went straight from the bathroom to his car, looking over his shoulder the whole time. He was surprised that his tires weren't slashed, but he didn't waste time thanking the universe before driving home.

The streets were clear behind him, but the interaction with Colton followed him home.

Jim didn't know about any work-rehabilitation program that Colton had been hired under. Kyle never mentioned anything when they let him go, but if there was something, Jim was sure he would have taken care of it.

Why the hell would he believe anything Colton Reid said? Even if he had been hired under some grant program, he was most likely messing with him anyway.

And even if he was telling the truth, it was probably a misunderstanding. If it was really a government program, then who knew how many miles of red tape they could be tangled up in?

Probably a mistake. He'd ask Kyle about it tomorrow.

But what about that note?

That ate at him more than anything.

It was stupid and petty but ultimately not that surprising, knowing Kyle's history with Colton. A bad decision in the heat of the moment.

But was it an isolated incident? Colton had been acting like this was personal the whole time. Had Kyle made it that way?

Jim tried to shake the thought out of his head as he parked.

When he limped in the front door of his parents' house, Helen was watching television with his mom. If she noticed his early return, she was polite enough not to say anything. Gail offered to make Jim a snack, but he declined.

"I'm fine, Mom. You watch your show."

He pulled a Castle Danger Cream Ale out of the refrigerator and sat at the kitchen table by himself. The beer was gone before he realized it, so he went for another. Jim tried to push Colton Reid out of his head, but he'd set up camp and, just like in real life, wasn't keen on going anywhere.

Eventually, Helen stuck her head into the kitchen to say goodbye.

"Thanks for coming over," Jim said.

"I was very glad to come over," Helen said. "We got to talking for a while, telling stories. It was really good. Better than it has been for a long time, honestly."

"That's great," Jim said.

"It's a good night," Helen said. "You should go talk with her."

Jim looked up at Helen and realized what she was saying. With the way his mom's condition had been steadily deteriorating over the past few months, it was easy to forget that dementia could be a roller coaster.

Sometimes the clouds lifted, and he needed to take advantage of that because there was no telling when they would again.

"I will. Thank you."

Jim winced as he pushed himself up from the table and walked Helen to the door. His knee told him he was due for more ibuprofen, but he headed over to the couch instead. The local news was starting up, and Jim caught a preview of the sports segment, led by highlights from the Silent Creek High School gymnasium, as he eased down next to her.

"You guys have fun tonight?"

Gail turned away from the television and smiled. Jim knew immediately that Helen was right, because this was a real one, with something behind it. He hadn't realized how long it had been since he'd seen that. "We did. We got to telling old high school stories about people I haven't seen in a long time."

Jim smiled, and he could see her eyes were clearer than they'd been in a while. "That's great."

"What did you do tonight?"

"I went to the basketball game." The memory of Colton standing in front of him in the bathroom tried to elbow its way in, but Jim shoved it aside. "I left early because I was getting a headache."

"That gym was always so loud," Gail said.

"It was fun to see the place packed," Jim said. "Kelli is doing a really good job with those girls. They may be as good as we were."

As if summoned, his phone buzzed.

Missed u at the game. North Star?

Jim wanted to, of course, but he wasn't going to let this moment with his mother slip away.

Luv to, but better hang here with mom.

Jim's nerves danced as the three little dots flashed at the bottom of his screen.

Say hi to mom for me

He smiled again and put his phone away. He leaned back on the couch to wait as the news came back from commercial. As promised, the Silent Creek High School girls' game led off the sports segment, and Kelli popped on the screen. The quick shot of her clapping encouragement in her purple SCHS polo shirt felt like it was directed at him.

Another genuine smile blossomed on his mom's face. "I like her."

Jim's chest filled with warmth at the sentiment, and for a brief second it chased away the stress that had invaded him. "Me too."

Jim had left—or more accurately, fled—the gym early enough he didn't realize the number the Beavers had done on their opponents. He and Gail watched a montage of layups, three-pointers, and steals interspersed with shots of a crowd in purple and white going absolutely wild for the home team.

The final score was 87–51. They cut back to the studio, where the middle-aged sports guy told the mid-twenties anchor that the win took Silent Creek to 7–0 on the year and they were the best team he'd seen from the area in years. She agreed that it was an exciting turn of events in Silent Creek, and they moved on without mentioning the score from Kyle's game. Jim flipped over to channel three, then channel six, in an attempt to see what they said, but they had both moved on to the weather.

Jim pulled out his phone again.

Just saw highlights. Big win!!!

A little heart appeared over his message and gave him all the feels yet again.

"Is that her?"

Jim nodded sheepishly. Even though he was well into his thirties, he still found talking girls with his mom awkward.

Gail leaned her head back into the couch. "I miss your father."

The words rocked Jim. Even in the best of times, Gail McCann had never been what he would have called affectionate. Heck, Jim wasn't even sure if he'd ever seen his parents kiss.

"I know he was ornery sometimes, but . . ." Jim saw a tear shine in the light of the television. "I hope you find someone to miss someday."

Every emotion that existed swirled through him as he watched his mother miss her husband. With no idea what to say, but positive nothing would fit the moment, he leaned over and hugged her.

She hugged him back, and he could feel her wipe her eyes before she pulled away so he wouldn't see it.

It was the Minnesota way.

They let go and settled back on the couch.

"*Ornery* was a good way to describe him," Jim said, and it brought an emotion-fueled laugh from both of them.

"I know he was hard on you sometimes, but he always wanted the best for you," Gail said. "He mellowed as he got older."

"He must have," Jim said. "Honestly, I can't believe you had him eating salads at the end."

Gail smiled again, but it didn't have the same wattage as before, and that broke Jim's heart. Because as great as the last few minutes had been, the smile reminded him that these times couldn't last.

"Remember, you and Kyle were telling me about it a while back?" Jim knew you weren't supposed to ask those suffering with dementia if they remembered things, but he couldn't help it. He didn't want to lose the moment. "He'd bring you stuff from his wife Carrie's garden to make the salads?"

Jim saw the memory click, and it gave him a wave of relief, even if he knew it was temporary.

"His wife always had the best lettuce," Gail said. "Your father, though, he still fought it. Said eating those salads actually made him feel worse. I said it was probably because his body wasn't used to all those vegetables."

She laughed at the thought, and it quickly turned into a yawn.

"Tired?"

Gail nodded. He didn't want her to go to bed, to let this moment end, and he could tell something inside her didn't either. It was like she knew it may be the last time it was like this.

She yawned again.

"You can go to bed."

Gail patted him on the good knee and got up. "Don't stay up too late yourself."

Jim watched her walk across the living room and head down the hallway.

"See you tomorrow," Jim said, even though he knew he wouldn't.

At least not like this.

Chapter Twenty-Eight

Jim sat at his desk, digging through his father's old files, looking for anything involving the hiring of Colton Reid.

But there was nothing.

The longer he searched with no results, the easier it was to dismiss what Colton had said as some dumb lie to get under his skin.

If that's what it was, it worked. But Jim kept digging.

Kyle was over in his own office on the other side of the reception area and probably could answer any question Jim had, but he couldn't ask.

Because what if what Colton had said was true and Kyle knew about it?

Jim kept telling himself he was overthinking it, but it was like a little wooden sliver buried in his skin. An irritant that wouldn't go away.

He put his head down on his desk and kept it there for a while, the thoughts and emotions of the past month swirling over him like a hurricane and blotting out any coherence he tried to hold on to.

Jim heard the phone ring out at the reception desk, then the murmur of Theresa's voice.

He sat up and kept digging.

After another thirty minutes, Jim pulled out a thin hanging folder marked *GOGP*. He opened it up and hit pay dirt.

Inside was a group of documents regarding the Growth Opportunity Grant Program from the US Chamber of Commerce.

Jim read through the sheets detailing exactly what Colton had talked about, a government program incentivizing companies to hire parolees and recently released felons in their area. For every program enrollee they hired, companies got significant tax breaks, along with grant money to cover their salary.

How the hell did Jim not know about this? If anything, knowing about that grant and tax breaks would have been nice when making the decision to fire Colton.

But more importantly, if what Colton said about the phone call was right and they were still sending the money, McCann could get in serious trouble. The last thing they needed was the IRS climbing up their ass.

Jim flipped through and found a few pages with signatures on them.

Andrew Garman

He opened up Google and found a page about the GOGP. A few more clicks and he had Andrew Garman's phone number.

Jim punched the numbers in and waited nervously as the phone rang on the other side of the line.

"Garman here."

The guy's voice gave him a jolt. Jim realized he should have planned out what he was going to say.

"Hello?"

"Yes, hello, Mr. Garman," Jim sputtered. "Jim McCann here."

"Hello, Mr. McCann, it's good to speak with you again."

Jim was thrown for a second, then realized the problem. "No, sorry. You're probably thinking of my father, he's . . . he's no longer here."

The news must have thrown Garman for a loop, because there was an awkward pause before he spoke again. "Oh . . . I'm so sorry. I didn't realize."

"It's fine." Jim didn't bother with an explanation. "I should've been clearer."

There was another pause.

"So, what can I do for you, Mr. McCann?" Garman said. "I assume everything's still going well with Colton Reid?"

"What?" The word was out of Jim's mouth before he had time to think, and Garman didn't miss the tone.

"I checked in with him the other day, and he said things were fine, and your father always seemed quite happy with the way things were working out." Garman's tone switched from conversational to cautious. "Have things changed?"

Jim tried to answer, but his words fought like he was pushing them toward a cliff's edge.

"Mr. McCann . . . you still there?"

"Yeah, sorry . . ." He forced a very fake laugh in an effort to buy time. "Things are a little crazy around here—you know how it is. But, yeah, things are fine." It sounded weird coming out of his mouth after everything that had happened over the last few months, but he figured it was the best way to stall. "I'm going over some paperwork about this and thought I'd call and ask a few questions about it. As I alluded to earlier, my father passed on a few months back and I've taken his spot here at McCann. I'm still trying to get up to speed on a few things around here, you know. Propane wasn't really my business before this."

Garman's voice perked up a bit, probably because people in bureaucratic government jobs often love the chance to explain what they do.

"That's perfectly understandable, Mr. McCann. What questions do you have?"

Jim scanned the papers in front of him again. "So, I guess, how's this work?"

Garman cleared his throat on the other side of the line.

"Well, we place recently released parolees in jobs to give them stability and purpose in hopes of giving them a second chance on life. As their employer, you get up to $30,000 a year, paid out quarterly, to help cover the cost of employment."

Jim looked at the numbers again and probed carefully. "And you're still paying for Colton Reid?"

"The grant lasts up to five years, so, yes, you are eligible for two more years of payment, assuming Mr. Reid's continued employment, obviously."

"Obviously."

"You know, I've actually got another potential GOGP opportunity in your area." Jim thought he heard papers rustling on the other side of the line. "His name is Charles Blount, and he's going to be living in Austin. He's got some mechanical experience, so he might actually be a pretty good fit if you have any room. Is it something you'd be potentially interested in again?"

There was a long awkward pause.

"Oh . . . um, I don't know," Jim said.

"That's fine—you don't have to decide right away. Mr. Blount won't be released for another few months, but he seems like a good candidate, so I thought I'd check. There are a few advantages to adding a second employee through GOGP. First, we already have your information from last time, and since it has been less than five years, we don't need to do another site visit. The grant would be the same, but you'd be eligible for additional tax credits for adding a second eligible parolee."

Jim still didn't know what to say.

"If that sounds like something you'd be interested in, I'd love to set up an interview in the coming week if possible."

"Yeah . . . well, maybe." The words tumbled out of his mouth without much thought to order or coherence. "I'll have to discuss it with a few others around here, to see what our status is . . . if we have room to bring someone on."

"That sounds great," Garman said. "If you'd like, I can check back with you in a week or two, but if you make any decisions before, then feel free to give me a call whenever."

Jim thanked him and said goodbye. His head swirled as he reached out and gently placed the phone back in its cradle.

It was probably a mistake.

But at this point, there was only one way to find out. He headed into the reception area and crossed over to Kyle's office.

"Hey, Kyle. Got a second?"

He was already up from his desk and pulling the coat out from behind his office door. "Actually, I'm about to head to practice."

"It'll just take a sec," Jim said. "I'll walk you out."

Kyle shrugged and grabbed a few mints from the bowl Theresa kept for visitors on her desk before heading to the door.

The brace under his chinos tugged at them as Jim followed. He was hit with a blast of cold air as soon as the door opened and they stepped outside.

"What's up?"

Jim hadn't thought of a way to ease into things, so he jumped in with both feet.

"I saw Colton at the game last night."

The shock on Kyle's face was instant. *"What?"*

"He was on the visitors' side, staring at me. When I tried to leave, he followed me into the bathroom."

Another gust of wind whipped through the parking lot, so they headed around the corner of the building for a little shelter.

And privacy.

"You okay?" Kyle asked. "Did he do anything?"

Jim thought about the punch in the gut. The letter with Kyle's taunting scribble across the bottom that Colton had stuffed in his back pocket.

"He said he got a phone call from the GOGP asking about how his job was going," Jim said. "You told them he's not working here anymore, didn't you?"

The flash across Kyle's face was quick, but Jim saw it.

"Of course."

"Then why are they calling and asking him how it's going?"

Kyle rolled his eyes and chuffed a laugh that came out in a little frozen cloud. "I'm gonna bet they didn't and he's messing with you."

Jim shrugged. "That's what I thought at first, but I called them up to make sure, and they think he's still here. Hell, they offered us another one because things seem to be going so well."

"Sounds like a typical government program to me," Kyle said. "Some pencil pusher didn't tell another pencil pusher, and it fell through the cracks. Happens all the time. Left hand doesn't know what the right is doing."

"Maybe, but if that's the case, we'd better straighten it out, don't you think?" Jim chose his words carefully and kept his eyes on Kyle's as he spoke. "Because if we're getting paid for something that we're not doing, that could be a big problem down the road, no?"

Kyle blew some warmth into his hands and shifted back and forth like a bored middle schooler. "If you want, I'll call them tomorrow and straighten this whole thing out. It's not a big deal. But we can talk about it then, because I've got to get to practice."

Kyle walked back around the corner to his Grand Cherokee parked in the spot next to Jim's. He was halfway around the driver's side when Jim followed.

"Why didn't you tell me about it?"

Kyle stopped, fingers on the door handle. "About what?"

"You never said anything about a government program when you told me to fire Colton," Jim said. "You told me we didn't need him, right? That we'd hired him when we were desperate and now that we weren't, it was time to let him go."

Kyle's brow furrowed a bit, and his eyes narrowed. "Yeah."

"How come you didn't mention anything about this GGP program or whatever it is?"

Kyle rolled his head back. "I don't know—I just didn't. What difference does it make?"

Jim stared at Kyle, not knowing what to say next.

"What?"

"Why did we fire Colton?"

Kyle looked at Jim as if he'd asked why he wanted a parachute before hopping out of a plane. "Are you seriously asking me that? I . . . I don't even know how to respond."

"You said we were overstaffed when I got here, but I was talking with Brent Halverson at the Stewartville game, and he said they were stretched thin."

Kyle rolled his eyes. "Those guys bitch about everything. We could hire a dozen drivers and they'd complain that they're overworked." His voice had raised enough it could still be used among friends but certainly not when you were talking to your boss.

"Even if that's true, with this grant thing, he didn't cost us a dime, so who cares if we need him or not?" Jim was trying to keep his voice professional but failing as much as Kyle was. "He could have sat in the shop all day, and it wouldn't have made any difference."

"Yeah, have Colton Reid hang around all day, that's a great idea. Maybe let him start a day care out in the shop?" Kyle stopped and gathered himself. "I'm not the boss around here. Your father wanted him gone, so we got rid of him."

Hearing that again pushed Jim beyond the realm of politeness.

"I don't believe you." He could see Theresa at her desk in the background, barely hiding the fact that she was eavesdropping. "That Garman guy offered us another one because my dad told him it was going well. Besides, there's no way James McCann would turn down a free employee. Never in a million years."

Jim reached into his pocket and pulled out the paper Colton had stuffed in his pocket when he'd been fighting for breath in the bathroom. He unfolded it and slapped it down on the hood of Kyle's SUV. "What the hell was this?"

Kyle put his hands up in exasperation. "What do you want me to say? That I was glad when we fired him? Fine, you got me. I fucking *loved* sending him that letter. Is that what you want to hear?"

Jim's fingers tightened around the letter, crumpling the paper again, and jammed it back in his pocket.

"All the shit that's happened started after *you* told me to fire him, so tell me this isn't because of some stupid high school grudge of yours."

Kyle's eyes darkened. "A stupid high school grudge? Are you actually saying that after everything that's happened?" He cut himself off with a laugh, but there was nothing light about it. "He's a rabid dog."

Jim stared across the hood of Kyle's vehicle.

"Yeah, and you're the one who let him off the leash."

Kyle held Jim's eye contact for a second, then tapped the roof a couple of times and smiled. "You know what, I can't do this right now. I've got practice."

He yanked the car door open, got behind the wheel, and slammed it hard enough it echoed over the wind.

Jim stood there, watching him drive away, and tried to make sense of everything that had happened since he returned to Silent Creek.

Chapter Twenty-Nine

The dark cloud that formed during his talk with Kyle followed Jim home, then hovered around the house the rest of the night. It loomed over him while he helped his mom with dinner and didn't go away when they sat down to watch TV after.

Since he'd come back to McCann LP, Jim had put all his faith in Kyle. He'd leaned on him for every decision he made, and counted on his advice as something he could stand on until he got his feet under him.

Jim wanted to trust him. To believe this was nothing more than a shit situation full of mistakes and misunderstanding, but he could feel the foundation crumbling beneath him.

He needed something solid, and then his phone rang.

"Hey." Kelli's voice was a balm on the road rash that covered his psyche that night. Part of him wanted to tell her all about what was going down at work, to ask for her advice on how to handle his growing suspicions regarding Kyle, but he didn't. Jim didn't want to stain the moment by dragging in his baggage. He wanted to escape it, even if he knew it would be waiting for him in the morning.

He asked her about her day, and she told him about the abstract self-portraits she had the second graders working on. Watercolors, crayons, and finger paints alongside printed out quotes she'd secretly written down from each of them throughout the year.

It sounded great, and Jim could've listened to it all night, but it got late quickly.

"I should let you go," he said. "It's a school night, after all."

"Yeah, probably better."

"I think I'm gonna bring Mom to the game tomorrow night," Jim said. "Might be good to get her out of the house, and I think she'll get a kick out of seeing you coach. I don't know if she's been in the gym since I played."

"If we play it," Kelli said. "They're talking about a big storm kicking up tomorrow night. Already some talk about postponing."

Disappointment punched Jim in the gut, and it hit harder than he would have expected. "Bummer."

"We'll see," Kelli said. "You know how pointless it is to try and predict the weather around here. Might be nothing at all."

"Let's hope so."

They said goodbye and hung up.

The dark cloud from earlier wasted no time in rolling back in.

Jim headed back into the living room and sat by his mom on the couch. The news was on, and they'd bumped weather to the top of the hour. Like Kelli said, they were predicting the season's first blizzard to hit Silent Creek tomorrow. Flurries would start in the afternoon, but the main brunt wasn't supposed to hit until early evening.

Right around when Kelli's game was supposed to tip off.

Jim remembered a trip back from Albert Lea during his sophomore year. A snowstorm had kicked up during the game and raged through the entire ride home. Being inside the bus shielded him from what was going on out on the road, and none of the players realized how bad it was until they pulled over in the middle of nowhere. Jim looked out the window and saw a pair of taillights glowing from the ditch.

Luckily, nobody was hurt, but a family of four caught a ride with the team back to Silent Creek. It shattered the little bubble Jim had been in. He'd barely started driving himself and never in anything close to adverse conditions. The whole ride home he'd stared out the window, watching the glowing snow stream across the road in front of them.

It was a good lesson in the hazards of Minnesota winters and helped ease the disappointment of Kelli's game's possible cancellation.

Better safe than sorry.

Chapter Thirty

Clouds had rolled in by the next morning, their bluish-gray tint promising a white night for the entire Silent Creek area.

Theresa said Kyle called to say he had to meet with the school's athletics director and superintendent about that night's game and wouldn't be in for a while. Part of Jim wondered why he couldn't take care of it with a phone call, but the rest of him was happy Kyle was out of the office.

He'd barely slept the night before, unable to put his suspicions to bed. He hoped Kyle would make a phone call to Garman over at the GOGP first thing this morning and straighten everything out.

Kyle's absence wasn't helping his case.

Jim looked back through their records at the grant payments received. They'd gotten two since Colton had been fired. The first was a few weeks after, and if that were the only one, Jim would've been more apt to believe it was a paperwork error like Kyle claimed, but the most recent was a week ago, which made it that much harder to blow off.

He really wanted it to be a mistake, because as the owner, it would be hard to convince anyone that he didn't know about that kind of fraud. Especially when it technically started right after he'd arrived.

The thought threw another log on the bonfire of nerves burning in the pit of his stomach.

He couldn't wait for Kyle. He'd call Garman himself, tell him about the mistake, and pray to God his ignorance helped his case.

He was about to close things up when a name on a spreadsheet caught his eye.

VanVeldhusen Fleet Solutions

Jim froze, staring at the entry. It was a unique name, which was probably part of the reason Jim remembered it. But even if it had been Smith, he would never forget the anger in his father's voice every time he said it.

VanVeldhusen had been a longtime vendor for McCann. It's where they'd bought equipment for their LP and gas trucks when Jim was a kid. The only reason he knew this was because the owner, Mark VanVeldhusen, worked as a high school basketball referee all over southern Minnesota.

It was a small fraternity, so Jim got familiar with most of the guys on the circuit while he was playing. VanVeldhusen wasn't a particularly good or bad referee, so he should have been nothing more than a nameless face from his playing days.

But one night in Duschee during Jim's senior year, VanVeldhusen and his partner (whose name Jim didn't remember) decided to call a tight game. Not a big deal, normally. As long as the calls were consistent, he could deal with it, and it usually ended up helping Jimmy in the long run. A point from the free throw line was as good as one from the floor.

That Duschee squad was feisty, and the Beavers were struggling to put them away, so Jimmy was on the court with four fouls late in the fourth quarter. With about two minutes on the clock, Jimmy used his long arms to tip away a lazy pass and streaked down the court for a thunderous dunk that should have put the game away.

But before Silent Creek could celebrate, VanVeldhusen's whistle blew as he called a technical foul on Jimmy for hanging on the rim.

It was his fifth foul, which kicked him out of the game. Coach Frederick went nuclear and picked up two techs of his own to join Jimmy in the locker room. Duschee got six free throws and the ball, effectively pulling out the dagger that Jimmy had delivered.

As mad as Coach Frederick had been, James McCann was worse after the game. It had been a borderline call that most referees wouldn't make at an extremely consequential moment of the game, but if you were going strictly by the rule book, VanVeldhusen was probably correct.

That didn't matter to his dad.

James McCann canceled their contract the next morning.

The fact that company's name was in the McCann ledger again was surprising to say the least.

Jim looked back through the records. There were invoices from anywhere between $7,000 and $9,000 each month for the past six, but nothing before that.

They'd started up the month after his father died.

That in itself didn't seem strange. Maybe Kyle went back to them after James had died in order to score better prices? Jim looked up the supplier his dad had used all those years and saw the difference was negligible.

Huh.

Jim scrolled through each month's ledger and saw they were still paying their old supplier, too, even after VanVeldhusen had come back on board.

That's gotta be a mistake.

But that wasn't the only new account that had shown up the month after his dad died. Some of which he'd never even heard of.

Maverick IT

Charlson Consultations

Kjellguard Mechanical

None of the bills were so big they'd stand out, but none had itemized invoices either. In all, the new accounts totaled almost $15,000 a month.

Jim pulled up an invoice for a massive supply of truck parts. Air filters, oil filters, replacement belts.

Anger replaced Jim's suspicion as he printed out a copy and grabbed his coat. Maybe it was all a misunderstanding, maybe it was as bad as it looked, but digging through files wasn't going to give him any hard answers.

"I'm going to run out to the shop," Jim told Theresa and powered through his limp out the front door, invoice in hand.

The clouds didn't look like they had anything particularly special in store, but the wind carried the smell of a coming storm that betrayed their intentions.

The four bay doors on the garage were closed due to the cold, so Jim came in through the side door. All the trucks were out trying to get their deliveries in before the storm hit, leaving the shop empty.

Brent Halverson sat at the metal desk pushed up against the far wall. He glanced up at the sound of the door opening and waved.

"Hey, boss."

"Got a question for you, Brent." Jim didn't hesitate, talking as his footsteps shuffled off the concrete floor and echoed around the empty garage. "How are we doing on parts out here? Back when that thing with the trucks happened, we didn't have any spare belts on hand and you were telling me about being pretty light on supplies in general. Kyle ever get that straightened out for you?"

There was a pause that gave Jim the answer before the words were out of Brent's mouth. "I asked him about it last week, but he said the supplier was still back-ordered on a lot of stuff."

Jim looked down at the paper in his hand that said they should be fully stocked.

"Sorry about that. I'll have a talk with him when he gets in."

"While you're asking, check when the new impact driver is coming. We're down to one, and it's practically held together with duct tape. I'm about ready to bring in mine from home."

Jim scanned down the list in his hand, saw two Craftsman V20 half-inch impact wrenches at $249 each, and muttered a curse under his breath.

"I didn't mean to complain or nothing . . ."

Jim looked down at his head mechanic and tried to keep the anger from his face. "No, you're good. If something isn't right out here, I want you to let me know so we can make it right, okay?"

"Sounds good." Brent sniffled a yawn as he answered. "Ope . . . sorry 'bout that. We got a fire called in last night, so I was up and geared up at 2:00 a.m."

Brent was one of a handful of guys in the garage who moonlighted as volunteer firefighters, but in a town the size of Silent Creek, that usually didn't mean a lot more than driving the trucks in the Fourth of July parade.

"I hadn't heard," Jim said. "Where?"

"Out at Reid's place."

Hearing Colton's name sent a warning flare up in the back of Jim's head. "Colton Reid?"

Brent nodded and yawned again. "Sorry . . . yeah. This shed or barn thing he's got out there went up. Lucky we got there when we did because we were able to keep it contained. He's got a trailer he's in now, but his dad's old house is still up out there, too, and that thing's nothing more than a pile of tinder. If it was windy like it is now? Shoot, things could have gotten scary in a hurry."

Jim nodded like he wasn't intimately familiar with the old house out on Colton's property and just how scary things could get out there.

"Any idea how it started?"

Brent shook his head.

"I guess he keeps his dog out there, so probably got an old heater or something that did it." He leaned back in his chair and looked up at Jim. "You should see that thing. When we pulled up it went nuts, barking and snarling. Literally kept us in the truck till Reid came over and got hold of it."

Again, Jim was very familiar, but before he had to think of anything else to say, the huge garage door to their right started lumbering up and one of their trucks pulled into the bay next to them. Brent popped out of his chair and headed over to talk to the driver.

Jim gave them a small wave and started back to the office, the story about Colton's fire battling for space in his head with the proof that whatever Kyle was doing with the books at McCann, it most certainly wasn't on the level.

Jim walked past Kyle's still-empty parking spot and through the office door.

"Heard anything from Kyle yet?"

Theresa shook her head. "Not since earlier this morning."

Jim stepped into his office and tapped out a quick text.

We need to talk

It took a minute or two for Kyle's response to come.

Figuring out tonights game

Jim felt the brush-off. Kyle was the head coach, but canceling a game was above his pay grade. There was no reason he needed to be at the school.

Needs 2 be today. Come out to office

Three dots appeared briefly, then disappeared.

Chapter Thirty-One

Nerves chewed through Jim's guts as he stewed in his office, waiting to see if Kyle would show up—and trying to figure out what he was going to say if he did.

Part of him wanted to believe there was some explanation, some reason this all looked so bad but really wasn't, but the more he dug through their financial records, the more that hope died. He combed through their ledgers, cross-checking invoices and noting more discrepancies.

The DJs on the radio spent the day updating listeners on the forecast, and it kept getting bleaker. Around noon, Jim got a text from Kelli saying the game was canceled.

Yet he still hadn't heard from Kyle.

By three o'clock, the winds were rattling the building the same way doubt was shaking Jim's faith in his friend. He told Theresa she should head home early while the roads were still drivable, then walked out to the garage to tell Brent and the rest of the guys the same thing.

Nobody expected propane delivery in a blizzard.

Jim kept a wary eye on the sky during his walk back. The clouds had turned dark enough it looked more like a summer rainstorm was bearing down, but the bite of the wind left no doubt about what month it was.

He should go home too. Kyle wasn't coming—after their talk yesterday, maybe he knew it was a matter of time before Jim figured out what he'd been up to.

And what about the fire out at Colton's? He didn't think Kyle would be stupid enough to have anything to do with that, but the timing was incredibly suspicious.

Jim headed over to his car and noticed the first flakes of snow starting to catch in the nooks and crannies.

Under the windshield wipers.

Around the door handle.

Alongside the headlights.

He absentmindedly brushed away the little bit that had stuck to the hood and noticed the back end seemed to be hanging low. Jim peered around the front fender and saw his back tire flattened against the gravel below.

"Shit."

He knelt down for a closer look, expecting to see a slash across the side, but it appeared surprisingly intact. The wind howled against his back as Jim ran his hand over the tread, hoping to find the head of a screw or something that would be a rational explanation, but there was nothing.

He tried to dismiss his suspicions—there are a million ways for a tire to go flat—but paranoia was hard to shake.

Brent's truck crunched past, and he gave a quick double tap on the horn before heading out. Jim looked over at the shop to see if anyone was still there, but it was already buttoned up and the cars out front were gone. When the boss says you can knock off early, nobody waits around to see if he changes his mind.

It wasn't until Brent had disappeared down Highway 14 that Jim realized he was alone out there with no way of getting home.

Jim pulled his jacket tight across his chest and turned back to the office. He opened the door as a gust of wind whipped around the building and tried to wrench it from his hand. It banged hard enough against the wall Jim was sure the glass would shatter. He wrestled for control of it and pulled it shut behind him.

Jim brushed the dusting of snow off his arms and looked out into the parking lot as the skies released the rest of it. It looked like a swarm of tiny white locusts had descended on McCann LP, blotting out what little late-afternoon sun was left. The snow was thick enough Jim could barely see his car, which was sitting twenty feet from the door.

The storm had arrived.

The radio still babbled gently in his office, but Jim could barely hear it over the sound of the wind. He felt like he was tucked into a little cave as the weather raged outside, and it wasn't going to let up anytime soon.

He pulled out his phone to call his mom. As the landline rang, he thought about her cell phone lying on the ground out at Colton's.

No. If he'd found the pills, he'd have her cell too.

After a few more rings, there was a click and a man's voice came on the line.

Not Colton's, but his father's.

Hearing James McCann's voice again was a shock, and it took his brain a few seconds to understand that it was an old outgoing message on his parents' ancient answering machine, telling him to talk at the beep.

"Um . . . Mom? Just wanted to let you know I caught a flat and will probably be a little late getting home." He sat there for a second, listening to the silence on the line and staring out the glass door at the storm. "It's Jimmy."

He hadn't referred to himself that way since he'd left Minnesota, and his old name hung in the empty office as his brain slowly caught up to the fact that his mom hadn't answered the phone.

Jim immediately hit redial, tamping down the panic that grew with every unanswered ring.

He hung up again when his dad's voice came on.

There were a million reasons his mom wouldn't answer. She could be in the basement doing laundry. She could be taking a nap.

She could also be out wandering in the storm.

Or, with all the stuff that's going on with Colton, something even worse.

Jim called Kelli, and thankfully she picked up on the first ring.

"What's up?"

"Hey, could you do me a favor?" Jim turned away from the door and tried to keep the worry out of his voice. "Can you go check on my mom? I'm out at McCann and caught a flat, so it's probably gonna be a bit before I get home. I tried calling, but she didn't pick up. I know she's fine but—"

"Absolutely." Her answer was immediate. "I'll go right now."

Jim felt a rush of relief. "Thanks so much. I know she's probably fine, but . . ."

"Of course. It's no problem at all," Kelli said. "How long till you're home?"

Jim turned to look outside again, where the storm had somehow gotten worse. He couldn't see his car at all, and he could already feel his fingers freeze at the thought of trying to put a spare on in this weather.

"It's gonna be a bit," Jim said. "The guys are all gone, but if I can get it over to the garage, I can put the spare on in there."

He heard a rustle on the other end of the line before a door closed, and he realized she was already headed out to his mom's house. "Can't you leave it there and have Kyle give you a ride?"

"He's not here." Jim said. "I figured he went home after that meeting you guys had."

"What meeting?"

"About canceling the game?"

Kelli laughed. "They don't involve us in that."

"Uh-huh," Jim muttered. "Maybe it was something else, then. Anyway, thanks for checking on Mom."

"Happy to." The faint click of a turn signal came in behind her voice. "I'm sure she's fine, but I'll text you when I get there."

Jim thanked her again and ended the call. Kyle's office door stood open on the other side of the reception area, where the fluorescent lights were seeping in to create a mosaic of weird shadows in the dark room.

Jim walked over and chased them away with the flick of a switch. He didn't know what he expected to find, but the pull of curiosity had its hand on the wheel.

Kyle's office was neatly ordered, which wasn't a surprise. A small stack of papers sat in front of a framed picture of him and Carrie on his desk, and a Silent Creek Beavers poster hung on the wall.

Jim headed around the desk and sat down. A long lateral file cabinet stood against the wall behind him, and Jim pulled it open. He leafed through the rows of paperwork, not sure what he'd expected to find but keeping an eye out for anything that might match up with the strange accounts that had popped up earlier.

Nothing.

He scooted back to the desk and pulled open the top drawer. Pens, pencils, paper clips . . . nothing more unusual than a tin of mints.

Jim moved a few things around and saw a Post-it stuck to the bottom of the drawer. It had a massive string of letters, numbers, and symbols printed on it. He pulled it out and studied Kyle's blocky handwriting. Jim thought about his own computer password stuck to the bottom of his monitor but couldn't imagine Kyle typing this whole thing in every morning.

It had to be something else.

Jim pulled out his phone and took a picture before sticking the note back under the drawer.

He moved on to the bottom drawer, but it was locked. Jim went back to the top drawer, looking for a key, but couldn't find one.

Under normal conditions, a locked desk drawer wouldn't raise an eyebrow, but they'd left normal conditions dying along the side of the road weeks ago.

Before he could decide how aggressive he wanted to be in getting that drawer open, the front door opened out in the lobby.

Jim pushed away from the desk right as Kyle stepped into the doorway.

"What the hell are you doing in my desk?"

Chapter Thirty-Two

Jim stared at his best friend as a dozen responses jockeyed for position in his head. It felt weird beginning this conversation on Kyle's turf—it definitely felt like a Boss's Office kind of thing. But if there was an innocent explanation, the proof would probably be in the files behind him.

And if there was proof the other way, it might be there as well.

Jim motioned to the single chair against the wall to his left. "We need to talk."

If Kyle didn't like where this was going, he certainly didn't like being asked to sit in a visitor's chair in his own office. He didn't move.

"Okay."

Jim wasn't having that conversation with Kyle looking down at him, so he stood up and used his height to shift the dynamic. "After we talked yesterday, I started looking through the books to make sure we hadn't gotten any more payments from the GOGP and found some other . . . discrepancies."

He watched Kyle's face for a reaction at that word, but didn't see one, nor did he get any other sort of response.

"There seem to be some new accounts we're paying on that feel like double-ups and some that I can't even find out what we're getting, service-wise. You've got invoices for stuff we don't have in the garage. So I gotta ask . . . What the fuck's going on?"

Jim saw the defensive mask slip over Kyle's face. "I don't know what you're talking about. I told you that thing with Colton was just a government mix-up. I called the guy this morning and—"

"*Did* you?"

Kyle didn't look like he appreciated the interruption, but Jim found himself not caring. "Yes, I fucking did, and we got it all straightened out. As for the other stuff, I don't know what the hell you're talking about."

"I'm talking about you making payments that I can't see the benefits from."

"Maybe that's because you don't know shit about this business, ever think of that?" Kyle's voice was loud enough it beat out the howling wind and echoed through the empty lobby behind him. "It may still say McCann out on the sign, but I'm the one who's running this place. Without me, it would've been dead *long* before your dad, but does that mean anything? When the time comes you parachute right into the big chair with absolutely no experience and no knowledge just because you're the boss's son, and once again I've got to hold your hand the whole way. And what do I get for that? For keeping your company afloat for years? You to come into my office and accuse me of something just because you don't understand it? Are you fucking kidding me?"

Jim swallowed the anger that was bubbling up in his chest, waiting to spew out over everything in front of him, and spoke with a forced calm. "You're right, I don't know all the ins and outs here, but I'm smart enough to know when something doesn't smell right. You say I'm wrong, fine. Let's sit down right now and go through some things. You show me that I'm wrong, and I'll apologize. But there's a whole lot of smoke to explain to me right now."

"I don't have to exp—"

The door out in the lobby opened again and cut him off as Kelli walked in and stomped the snow from her boots. "Okay, I'll admit it's pretty nasty out there."

Kyle ignored Kelli and held Jim's eyes as he spoke. "It's only gonna get worse."

Jim pulled away and looked past him into the lobby. "What are you doing here?"

"I figured you could use a ride, although it looks like you already called an Uber." Kelli chuckled as she pulled her stocking cap off and shook out her brown hair.

"He just showed up," Jim said.

"No biggie, you can ride with him . . . or you can ride with someone who learned to drive up on the Iron Range, where we have real winter. Your call." Kelli laughed again but noticed she was the only one who did. "All joking aside, I'm a little surprised you're still sending trucks out in this."

Jim looked over at Kyle and saw the same confused look that was surely on his own face. "I told you I sent everyone home a while ago. We're not doing any deliveries in this stuff."

It was Kelli's turn to look confused. "Well, somebody's got a truck over by the tanks."

Kyle looked back at Jim, the defensive hostility that had filled his eyes a second ago gone. None of their drivers would be out there filling a tank in the middle of a blizzard.

But a former one would.

Kyle hustled over to the door and looked out into the storm. The wind died down for a second, and he looked back at Jim. "I see taillights."

The thought of Colton doing something with one of their tanker trucks, or even worse, the storage tanks out there, jumped ahead of everything Jim and Kyle had been arguing about.

His dad's voice echoed in his head.

Because if there is an accident at Kyle's dad's office, it won't blow up half the town.

"We gotta call the police," Jim said.

"They'll never get here in time." Kyle looked back from the door. "I don't know what the hell he's doing, but there's no way it's good. We've got to stop him."

Kelli stepped between the two men. "What are you guys talking about?"

Jim turned to her and tried to keep his voice calm. "It's Colton Reid. I told you he's been messing with us, but I haven't told you everything. It's been a lot more. Worse. He's . . ."

"Come on, we gotta do something." Kyle was looking out the door again. "If he's got that truck full of . . ." He didn't finish. He didn't need to.

Jim looked back at Kelli and saw fear creeping in.

Kyle swore under his breath and turned away from the door. He pushed past Jim and went into his office. A key was out of his pocket and into the drawer before Jim could ask any questions.

When Kyle stood back up, he was holding a black pistol.

Jim was speechless. Kelli was not.

"What the fuck?"

Kyle ignored her and grabbed Jim by the shoulder. "We can deal with everything else later, but right now the only thing that matters is Colton Reid is out there driving a freaking bomb. I don't know what he's planning on doing, but we sure as shit can't find out." His grip tightened on Jim's three-quarter-zip sweater. "You hear me?"

Jim stared at his former friend, head swirling with fear and distrust, and gave a curt nod.

Kyle released him and headed for the door. "Let's go."

Jim turned to Kelli and saw a million questions he couldn't answer in her face. "Stay here. I don't know what he's gonna do." He didn't wait for an answer before taking off and realized as he ran that he wasn't sure if he was warning her about Colton or Kyle.

Maybe both.

Jim followed Kyle out the door and put his hand up against the wind, trying to keep the unending shower of tiny snow crystals from peppering his face. He could see the outline of one of their LP trucks alongside their ten-thousand-gallon storage tank. A dark figure moved around the back of the truck.

"There he is!" Kyle yelled and ran off into the snow.

Jim's knee was balking at his disjointed attempt to catch up to Kyle, who was already a good twenty feet ahead of him, when a loud crack stopped them both in their tracks. Jim wanted to crouch down, make himself a smaller target, but his knee wouldn't allow it.

The wind died enough Jim got a clear look at Colton standing at the back of the truck, his arm extended in front of him. Kyle was up ahead, holding out his own gun but not pulling the trigger, knowing that Colton was standing in front of what amounted to a twenty-thousand-pound bomb.

With visibility suddenly clear and only a couple of hundred feet between them, there was little Jim could do but wait for a bullet in the chest.

But it didn't come.

Jim squinted against the fear and snow and saw Colton still at the rear of the LP truck. The back hatch, where the valves and hoses connected to the tank, was propped open, but Jim had to use his imagination to figure out what Colton was doing there.

All the worst-case scenarios were chased away when a flash of red popped out of Colton's hand. Jim reflexively braced for an explosion, despite knowing that if the truck went up, he'd be dead before he heard the blast.

Jim opened his eyes in time to recognize the road flare Colton had cracked open, then watch him reach back and throw it toward the garage. Instinctively he was happy to see it fly away from the tank but knew better than to think there wasn't some bad intent behind it he hadn't figured out yet.

The flare bounced on the ground about ten feet from the garage and rolled up next to the metal cage where they kept the twenty-pound tanks people swap out for their grills. The realization sent a jolt of fear through him, but he knew a small fire like that wouldn't do anything to those tanks. In theory they could explode if heated enough, but even the consistent flame of a road flare most certainly wouldn't be enough.

It was probably a distraction or something to give Colton a chance to slip away.

That said, it was still a good idea to remove an open flame from a propane dealership.

"Kyle—" Jim hollered through the snow but was cut off by another crack from Colton's gun. Neither he nor Kyle fell, but Jim saw a spark over by the garage and realized he wasn't aiming for them but in the same direction he'd chucked the flare. And while shooting a propane tank would most likely not cause an explosion in itself, if it punctured the tank and there was an open flame nearby . . .

Jim's eyes locked on the flare burning at the base of the tank and yelled at Kyle louder than he had in his life. "RUN!"

He got two painful steps back into the wind when another crack came, immediately followed by a sound so loud it replaced time and space as the only reality Jim could perceive. A blast of hot air slammed into his back and sent him sprawling face-first into the frozen parking lot.

The storm continued over Jim, but the thrumming in his ears blocked out most of it as he lay on the hard-packed gravel beneath him. He pushed himself up as his head cycled back through a hard reset. Fresh snow and a couple of rocks stuck to his face, but his back was warm like there was a space heater behind him.

Jim shook his head, and one of the rocks dropped off. He pushed up to all fours, causing a head-clearing surge of pain in his bad knee, so he rolled over onto his butt.

Over by the garage, fire rose at least fifty feet in spite of the storm. The wind twisted and swirled it around like a flaming tornado.

Jim wiped his arm across his face as a figure appeared in front of him, a black shadow framed by the fire behind. He tried to scramble away, but a hand clamped on to his sweater and yanked him upward.

"Come on." Kyle's other hand grabbed Jim's elbow and pulled him to his feet.

Jim took stock of his condition and his surroundings, slowly getting back to cohesive thought. His knee still ached, and he could already feel the warmth of a coming welt on his cheekbone where his face had met the ground, but other than that, he seemed fine.

"You okay?" Jim asked out of habit. Colton's arrival and the subsequent explosion had pushed his accusations of Kyle out of frame for the moment.

"He got in the truck and headed out back," Kyle said, ignoring the question. Beyond the burning garage, there were a half dozen storage tanks holding enough liquid propane to wipe everything between them and Silent Creek off the map. They were built like vaults and had multiple safeties, but they were designed to prevent accidents, not sabotage. Someone familiar with them or the delivery trucks would probably be able to do something catastrophic if they wanted.

And the massive fireball to their left was proof that Colton was plenty familiar.

"Let's go."

Jim started to follow but stopped after a step.

"Wait." He turned back to the office, squinting through the blowing snow for any sign of Kelli. Her car was still next to his, but he didn't see any movement. Jim started back to look for her, but Kyle grabbed a fistful of his sweater.

"She's fine," Kyle said. "We gotta find Colton."

"But—"

He was cut off by another *whump* from the fire when a second tank exploded and a burst of hot air slammed into them. The flames stretched up the metal siding of the garage and caught the roof above. There were at least a dozen tanks in the cage, but Jim had no idea how many were full and how many were empty returns.

Kyle yanked Jim around. "If we don't stop Colton from whatever the fuck he's gonna do with that truck, there isn't going to be enough left of any of us to identify, so we gotta go now."

The pull to go back and find Kelli, make sure she was okay, was strong, but Kyle's logic superseded all that. Jim nodded, and they headed away from the fire, toward the long row of tanks.

The wind picked up as if it were a warning, pushing them away, but Jim put his head down and limped on.

The storage tanks loomed ahead, giant white pills lined up a hundred or so yards away from the garage. Orange shadows danced off the nearest ones as the fire continued.

A third tank exploded in the flaming cage, but they ignored it and pressed on. Those twenty-pound tanks were firecrackers compared to the bombs that lay ahead of them.

Kyle worked his way ahead, the gun in his hand and two good knees pushing him forward at a faster pace than Jim. He made his way around the first tank, but there was nothing there. The rumble of the truck's engine seeped through the howl of the wind, so they kept going and found it idling between the second and third tanks.

They both stopped, hopefully hidden, and peered around the end of the tank.

The truck idled probably twenty feet away, taillights turning the blowing snow behind it red. The driver's side door was open, as was the back hatch, where the delivery hose had been pulled from the wheel and whipped around on the ground like an angry snake, white gas spewing out into the storm with an angry hiss.

"Shit." Kyle sprinted out to the truck, Jim behind him. "He's jammed the valve open."

Kyle ducked into the back of the truck, fighting with various knobs and levers as Jim stood next to him, fairly helpless with limited knowledge of how their trucks actually worked.

The flailing hose snapped its heavy metal nozzle into Jim's right ankle, forcing him to put all his weight on his bad leg and almost sending him to the ground. He hopped out of the way as Kyle managed to shut it down, and the hose fell limp.

"Got it." Kyle emerged from under the hatch and looked up at the cab of the truck, then back along the tanks.

Colton was nowhere they could see, but Jim could feel him out there somewhere. "What was he doing?"

"I don't know. Maybe the same thing he did out front but on a much bigger scale," Kyle said. "But in this wind the gas will dissipate pretty quickly, and you couldn't be anywhere nearby when you triggered it. It doesn't make sense."

Jim looked at the shadowy tanks around them and shuddered.

"Maybe it's a distraction," Kyle said. "Pull our attention away from whatever he's really trying to do."

A gust of wind blew around the tanks and sent a shiver down Jim's spine. Kelli was still alone in the office.

Or at least he hoped she was still alone.

"I'm gonna go check on Kelli."

Kyle looked behind him again and shook his head. "She can take care of herself. We need to make sure he isn't messing with the tanks." He reached into the cab and cut the ignition.

"I'm not gonna leave her alone with that psycho out here," Jim said.

Kyle slammed the door and turned into the wind to face Jim. "We can't leave that psycho out here without knowing what the hell he's doing."

"But—"

Kyle grabbed him by the sweater. "If these things go up, it'll blow up the whole fucking town, you understand?"

Jim yanked away from Kyle's grip and felt his hand ball into a fist. Kyle must have seen the look in his eyes because his voice softened. "Jim, think for a second. If he blows one of these, nothing else matters 'cause we're all dead anyway. But however he's gonna do it, he'll have to be pretty far away when he triggers it, which means he's not heading to the office. That means we've got time to stop it. Kelli's fine. If she's got any brains, she's already called the cops, so we just have to make sure Colton doesn't do anything crazy before they get here."

Jim didn't like it, but Kyle was probably right. He gave a resigned nod, and Kyle stepped behind the truck.

"You head up that way and I'll go back here," he said. "You see that fucker, holler."

Jim noticed he'd pulled the gun out from his waistband. The explosion and everything since had rattled his mind enough that seeing Kyle pull that from his desk felt like a different lifetime. Its presence had unsettled him, but at this point he was afraid they'd need it.

Kyle disappeared around the truck, and Jim headed the opposite way. He made his way around the tank and peered down the next row. Nothing. He kept going.

Somehow the snow came down harder, and the wind cut through the adrenaline and three-quarter-zip sweater Jim wore to remind him of the cold for the first time since he'd limped out from the office. It not only brought back a biting chill but memories of what he'd found before all hell broke loose.

Right as his mind drifted back to his confrontation with Kyle, a loud bang came from somewhere in the storm and something sparked off the tank to his right.

Jim froze as a voice cut through the wind.

"Looks like trouble found you."

Chapter Thirty-Three

Jim watched as Colton emerged from behind the giant tank looming to his left. They were far enough removed from the burning pyre of propane out front that they were both in the shadows, but he could see a faint glow of orange on the snow out in the distance.

He saw a glint of metal from the gun in Colton's hand and put his hands up.

"I almost feel sorry for you." Jim could hear the smile in Colton's voice. "You can't stop poking the bear, can you? Every time I think I'm ready to move on, there you are. Just poke, poke, poke. And the thing about me is, I'm a big believer in justice. An eye for an eye." Colton nodded back at the flames that were twisting in the wind beyond the tanks behind him. "A garage for a garage."

Jim didn't know what he was talking about but was too scared to argue.

"And unlike some," Colton said as he gestured at Jim with his gun, "I don't send some toady out to do my dirty work."

"I don't know what the hell you're talking about." Jim had to practically shout over the sounds of the storm.

Colton laughed. "If that's the case, you may wanna get your boy back on the leash before he writes any more checks that your ass can't cash."

Things started clicking in Jim's brain, but Colton wasn't going to wait for Jim to put his thoughts together and pointed the gun directly in his face. Panic flooded Jim's system, and his fight-or-flight reflex chose neither.

Too scared to close his eyes, Jim saw a blur of motion fly out from the tank as Kelli slammed into Colton's midsection under his extended arm. The gun went off and sent a stray bullet into the night as she tackled him to the ground, where the gun skittered out of his hand on impact.

It was a perfect blind-side tackle, but once they hit the ground, Kelli had no chance of keeping him there. Colton used his size advantage to buck her off, and she bounced hard against the frozen dirt. Jim could swear he saw all the breath she had rush out on impact but couldn't take the chance of checking on her.

He dove to the ground in the general direction he'd seen Colton's gun fly when it left his hand. Jim swept his hands through the snow. Finding that gun was their only chance.

His fingers bumped into the barrel, but it spun away, and before he could grab it, a hand clamped down on the back of his ankle. Jim blindly kicked back with his left leg and connected with something. The hand let go, but he barely noticed through the pain that burst in his knee. Jim ignored it and reached for the gun again. His fingers found the grip this time, and he pulled it toward him and flipped over onto his back.

Colton was up to his knees but stopped when he saw the gun. Jim sat up with the barrel trained between Colton's dark eyes, finger tight around the trigger in case he moved.

Kelli was on her feet again but bent over with her hands on her knees, fighting for breath.

"You okay?" She stood up and nodded, her hands atop her head like she'd finished a set of wind sprints. Jim stayed on the ground. His knee wasn't going to let him stand up without taking the gun off Colton, and that wasn't something he was willing to do yet.

"Come over here." Jim looked at Kelli, then jabbed the gun at Colton. "You stay down."

Kelli treated Colton like a coiled rattlesnake and gave him a wide berth as she came over to Jim. "What now?"

Jim nodded and held a hand up for her. She grabbed it and pulled him to his feet, the gun fixed on Colton the whole time.

"You gotta get out of here," Jim said. "Get back to the office. Call the police . . . the fire department . . . everybody."

Kelli hesitated and glanced down at Colton. "You all right here?"

Jim could hear the warning in her voice. *Don't do anything stupid.*

"I'm good. Go get help."

She jogged off and disappeared into the blizzard almost instantly, leaving Jim alone with Colton.

And the gun.

"What now, boss man? You gonna shoot me?" Colton was on his knees, but he didn't put his hands up.

"I should after the hell you've put me through." The words were threatening, but even to Jim they sounded like posturing. They both knew he wasn't going to cut him down in cold blood. "You even know what happened to my mom that night? When you stalked her house like a fucking creep? She went out to see who was there and wandered off. Almost froze her fucking feet off because of *you*. Did you see her come out? Did you run off like a coward, or was that your plan all along? Lure a poor woman with dementia out of her house and see what happens? You're lucky it wasn't worse because I would've come at you a hell of a lot harder than we did."

"Hey now," Colton said. "I may be a spiteful motherfucker, but I never did shit to your ma. You think I'd go after the widow of the guy who actually gave me a job just 'cause she had the misfortune of shitting you out?"

"I don't care if it was your intent or not—it was your fucking fault." Jim felt the anger and frustration of the last few months pressurizing inside him. "If you weren't there, she would never have gone outside in the first place."

Colton looked up at him from his knees, oblivious to the snow whipping around them and catching in his rust-colored beard.

"Do what you gotta do, but I told you; I ain't never been to your house, and I didn't have nothing to do with whatever happened to your mom."

Jim stared down at him, looking for the lie in Colton's face. "She said it was *the guy you played basketball with*. Who the fuck else would that be?"

Colton looked to his right, then to his left, and came back with a smirk. "Pretty sure you've got another friend round here you played basketball with."

A gust of wind flew around the corner and slammed into Jim's back as Colton's words punched him in the chest. It couldn't be. For whatever the hell he'd done since, Kyle had been his best friend since they were kids. She *knows* his name.

Right?

"Well, speak of the devil," Colton said.

"You got him?" Kyle emerged from the same spot Kelli had disappeared to a few minutes before. As if on cue, another tank blew off in the distance, and the flames stretched out high enough they could see them over the tanks.

Kyle trained the gun he'd pulled from the locked drawer in his desk on Colton, and he circled over by Jim. He nodded at the one in Jim's hand. "That his?"

"Yeah."

"Perfect." Kyle reached out his empty hand.

Jim hesitated, his thoughts swirling the same way the snow did around the little enclave between the tanks where they stood. The gun was heavy in his hands, but he was suddenly afraid to give it up.

"Give it here."

Jim took his eyes off Colton and glanced at the office. "Kelli went to call the police." Before he could turn back, Kyle snatched the gun out of Jim's hand. *"Hey—"*

"It's all good." Kyle trained the gun on Colton as he stuffed his own in the back of his jeans. "I know how we can end this."

"It's already over. The cops will be here soon." Kyle didn't seem to hear him. His focus was on Colton. "Kyle . . ."

He stepped forward, gun aimed right between Colton's eyes.

"*Kyle,*" Jim shouted through the wind. "What are you doing?"

"We can shoot him in the head and leave him out here," Kyle said. "Crazy motherfucker who got fired came out and tried to blow the place up. They'll think it's a suicide."

Jim stared at his childhood best friend in disbelief. *"What?"*

Years of rage danced in Kyle's eyes as he stared down the barrel at Colton. "The cops won't do shit. You know that. And this fucker won't stop. You know that too. So we gotta stop him."

"We're not shooting him," Jim said, looking for any bit of logic that might break through the fog of anger inside Kyle. "They've got forensics and stuff."

Kyle cackled with more malice than humor. "Not in this shit. He'll be under a foot of snow before they find him. It's even his gun, for crying out loud. It's perfect."

Jim stepped forward and grabbed Kyle's shoulder. "You can't just shoot him like this."

Kyle's eyes slowly shifted over to Jim, but Colton spoke before he opened his mouth.

"Don't worry, he won't."

Jim looked down at Colton, kneeling in what was now a couple inches of snow.

"He don't have it in him. Never has." Colton looked up at Kyle. "Ain't that right, Kyle? You talk a big game when you got someone to hide behind, but when it comes down to it . . ." He shook his head dismissively. "How many years you been sitting on that hate but didn't have the balls to do anything till your buddy got back here? Even now you're still hiding behind him. You ain't got the guts to pull that trigger."

Kyle stepped forward and smacked Colton across the temple with his gun, opening a gash that dribbled blood down into his eye. He reached up and calmly wiped it away, leaving a red smear across his cheek.

Colton looked past Kyle at Jim; the hole in his smile popped as he spoke. "See?"

"Fuck you, Colton." Kyle stepped to the side and pressed the gun against Colton's temple as a huge gust of wind kicked up and threw a handful of snow in his face. Kyle paused a second to blink it out of his eyes, giving Jim enough time to act.

He leaped forward and yanked Kyle's wrist upward. The gun went off, and a shower of sparks flew where the bullet hit the thick steel wall of the tank next to them.

Jim added his other hand and wrenched Kyle's arm above his head, where he managed to send two more shots up into the falling snow. At six foot nine, Jim had all the leverage he needed, but right as he wrenched the gun away, Kyle kicked him in the knee. His leg gave out, and he collapsed to the ground, the gun spinning off into the dark.

Kyle stood over him, head snapping back and forth, as Jim struggled to ignore the pain and get back to his feet. "Where is he?"

Jim glanced around but didn't see Colton anywhere. He crawled over to the tank and braced himself against the base in an attempt to get up, but Kyle ran over and kicked him in the side of the knee again. A supernova of pain short-circuited Jim's nervous system and sent him crashing to the ground like a marionette with its strings cut. His head banged off the concrete support, and his vision filled with stars and pinwheels.

Somewhere above him, the angry storm was screaming.

"He got away."

A Red Wing Iron Ranger boot connected with his ribs, but he barely registered it.

"I had him, and you fucking fucked it up again!" Kyle kept kicking Jim as he screamed. Ribs, back, legs, whatever his rage could get.

"You have fucked me over and over and over my whole fucking life." His voice cut right through the storm, years of jealousy and resentment pouring out of him like a broken dam. "You never had my back in high school—then as soon as you got to college, you dropped me like a bad fucking habit."

Jim rolled over onto his back and tried to respond, but it hurt to breathe, let alone talk.

"I thought seeing you crash and burn at Minnesota was fucking karma, man, but you couldn't stay away, could you. I kept this place going for *years*. When you were out East doing whatever the fuck, I was here doing everything your dad asked me to do. We expanded. I turned this into a fucking monster. It was *mine*. But when your dad finally kicks, you show up and take the throne like it's your goddamn birthright. Like always. Jimmy Fucking Buckets gets whatever the hell he wants and leaves the scraps for me."

Jim looked up at the rage that had consumed Kyle, but he had no answer for it. He sucked in a frozen breath to say he was sorry, but the sharp pain in his side kept the words unsaid.

Kyle reached down and picked up Colton's gun off the ground.

The barrel was packed with snow, but Jim knew that wouldn't stop a bullet if Kyle decided to pull the trigger.

"Fuck you, *Jimmy*."

The chunk of snow fell from the muzzle as Colton reappeared behind them and yanked out the gun tucked in the back of Kyle's pants.

It happened in slow motion but was over in an instant.

He swung Kyle around by the arm and buried the gun under his chin. The gunshot tore through the storm and painted a grizzly swath of dark red across the twenty-thousand-gallon propane tank behind them.

Kyle's body collapsed in a heap next to Jim, who could do little but stare up at Colton and wait for a bullet of his own.

Instead, Colton knelt down next to Kyle's body. "Guy might be an asshole, but that don't mean he don't got decent ideas." He tucked Kyle's pistol into his hand. "Too bad for him he's too chickenshit to do them himself."

Colton then got up and disappeared into the blizzard.

Chapter Thirty-Four

Jim lay in a painful daze alongside that propane tank until some semblance of rational thought returned and his brain told him he had to get up. Kyle was dead beside him, he had no idea where Kelli was, and Colton was in the wind. His mind was so jumbled that he half expected Kyle to pop up next to him after he'd struggled to his feet.

But that wasn't happening. The mix of blood and brains already half frozen to the tank above him was proof of that.

Kyle had tried to kill him. Would have, had Colton Reid not come back.

He looked down at his old friend's body. The gun Colton had put in his hand—the one he killed him with—was already covered with snow.

"Jim!" He spun around and saw Kelli shambling toward him. She stopped when she saw Kyle's body. "Oh my God . . ."

Jim limped over and hugged her, using all his remaining strength to keep from collapsing into her and taking them both down. "Are the cops here?"

She pulled away and shook her head. Snow fell from her hair but was quickly replaced. "Kyle jumped me." Kelli reached back and gingerly rubbed the back of her skull. "He hit me with something . . . I was out. What happened here?" She looked down at Kyle. "Is he . . . ?"

"Yeah."

He felt Kelli's muscles tense and knew what the next question was. "Did you . . ."

"No." Jim's mind swirled like the snow around them. "He came after me too. Knocked me down and kept kicking." He put a hand on his ribs and winced. Kyle's voice came back to him in the wind. Ranting. Blaming him for everything. The chunk of snow packed into the muzzle. "Then it stopped."

Kelli wrapped her arms around him again while Jim looked behind them for Colton, half expecting him to emerge from the shadows and finish them off. Two shots and they'd be dead next to Kyle as the blizzard slowly buried them all.

Jim told himself he hadn't technically lied to her, but he knew he had. No matter what words had come out of his mouth, she believed Kyle had killed himself because of what was left unsaid. The door was still open for clarification, either then or sometime down the road when things had calmed down, but he knew that wasn't going to happen. The door to that vault had already slammed shut, its key tossed somewhere in the shadows where they'd never find it.

She slipped her hand into his and guided his arm around her shoulder for support, which he badly needed to get back to the office.

Away from what had happened.

The cold settled deep into Jim's bones. He shivered and put more of his weight across Kelli's shoulders. She wrapped her arm around his waist but said nothing.

The garage was half gone by the time they got there, and he saw flashing lights appear in the distance on Highway 14.

"I thought you didn't call?"

"I didn't," Kelli said. "Somebody must've driven past and seen the flames."

They limped across the parking lot toward the office, where they stopped and watched the fire trucks pull in. For an all-volunteer group, they worked like a well-oiled machine. Brent Halverson hopped out of one of the trucks to help two others uncoil a hose. Within minutes they had the water flowing. In the glow of the fire, Jim recognized Pete Jeffries and Blake Hagen holding the hose with him, keeping a steady stream on the flaming wreckage of the place where they all worked.

Jim and Kelli stood in silence, the massive fire across the way keeping them warm like a campfire. The flames cast eerie shadows across the grounds, and Jim kept scanning the periphery for Colton.

But he was gone.

After about ten minutes, a black SUV with flashing lights on top pulled in from Highway 14 and parked next to them. Chief Nelson got out and took a long look at the fire before noticing Jim and Kelli.

"What the hell happened out here?"

Jim felt Kelli squeeze his shoulder before he told his story.

Chapter Thirty-Five

Jim turned his SUV down the long driveway, the halogen lights illuminating the tunnel of trees ahead of him. The branches above had caught most of the snow that had fallen over the last week, but there was still enough on the ground Jim could see tracks stretch out in front of him like an airplane runway.

It was a skinny driveway, which was good because the instinct to abandon this idea and head home was getting louder. But there was no way to turn around until he got into the yard ahead, and by then it would be too late to abort.

If his last visit out here was any indication, Colton already knew he was there anyway.

The shadows bounced around the driveway as he crept over gravel and potholes, his headlights trumpeting his arrival to a place Jim had been warned about returning to.

Right as he thought about slamming his SUV in reverse and backing out the entire length of the driveway, the trees disappeared and emptied him out into the yard.

Jim rolled to a stop, put his car in park, and stared out the windshield. The old house loomed off to his right, while the charred remains of one of Colton's old sheds were bathed in his headlights ahead of him.

That morning, the police had finally given them permission to start reconstruction on the garage at McCann. Their investigation was over and all questions as to what had happened had been answered to their satisfaction, so it was time to rebuild.

To move on.

Jim reached down and adjusted the brace under his pants before opening the car door. It was a new brace, much stronger but still lighter than the one he'd been using. They'd made great advances in technology since he'd had his first operation. He was scheduled for surgery in two weeks, assuming the swelling from the past few days was gone by then. His doctor had chastised him for "running around" on it before coming in, but he'd somehow managed to avoid any additional structural damage after the initial tear. There was a lot of scar tissue that had built up over the years they wanted to clean out while they were in there, and his surgeon had said he could come out of this one better than he'd felt in years.

Jim swung his leg to the ground and got out, then hopped back and pulled open the rear door.

Jim reached inside and heard the voice he'd been expecting behind him.

"You get my invitation?"

Jim grabbed his crutches and slowly pulled them out of the back seat. "I'm just here to talk, Colton."

He kept one hand empty in front of him, as nonthreatening as possible, and used the other to prop himself atop his crutches. He realized he didn't need to worry. Even with two good legs, Colton never saw him as a threat.

"Aw, looks like somebody got a boo-boo."

Jim adjusted himself and closed the back door behind him. "Torn ACL." He nodded over at the hole in the porch steps. The top step was still broken from when he'd crashed through it, and his knee yelped in pain at the sight of it. "Did it right over there, actually. That time I was out here to hide those pills. Busted through those steps and *pop*, there it went again. Had to crawl across the porch and drop off the far side before you got out of your truck and saw me. Laid back there the whole time you were out here with your dog. Did you know I was there?"

A genuine laugh escaped from Colton's throat. "Honestly, I figured you were smart enough to get outta Dodge. Guess I should've let Bubble loose earlier. He'd have found you."

It was Jim's turn to laugh, and it sounded very strange in his ears, considering the situation.

"*That* dog's name is Bubble?"

Colton ignored the question, and his tone made it clear he didn't appreciate it. "What the fuck are you doing here?"

"I figured we should talk." Colton didn't respond, but he also didn't shoot him, so Jim gestured over by his trailer. "Should we go inside?"

"You're lucky I'm letting you stand out here."

"Fair enough." Bubble let out a string of barks somewhere behind them before Jim could begin, and he saw a satisfied smirk cross Colton's face in the glow of his headlights. He took a steadying breath of cold night air and started. "As you probably figured by now, I didn't tell anyone how things went down out at McCann. They think Kyle did it to himself, and as far as I'm concerned, that's for the best. Ends up he'd been stealing from McCann since well before my dad died. I figured it out pretty much right before you came out and tried to blow the place up."

Colton let out a snort. "Are you wearing a fucking wire or something?"

"Considering all the stuff I just said about what I've done, I think it's pretty obvious I wouldn't want anyone else hearing this conversation," Jim said.

Colton nodded.

"Anyway, I told them I confronted Kyle about it before all this went down, which is all true, by the way, and I even had a few fortunate text messages to back me up. It wasn't hard to convince them that he caused the explosion and fire, wanting to do as much damage as he could on the way out. The cops still have people going through the books, and they're finding way more stuff than I did, so the story rings awfully true."

"Your girl was out there too," Colton said. "What's she gonna say 'bout all that?"

"Kyle jumped Kelli before he came after me. Left her lying unconscious in the snow without knowing if she was alive or dead, so she's got no pity for him." Jim leaned forward on his crutches and blew some warmth into his hands. "As for what you were doing out at McCann, I told her what Kyle did to Bubble's house over there—and she was a little more understanding. I guess she's a sucker for anyone who may have gotten a raw deal in life. Especially when any hint of trouble could get them sent back to prison. That said, she doesn't know who pulled the trigger out there, and I think that's for the best. It's not a secret I want to burden her with."

"I'm sure that won't come back to bite your ass in the future."

Jim shrugged. "Maybe, I guess we'll find out, but I don't figure you'll tell her anytime soon."

"Oh, I'm full of surprises," Colton said. "I figured you'd know that by now."

"I do, which is why I wanted to give you this." Jim reached into his jacket pocket and pulled out a scrap of paper. He crutched over to Colton and handed it to him.

"The fuck is this?"

"When that guy called you asking about the GOGP program, did you even know what he was talking about? Did my dad say anything about it when they hired you?"

Colton looked up from the paper. "Not a fucking word."

"That's what I figured," Jim said. "As you may know by now, the business not only got some tax breaks but also $30,000 a year to cover their salary."

Colton laughed. "I should've figured they didn't hire me out of the goodness of their hearts."

"Not likely." Jim pointed to the scrap of paper in Colton's hand. "Anyway, that's the log-in info for a cryptocurrency account I made the other day. Completely untraceable. Kyle had a similar one where he dumped all the money he stole from McCann. I found his password right before you showed up. I put it back for the cops to find, of course, but not before I pulled some out and stuck it into that one there. I figured Kyle owed you."

Colton stared down at the long string of numbers, letters, and symbols scrawled out on the paper. "I don't know shit about crypto."

"Then I'd figure it out, because that's the money Kyle stole on your name. There's enough in there to give you a fresh start somewhere else. I don't think Silent Creek is a good place for the two of us, you agree?"

Colton stood there a minute, the cocky ambivalence that usually rolled off him gone for the first time. "Maybe not."

Jim turned and crutched back to his SUV, still running with the driver's side door open. He tossed the crutches in the back and looked at Colton again before climbing in sideways and pulling his leg in after him.

"I know it doesn't matter, but I'm sorry," Jim said. "Kyle was playing us both off each other from the beginning. The fire out here, blackballing you with other jobs, hell, firing you in the first place . . . that was all him."

Colton's eyes narrowed. "Might've been his idea to shitcan me, but it was still your signature."

"That's why I'm apologizing," Jim said.

He didn't wait for a response and closed the door. Colton stood in the glow of his headlights, scrap of paper in his hand, as Jim reversed into a turn and left him behind.

Chapter Thirty-Six

Walking into Williams Arena after all those years was a surreal experience for Jim. The last time he had been in the Barn was the final game of his junior season. He'd dressed, but hadn't played, which happened more times than not that year.

Jim remembered his knee hurting as he stepped up onto the raised court for the postgame handshakes and knew it would be the last time. The career that had started out so promising in this building ending on the bench.

Sabotaged by a knee injury that never healed correctly.

Jim held on to the rail as he walked down the steps to their seats but didn't notice anything in his left knee on the way down. He hadn't for a few weeks, actually. Roughly two-months post-op, Jim had been off crutches for a while and his knee felt good enough he didn't think about it anymore.

He'd probably never dunk a basketball again, but his surgeon had said—as long as he kept doing his rehab—he didn't expect it to give Jim problems.

"Well, hello, Jimmy McCann."

Jim looked up to see an older man wearing one of the gold sport coats the ushers always wore at the Barn, and it took him a second to recognize him.

"Hey, Phil! How you been?" Jim shook the usher's hand with gusto. Phil Haddy had been an usher at Williams Arena since long before Jim played for the Gophers and was universally known around the University of Minnesota Athletics Department as the friendliest guy on the planet.

"I remembered you were from Silent Creek, so I was wondering if we'd see you here," Phil said, then looked over at Gail and extended his hand. "Mrs. McCann, it's wonderful to see you again."

Gail smiled and shook Phil's hand, but Jim could tell she didn't recognize him.

If Phil noticed, he ignored it. "Can I show you to your seats?"

They chitchatted on the way down the steps, mostly talking about Phil's newest grandchildren.

Phil got them to the correct row and shook both Jim's and Gail's hands again before heading back up to his post. "Great seeing you again, Jimmy."

"You, too, Phil."

Jim watched him walk up the steps and marveled over all the people that basketball had brought into his life.

"Right here, Mom. We've got one and two." Jim motioned to the row of seats next to them and let his mom slide past him.

He was glad he could bring her to the game today, knowing it wouldn't be long before excursions like this would be too difficult for everyone involved. After talking to her neurologist, they'd decided Gail would be better off in an assisted living facility. Luckily there was an open spot at a place that specialized in memory care in Albert Lea, so it was close enough that Jim, and Gail's friends, could be regular visitors.

They settled in their seats and looked around the rapidly filling arena. The court was different, having been custom painted for the Minnesota girls' state basketball tournament, but there was still a line of maroon-and-gold banners in the rafters above. Jim looked up at them, finding the NCAA tournament appearance from his freshman year. Lots of people at the time thought that one would have been different—Sweet Sixteen, maybe more, but fate had other plans for them.

For Jim.

The purple-and-white members of the crowd erupted around them as the Silent Creek girls emerged from the underground tunnel that led to the locker rooms and ran onto the court for warm-ups.

Kelli came up behind her team and stepped onto the court in her customary purple polo and ponytail. Jim had joked that she should dress up a bit for her first state-tournament game, but she wanted the team to treat it like just another game, so she needed to as well.

After a little gentle prodding, she admitted to also being a little superstitious.

Jim looked at the crowd around them, and it filled his chest with warmth. Silent Creek had really rallied around the basketball program after everything that happened with Kyle in December. Rumors of his embezzlement swirled all through town, but people chose to ignore them and publicly think of his death as a tragedy.

For her part, Carrie never asked Jim and Kelli what happened out at McCann. With the amount of money that Kyle had taken over the years, she must have at least suspected something was going on. She was content to play the grieving widow, and Jim was happy to play along if that's how she wanted to deal with it.

In the short term, Jim agreed to help John Pederson coach the boys' team for the rest of the season in Kyle's absence. It was a welcome distraction but a tough assignment, considering the circumstances. They didn't win many games, but Jim knew that wasn't what a season like that was about. They bonded as a team and made it to the end together, which should prove beneficial for whoever took over as the coach next year.

More and more fans filled in around them, and by the time the horn blew, the Barn was packed to the rafters.

A large red-headed man sat two sections over.

Jim saw him as they sat down and was briefly hit with a familiar paranoia. He wasn't Colton; that was obvious right away.

Too skinny, no beard.

Jim hadn't seen Colton since he'd gone out to his farm after the explosion. As far as he knew, nobody had. The crypto account Jim set up had been emptied a few days after he'd given Colton the password. He'd been tempted to drive out to his place a few times and make sure he was gone but chose to leave all that behind.

Still, he sometimes wondered where Colton had gone, if he'd ever see him again, and what the hell would happen if he did.

Mostly, he hoped to never find out.

The horn blew again, and the teams headed back to their benches to line up for player introductions. Jim caught Kelli's eye, and she gave him a quick smile and a wink before the PA announcer's voice boomed through the arena.

"Making their first ever Minnesota girls' high school state tournament appearance . . . led by Head Coach Kelli Alexander . . . the Silent Creek Beavers!"

Acknowledgments

As always, the first thank-you goes to the greatest agent in the universe, Abby Saul. You are always there to answer my ridiculous questions or to remind me that I can do things I once thought were impossible. I would not have a career if not for your guidance.

The whole team at Thomas & Mercer is a dream to work with, and I want to give extra-special thanks to my editor Liz Pearsons for believing in me and this book.

Thanks to my production manager Miranda Gardner for shepherding me through the process and getting this all to come together. Big thanks to my copyeditor Alicia Lea, proofreader Megan Westberg, and cold reader Heather Buzila for once again patiently pointing out the exact same mistakes over and over and over. Thanks to my author liaison Darci Swanson for being there to answer any and all questions.

Gabino Iglesias is one of the greatest writers currently scribbling, and I'm beyond honored to have worked with him again. When I was drafting the final, bloody scene of *Silent Creek*, all I could think was *Gabino's gonna read this, so make him proud!*

Thanks to David Drummond of Salamander Hill Design for another fantastic cover.

Thanks to my Lark Group buddies, Tara Tai, Brianna Labuskes, Elle Grawl, Meredith Hambrock, Mindy Carlson, Jason Powell, Terah Harris, Kris Calvin, Daisy Bateman, Stephanie Thérèse, Sarah James,

Amy Hagstrom, Logan Steiner, Summer Olsen, and Carol Dunbar. Go buy their books. #TEAMLARK4LIFE

Speaking of books, I want to shout out all the authors who have inspired me with their work over the years—Stephen King, S. A. Cosby, Zoje Stage, Chelsea Cain, Joe Hill, Jess Lourey, Gillian Flynn, Caroline Kepnes, K. T. Nguyen, Jordan Harper, Amina Akhtar, Megan Abbott, and dozens more I don't have room to thank.

Finally, I want to thank my family. There is no way I could have even attempted writing without the support of my wife, Erin, and I get inspiration from my daughters every day.

About the Author

Photo © 2022 Alyssa Dey

Tony Wirt was born in Lake Mills, Iowa, and got his first taste of publication in the first grade, when his essay on *Airplane II: The Sequel* appeared in the Lake Mills Elementary School's *Creative Courier*. Since then, he has published three thrillers: *Pike Island, Just Stay Away,* and *A Necessary Act. Silent Creek* is his fourth novel.

Wirt graduated from the University of Iowa and spent nine years doing media relations for the Hawkeye Athletic Department. He's also worked as a sportswriter, a movie ticket taker, and a Dairy Queen ice-cream slinger who can still do the little curly thing on top of a soft-serve cone. He currently lives in Rochester, Minnesota, with his wife and two daughters.